SUNNILAND

A Novel

SUNNILAND

A Novel

Stephen O. Sears

Editors: Dianna Graveman and Joshua Owens

Cover Design: 3SIXTY Marketing Studio

Interior Design: 3SIXTY Marketing Studio - 3sixtyprinting.com

Indigo River Publishing
3 West Garden Street, Ste. 352
Pensacola, FL 32502
www.indigoriverpublishing.com

Ordering Information:
Quantity sales: Special discounts are available on quantity purchases by corporations, associations, and others. For details, contact the publisher at the address above.

Orders by US trade bookstores and wholesalers: Please contact the publisher at the address above.

Printed in the United States of America

Library of Congress Control Number: 2019938716

ISBN: 978-1-948080-93-4

First Edition

With Indigo River Publishing, you can always expect great books,
strong voices, and meaningful messages.
Most importantly, you'll always find . . . words worth reading.

Acknowledgments and Disclaimer

Everglades City and the surrounding swamps and mangrove islands are real places. Oil was discovered in 1943 in the Everglades of southwest Florida. The German U-boats sank over one hundred tankers in the Gulf of Mexico and Caribbean Sea during 1942 and 1943. These historical settings and facts are used fictitiously in this novel. All other names, characters, places, and events are solely the product of the author's imagination. Any resemblance to actual persons, living or dead, and actual events and places is entirely coincidental.

The author would like to thank the geologists and engineers at the University of Florida, Penn State, Shell Oil Company, and LSU who worked with him and shared their knowledge of geology and petroleum engineering, especially the geology of the Florida peninsula. He would also like to thank Dianna Graveman for her meticulous and creative editing, and the detail editing team at Indigo River for a final review.. And he is especially grateful to his wife, Barbara, for her patience and support during the writing and revisions to this book.

Prologue

ir crews stationed at the Naples field had noticed the straight, narrow clearing extending from the Barron River into the swamp, a linear feature superimposed on a landscape of winding waterways and irregular patches of green. Extending a half mile through a savannah of brown grass growing in shallow water and interrupted by stands of cypress trees, it appeared as a scrape on the tropical landscape, as if a giant hand had drawn a razor across the surface of the Everglades.

The marsh grass that had been cut and pushed aside to produce the clearing consisted of thin, tough stalks growing from the water bottom, rising above the surface in dense patches and branching into elongate leaves at the top. Standing erect in a rowboat, feet level with the water that surrounded the aquatic plants, barely gave one enough elevation to see above the reeds. Small ponds and bayous interspersed in the savannah formed a maze where an interloper could founder a few hundred yards from his intended destination. An observer slogging along the linear clearing would be given a new perspective of the marsh and allowed a glimpse into the disconnected channels, isolated ponds, and puddles of clear water, a perspective similar to that of a passenger in an elevated train looking down alleys and through the windows of apartments.

The center of the cleared path was a board road resembling an elongated wooden dock, stout enough to support a locomotive. Constructed of enormous cypress plants bolted to piles sunk deep into the swampy bottom, it began on the Barron River, upstream from Everglades City. It ended in at an artificial island, several acres in size, created by dredging mud from the swamp floor and filling in a small lagoon. The result was a pad of dirt a few feet above the water in a part of the world where dry land was essentially nonexistent.

To the local inhabitants, the board road appeared to be a project dreamed up by a fool, leading to nowhere. But it had been a source of much needed cash for the trappers, fishermen, and Indians who lived south of Immokalee and seldom encountered anyone who wanted labor in the Everglades. It was difficult to find able-bodied men in the fall of 1942; the draft and the high wages in factories had shifted to produce weapons and airplanes, depleting the southwest Florida workforce. Those who came from higher ground were soon driven away by the hellish nature of working in a tropical swamp. Sightings of alligators and snakes instilled fear even in men who had lived since birth in the woods, the noiseless appearance of reptiles in the surrounding water tapping into a reservoir of dread they were unaware of until arriving in the Everglades. The arrival of mosquitos in the evenings, so numerous they formed a black blanket on an uncovered arm, made existence unbearable after sunset. So the natives of the uninhabited country of the Ten Thousand Islands, capable of surviving and working in the beautiful but harsh country of the southern tip of the Florida peninsula, found a job waiting for them if they wanted it.

The itinerant work force labored on the project until an afternoon in late October, when the crew chief called the men together. The small crowd, cooled by an onshore breeze bringing cooler and drier air to the southwest Florida coast, gathered at the end of the board road.

"We're done," the chief told them. "I've got your final pay envelopes here. We won't be needing you after today. The boat will take us back to town." He passed out the small yellow envelopes, each containing a few bills and some coins, to the assembled crew. Together they boarded the small barge that had been carrying men and supplies to the construction site and rode silently back to Everglades City. A new gray painted pickup truck greeted them at the dock, the driver leaning on the fender with his arms crossed. The crew chief stepped on the dock, threw his duffel bag into the back of the truck, and opened the passenger door. The truck departed immediately, heading north on the road to Naples. Someone later said he had gone back to Louisiana. In any case, he was not seen again in southwest Florida. The men who constructed the board road and the locals who saw him in the hotel where he stayed had repeatedly asked about the purpose of the road since the construction began. He had said nothing, brushing off questions with brusque replies and changing the subject.

No one searched for laborers. The local men went back to scratching a living from the swamps and bays, the board road was abandoned, and the chatter at the general store was a mixture of ridicule and incredulity.

Eddie, one of the trappers who had welcomed a chance to earn some hard cash during the slack demand for furs during wartime, hoped the crazy people might come back and build another road. He had survived alone in the Everglades after his mother left him in a lean-to cabin built on a shell midden and boarded a skiff with the rum runner Josie, telling Eddie she would return in a couple of days.

She never did. Josie had been found alone, shot in the back of the head, floating in his boat a few miles offshore. Some believed he had been robbed of a load and killed for his trouble. Others said he had short-counted the buyer from Miami on the number of bottles of Cuban rum. In either case, it had been fatal to Josie, and Eddie's mother was nowhere to be found. At ten years of age, Eddie could run a trotline for red drum, net mullet, and shoot the birds who landed on the shell midden in search of crabs and sand fleas. He had survived alone for a month on the island before a deputy and a welfare worker came to find a mostly naked, sunburned, scrawny child sitting cross-legged on a piece of driftwood and cleaning a duck.

Several years of living in town with foster parents, interrupted by escapes to his lean-to in the swamp, ended when he was fifteen. No one bothered to follow him the last time he paddled away in his dugout canoe.

At times he appeared in Everglades City to sell mullet, mink pelts, and alligator skins. A few attempts at guiding tourist fisherman had resulted in a lot of fish caught and requests for more bookings, but Eddie usually forgot about an upcoming charter so that after a while no one contacted him. His house on stilts, raised above the high-water mark, was a disagreeable place filled with smoke and drying furs. Women never wanted to visit, and the house was about to fall down. A small still concealed in the nearby swamp provided a clear, almost lethal source of alcohol that left him inebriated most days. The crew chief had fired him twice, the second time when he mistook a spike half-driven through a cypress plank for a snake and chopped it with an axe, shattering the blade. But he had gotten back on after no one else wanted the work. He had spent most of his paychecks on bottled liquor and some meager groceries to supplement his diet of fish, oysters, and small game. Now, with no more prospects of employment, he loaded a pair of traps into his dugout canoe and paddled away from his house.

Chapter 1

Vacations to Florida in February 1943 were uncommon, especially for young men who looked as though they should be serving in Africa or the Pacific. Five years earlier, the train had frequently carried young couples enjoying the perquisites of inherited wealth or jobs on Wall Street to winter vacations in Miami, but that had largely stopped in 1942.

The couple looked like an advertisement for train travel before the war. The young man was in his late twenties or early thirties, about six feet tall with light brown hair, looking physically fit but without the muscular development caused by manual labor. He was dressed in an expensive sweater and gray slacks, and his clothes were too warm for the temperature of the dining car. Steam heat had been welcome when the train left Grand Central, but it seemed difficult to turn off, and the radiators were now maintaining a temperature of about eighty degrees. It was lunchtime, and he was eating a pork chop accompanied by a glass of beer. His companion was a slim, pretty woman of about the same age, dark-haired and six inches shorter. Wearing a light sleeveless dress, she had adapted to the change in climate and looked comfortable as she finished her salad, lifting a glass of white wine.

The train stopped in a small town, identified by block letters that read "WALDO, FLORIDA" on the sign above the wooden platform. About twenty young white men and boys, dressed in worn work clothing and carrying small bags, were lined up waiting for a northbound train. They were being pushed, yelled at, and kicked by two sergeants in Army khakis, who threatened them with severe but unfamiliar consequences if they moved out of the haphazard formation. The young man in the dining car identified them as new inductees into the US Army, sworn in hours ago and now en route to one of the huge basic training bases in Georgia and South Carolina. Some appeared frightened, a few smirked, but most just looked depressed as the reality of military life began to sink in. The sergeants had made it clear they could no longer decide for themselves when to sit, talk, or light a cigarette. Watching them shuffle and twitch, Jerry MacDonald felt familiar pangs of guilt that dampened his mood. A combination of chance and skills had left him in civilian life, while his contemporaries reported to the barracks at Fort Benning and Fort Jackson.

The car lurched as the train began to move, and the group of future soldiers disappeared from view. Jerry and Maria had boarded the train in New York City yesterday evening, settling into a double Pullman berth and missing breakfast to sleep late in their compartment. Lunch in the dining car was the first they had seen of their fellow passengers, and a familiar mix of curiosity, envy, and hostility was apparent in the attention they were receiving. The car swayed as it rounded a curve, and a man wearing the uniform of an Army colonel grabbed the edge of their table to steady himself. He was about forty years old and soft-looking, but with a slat of ribbons over his left breast pocket and a face that exuded authority. Removing his hand from the table and standing erect, he looked down at the young couple.

"Going down to Miami?"

"No," Jerry replied. "We're transferring at the next station and going southwest to Everglades City."

"Oh, going fishing at the Mangrove Lodge?" the officer asked, a touch of derision evident in his manner. He stared at Jerry, accustomed to deference from young men and expecting an answer.

"No," said Jerry. He thought about explaining why they were there, but he didn't like the man or the interruption to their lunch, and it was none of his business anyway. Maria looked at the colonel and smiled, causing him to nod and move on.

"I always wondered what Florida looked like," she said. "I thought there were palm trees and beaches."

Jerry looked out the window at the flat landscape, clumps of green palmetto bushes about four feet high dotting a prairie of brush. It didn't look the least bit tropical. He knew they had traveled through the piedmont of North and South Carolina during the night, and he had awakened as the train passed west of the sea islands of Georgia. "There's a lot of variation in the state. I don't think this is what we'll see in the Everglades."

In normal times they would have purchased a car and driven to Florida, but with gas rationing and tire shortages, even Pride Oil Company could not guarantee their trip would be made without incident. Rail service was reliable, Maria seemed to be enjoying the ride, and at least there was a dining car. As they crossed the state line into Florida, Jerry relaxed, feeling more certain that he was going to eventually arrive in the small town of Everglades City, a village on the Gulf Coast south of Naples.

SUNNILAND

In 1940 their journey would have been a paid-for semi-vacation. Living in a spacious apartment in Queens, the couple was thoroughly immersed in the life of New York City. Eating picnic lunches from Chinese, Italian, and Jewish restaurants in Central Park, going to the theatre, and searching for fashionable clothes at cut-rate prices had become part of their routine. They had originally come from two different worlds, and their friends were an eclectic mix of lifelong city dwellers and transplants who had come to work in the tall buildings that housed the headquarters of giant companies. They awoke early and read the newspaper while eating breakfast in the kitchen with one small window that overlooked the busy avenue. But for two years, their morning ritual of reading the New York Times had been dominated by descriptions of British and American forces being driven back by German and Japanese troops. The conquest of Guadalcanal and the Allied invasion of Africa were two of the few bright spots in the dreary recitation.

Their trip had been the result of a command, not offered as an option, but Jerry knew that it was a worthwhile endeavor. A visit to a Navy recruiting office had resulted in the offer of a commission last year. Serving at sea would be a welcome change from the dusty plains he had grown up in and appealed to his wanderlust. But Pride Oil had him declared essential to the wartime effort and persuaded him to stay in New York City.

"There are a lot of people who can serve in the Navy. But a ship can't go anywhere without oil. If this goes on more than a year, the refineries will start having shortages. We need you here—half of our geology staff has already left," Mike Woods, the Vice President of Exploration, had told him.

Jerry had reluctantly agreed and started work on the South Florida prospect, examining records from older, shallow wells and studying the geology of the Florida peninsula. Well paid, doing interesting work, and living in the most interesting city in the world with Maria, he felt life had treated him well. But he still wondered if he was doing the right thing when he saw the headlines displayed on the back walls of the newsstands, all describing one battle or another across the globe. His classmates from the small high school he had attended, as well as contemporaries at OU, were serving in the Navy and the Army and the Marine Corps. *They'll have some stories to tell after the war,* he sometimes thought. As the train gained speed across the northern Florida landscape, his mind drifted across the events that had led to this South Florida expedition.

His life, his job, and his new marriage had all been moving along a predictable path until he was summoned to the thirty-ninth floor at Pride Oil one morning. The secretary, Ellen, smiled and flirted with him while he waited outside; he had dated her for a while before marrying Maria. A graduate of Katherine Gibbs, Ellen was originally from a small town in Georgia. Her family had saved money to educate her, proudly waving goodbye when she boarded the train to New York City after graduating from high school in 1936. Pretty, smart, and hardworking, she had started in the typing pool at Pride Oil, spending long days pounding the keyboard of manual Royal typewriters, transcribing the words and scribbles of the executives and the technical staff into letters and reports. It was hard work but fun, and the after-work hours were often occupied by nights out with the other girls and the young accountants, scientists, and engineers who brought their manuscripts to the typing pool.

Ellen didn't realize how much the camaraderie meant to her until the pool supervisor, a middle-aged woman who had begun as a stenographer in the same place, told her one afternoon that she had been selected as an assistant secretary to Mr. Woods. It meant a promotion, a nice raise, and a polished desk on the top floor of the

Pride office tower. But she was isolated, spending most days alone, and when the young men showed up to see the vice president, they were too nervous and intent on making a good impression to flirt or ask her out. Ellen liked her job and wanted to keep working, but she also wanted to meet someone who would ask her to marry and start a family. She had thought that might be Jerry MacDonald, but he stopped their budding relationship when he met an Italian girl named Maria on the subway. Ellen had been invited to the wedding, and she liked Maria. But it was disheartening that Jerry had picked a dark-haired beauty with an Italian accent, lacking in the social graces Ellen had painstakingly learned at Katherine Gibbs, over her.

Now she looked up as the door opened to the corner office, a room isolated from the noise and activity of the rest of the thirty-ninth floor, revealing the perks of higher-executive rank. The plush carpet, a rich brown color, had been replaced last year although it was barely worn. The walls were a light beige, and a painting Jerry knew cost a year of his salary hung on the wall. A polished wooden desk occupied the back half of the room. Tall windows on two sides looked down the island of Manhattan toward the Statue of Liberty, and three mahogany doors occupied the third wall. One concealed a closet, one led to a private conference room, and one was a private bathroom, which spared the vice president the necessity of walking down the hall with his male subordinates.

Inviting him in, Mike Woods motioned to the conference room. He watched Jerry take a seat at the side of the table. The questions were abrupt but anticipated.

"Did we get a log yet on the Cornucopia prospect well?"

"Yes, we ran an E log yesterday. It looks like we have a dry hole—only about a tenth of an ohm meter. But we did find a permeable sand on the SP; we need to look at drilling updip."

"I understand we have finished the location on the Sunniland well. When do we spud?" Woods asked.

"Should be in a couple of weeks."

"Any change in the bottom hole location from the gravity survey?"

"Yes, it looks like the crest of the reef may be about five hundred yards north of where we originally mapped it. But we can still penetrate any oil column from the current surface location," said Jerry.

"Who is the wellsite geologist?"

"It was going to be Drew. But he's been ordered to report for his draft physical this week and may not be available. I'm looking for someone who we can be sure will be on site all the way down.

I want you to go." Woods said. " We've had a hell of a time getting this prospect together. When can you leave?"

"I'm not really a well-site geologist, as you know. I put together the regional stratigraphy and mapped the top of the Sunniland. But I've never sat a well."

"Time you learned. At least you know what a wellhead looks like. Make some arrangements and let Ellen know when you are leaving. Keep me informed." The vice president stood up, indicating the discussion was over.

Mike Woods had risen to his position through the ranks, starting as a geophysicist conducting gravity and seismic surveys in remote parts of the world. Smart, profane, direct, and expecting respect, he didn't fit the profile of the polished Ivy League graduates who inhabited most of the corner offices in Pride's Manhattan neighborhood. Most of the staff thought he would eventually take over when Mr. Pride retired.

Jerry left and paused in the outer office at Ellen's desk. "Can you help make me some arrangements to go to Florida? I've never been there."

"Sure. Is Maria going?"

"Don't know. I'll ask her. But I don't think so. Why is this well so important all of a sudden?"

"Mr. Pride got on him about the Florida prospect yesterday. Someone from Washington came by, and I guess the country really needs more oil for the war. So he told Mike to do whatever it takes to make sure this well gets down."

Finishing his lunch in the dining car, Jerry saw a landscape of small, isolated lakes interspersed with wooded areas and hills. They were passing south of the university town of Gainesville and were now headed almost directly down the center of the state. Occasional cuts in the hills where rock had been blasted away to create a level bed for the railway showed white rock with fragments of shells. Contemplating the geology that flashed by at sixty miles per hour distracted Jerry from his reverie.

Oil had not been discovered in the state of Florida, but the geology was similar to West Texas, and a local landowner and politician, Barron Collier, had been advocating more drilling for years. Pride Oil had been awarded some hard-to-get leases, built a location, and was ready to start drilling. Seismic and gravity data showed the potential for some reefs similar to those found in the Texas Hill country near San Antonio. The next step was to drill a well to eleven thousand feet and find out what was there.

Chapter 2

As the sun rose over the marsh and the small town of Houma, Joe watched the derrick of the LT-105 drilling rig slide onto an ocean-going barge. They had finished the well, a dry hole, a week before and rigged down for transport. Black paint stained with rust marked the sides of the flat steel rectangular hull that was wedged hard against the dock with steel cable, decked over with nonskid steel interrupted by dogged down hatches. The bow was an inverse ramp, sloping up from the water to a blunt nose a few feet thick at the front of the vessel. Wooden rollers supported the skeleton of the derrick, a matrix of steel beams reinforced by smaller members crossing at odd angles from one side to the other. Erect and in place, it had looked like a radio tower or the column of a suspension bridge. Lying flat on the deck of the barge, it resembled a section of a railroad trestle. Auxiliary equipment, the tanks, mud pumps, shale shaker, and other components were already on the barge. The derrick was being carefully winched across the gap between the barge and the dock, its length almost greater than the deck.

SUNNILAND

"Hold!" A roughneck in black overalls signaled that the derrick was in position, running from bow to stern on the barge, making passage around it difficult. Two men dressed in stained work clothes rolled a gas cylinder connected to a welding torch near the base of the derrick. Pulling down the almost black welding shade over his face, the larger man lit the torch, holding a welding rod in the other hand. Bending over near one of the reinforced corners of the derrick, he touched the flame to the steel, causing a flurry of sparks and creating a single iron unit of the derrick and the deck. He moved toward the bow and repeated the process until the two steel structures had been welded together at twenty different points.

The operation had been performed by the crew many times before, although usually on a small inland barge intended to move the equipment to a nearby location. But this time a contract had been signed to move the rig to Florida and drill a wildcat well for Pride Oil Company. A few dry holes had been drilled in the area where they were headed, but no discoveries had been made. Trucks loaded with drill pipe, spares, and a variety of bits were backed up to the dock—they would not be in oilfield country where they were going. Anything not carried on the barge would have to come from the warehouse in Oklahoma—a two-day trip by rail.

Joe was dressed in dirty red overalls, an average-sized man with a face worn by years of exposure to sun and harsh climates at drilling locations around the world. He had never been to Florida and didn't really care to go, but he went with the rig and that was where it was headed. His position was tool pusher, responsible for the daily operations of the rig. He had made his way from the rig floor to the derrick, and then to his first chance several years ago to be the man in charge. Joe intended to make sure the rig got to Florida and drilled the well that Pride wanted. Whether it found oil or not was beyond his control; he wasn't a geologist. Getting the hole down to the right depth in the right place was what the LT company and Pride Oil expected of him. The seemingly impossible task—drilling a ten-inch hole to a depth of two miles and hitting a target a few hundred feet in diameter—was something he knew how to do. The complexities of guiding the well, controlling the pressure, and keeping the hole open were all problems with possible solutions. The unknowns were the pressures and the kind of rocks he would encounter. A wrong decision or a moment of unawareness could lead to a loss of the wellbore, with potentially fatal consequences for the rig crew.

This hasn't been a bad little town, he thought, looking down the road covered with white shells toward the village of Houma. *Wish I could have brought Cindy down to see it.*

Once married to a woman who took up with a friend on one of his long absences, Joe had been leading the single life of military men, sea captains, long haul truckers, and others whose lives were spent on the frontiers of the earth, locations that had few accommodations and less entertainment for young women. Visits back to the LT headquarters in Oklahoma were brief, and not conducive to forming friendships or romantic relationships. Not expecting or wanting to marry again nor seek emotional involvement with a woman, Joe resigned himself to a solitary existence he expected to last.

But his life changed in the late fall of 1938. He had been kneeling on the floor of a Ponca City hardware store, searching for sixteen-gauge shotgun shells on a lower shelf. Pulling boxes off the shelf in the dim light to better read the labels, he noticed a pair of small feet in black low-heeled shoes, toes touching the pile of boxes he had placed on the floor. Raising his eyes, he perceived a pretty woman with blonde hair (which he reckoned was dyed because she had dark brown eyes), cut short around her small face, looking at him and smiling. She watched him shift his gaze back to the boxes of shotgun shells.

"Going quail hunting?" she asked.

"Oh. Thought I might be in your way. I'll put back the ones I don't buy. I guess so. Friend of mine can get us on some land around here and has a dog. We ride along until we see a quail, then let the dog chase it up."

"I've done that," she replied. "My brother has a truck with a seat up high behind the cab. I like riding up there on a fall morning and looking across the prairie. Don't like eating quail too much, though. Are you new around here?"

"I live most of the time on a rig. But when I'm not, I have family in Oklahoma and I work for LT; they have their office here. Don't own any property, but thinking about buying some for when I'm here. Maybe a small farm." Not used to talking to pretty women, Joe wanted the conversation to continue but expected her to say "Have a good morning" and walk on.

"My name's Cindy," she said instead. "I've spent most of my life here in Ponca City. What's yours?"

"Joe."

"Well, Joe, I usually have some coffee across the street about now," she said. "Want to join me?"

Cindy still lived in Ponca City, and Joe didn't question what she did when he was in the field drilling wells. He always gave her at least a few days' notice when he was going to return, and he always found her single, living alone, and welcoming him to stay with her until he moved on to a new part of the world. Joe thought that one day he might get an office job with LT so he could stay in Ponca City and make something permanent with Cindy. But it hadn't happened yet.

Now he looked around for the rest of his crew, down to four men. Billy had been drafted last week, and Rick had left for Oklahoma, declining to go to a snake-and-gator-infested place like Florida. That didn't make sense to Joe, since the swamp around Houma had at least as many snakes and gators as he expected in Florida, but the roughneck had had enough. He still had his derrick man, Jacque, plus Bobby and two others, but he would need to recruit and train a new floorhand when they got to Florida. The new man, whoever he was going to be, could look forward to being called the "worm" by the crew with drilling experience, an expression that came from the belief that there is nothing lower than a worm. It was an oilfield tradition around the country. Joe would also have to find a motorman to keep the diesel engine running, but the company had promised to send someone from Oklahoma to meet the rig. If they didn't, there were lots of ranches near the well location that should have some men familiar with farm equipment who could be hired. Unless they were all in the Army or the Marines.

Crack! The sound of the thirty-caliber rifle startled him and made him put his left boot in a puddle of brown water.

"What the hell are you shooting at?" he asked Jacque, who was pointing the weapon at a small area of open water next to the barge. The shooter was Cajun French, descended from the settlers who had been forcibly removed from Nova Scotia by the British and had eventually arrived in the French possession of Louisiana. His ancestors had lived in the swamps west of New Orleans all his life, a place not very different from the Everglades. Jacque had been born to a mother who did not speak English, growing up in a village that was entirely French-speaking.

"Muskrat. The pelt is worth fifty cents."

"Good luck with that. You just spent a nickel on the cartridge. Stop shooting until we get the derrick welded down. We have a lot of water to cross."

"This place is a gold mine. You never see anything but a cow or a twister when drilling in Oklahoma. I've already got twenty pelts in the boat."

"Well, get them off and cash them in, because we're leaving in about two hours."

Jacque worked the bolt on the rifle, ejecting the empty casing, and put the gun in the drilling trailer. Stepping into a pirogue, he paddled off to the general store with his pelts. "Back in about an hour."

"Make sure you're sober. We still have to secure these sacks of cement before we get to open water. And stay out of the Dreamers Bar. The last time you were there you got your head thumped pretty good."

Joe returned his attention to the final loading of the drilling supplies, inspecting the steel cables that lashed the equipment to the deck. It was past noon when a large tug, bearing the unromantic name of Mr. John, pushed the barge down the bayou toward the open water. Looking out the window of the drill shack, a drilling trailer that was attached to the rig floor on location but that now was loaded at the aft end of the barge, Joe saw a flat expanse of grass extending toward the horizon in every direction. Small winding creeks broke off from the main bayou they were navigating and led into the marsh. Rounding a bend, they startled ducks in a small open pond that flushed upward with a sound that reminded them of pheasants at home but from hundreds of birds instead of ten. As they moved south, the color of the water changed from brown to green as the incoming tide moved the fresh water back. Sightings of alligators were replaced by schools of mullet jumping in open bays, and a pair of porpoises escorted the vessels. Approaching the pass to the Gulf, they could see sticks marking the channel but no numbers indicating what they might mean. The tug captain seemed to know, and he worked his way through a channel deep enough for a seagoing vessel. Clearing some rock jetties, they encountered a four foot swell that broke against the flat bow of the barge. It was enough to soak everyone on board.

"Captain, we want to move to the tug."

"That will be fine. Welcome aboard."

The rig crew jumped the gap between the stern of the barge and the tugboat, relieved to take shelter in a dryer place. The cabin of the tug reflected an ocean going vessel with steel doors, reverse-angled windshield, and a watertight pilothouse—well suited to the sea conditions they would encounter on the way to the town of Everglades City, located at the southern tip of the Florida peninsula.

Chapter 3

C hanging trains at the small town of Orlando, the MacDonalds traversed the state of Florida north of the huge Lake Okeechobee. The train had passed the ranches of the Lykes brothers and other cattle barons, and the cows grazing on the subtropical savannahs reminded Jerry of the country near the huge King Ranch south of Corpus Christi. The people they saw working the fields and orange groves, walking the roadways, and idling near the small stations included descendants of former slaves, Seminole Indians, cowboys, and brown-skinned men and women who spoke a language Maria guessed to be Spanish. She had grown quiet as they left the glitz of the East Coast, surprised by the wilderness they encountered and the diversity of the population.

Maria had been delighted by Jerry's deferment and the prospect of his spending the wartime years in New York City. She had grown up in Queens, the third child in a large, noisy, quarreling Italian family, the niece of a bar owner whose establishment was frequented by hard men and small-time hoodlums. Located on a nondescript street, smoke-filled and noisy, the floor littered with newspapers and horse-racing sheets, the place made enough money to support Maria's family through the Depression. Maria remembered the one window. Filmed with cigarette smoke and the exhaled breath of thousands of customers, it was covered with snow and ice in the winter and became a translucent square of light during the spring rains. On a clear afternoon, it looked across the street to a dry cleaning establishment with "DRYCLE NING" outlined in light bulbs on a homemade sign in the window. Her mother had often brought her to the establishment as a child, saying, "We're going to go visit Uncle Ignatius's place." The adults let her play the slot machine while some aspect of the family business was discussed in low but passionate Italian. The rough men sitting by themselves on stools, drinking and arguing, mostly treated her with affection as one would a member of a larger family. She learned that some were cousins, related to her in some indistinct way.

Afternoons during her high school years were spent working in the bar, learning to make drinks and push away rude or lecherous drunks. As she grew older she found that most unwelcome encounters could be resolved with humor and an occasional slap, but when things got out of hand, a glance at one of her cousins resulted in the miscreant receiving a thump on the head and a toss out of the door. Occasionally Maria went out with customers who were often destined for prison before reaching thirty, but she found no one she wanted to become involved with in a permanent way. Smart, pretty, and tough, she was confident she could take care of herself. Her life had good moments and bad. She couldn't complain, but she hoped there was going to be more in life than what she had experienced so far.

Wednesday afternoons were time off, and she often took the subway into Manhattan to see a different world. Standing on a crowded train, grasping an overhead strap with three other people, she sensed the good-looking young man next to her trying to give her some space, not typical behavior of most men standing next to a young, pretty woman on the train. She smiled, and that was enough to start a conversation, including a mention of her role in her family's saloon business.

The encounter made her feel good about the day, a bright spot in her week. Not expecting anything to come of it, Maria was surprised to see the young man walk into the bar the following day. Six months later, the two were married. Her family's first reaction had been passionate opposition to her marrying someone who spoke no Italian and who was more used to potatoes than pasta, but eventually they grudgingly accepted him, especially after learning he was Catholic. He ignored the shady nature of the family business, formed tenuous friendships with her cousins, and convinced her parents he would take care of her.

The young couple's arrival in Everglades City had been uneventful. The town was quiet, with a few rich tourists visiting the Mangrove Lodge, but otherwise left to the locals in the summer heat. Located on higher ground created by a natural levee of the Barron River, the town subsisted on fishing, both commercial and by the tourists who came from around the world, drawn by the phenomenal inshore fisheries. Separated from the open waters of the Gulf of Mexico by a network of islands and bars, the town was a fragile plot of civilization amidst the untouched wilderness of the Everglades. Appropriately named, Riverside Drive paralleled the water, the rows of building interrupted by side streets running back into a small village. The houses, hotels, and restaurants were built on stilts, raised several feet above the ground to avoid inundation from the periodic visits of hurricanes and tropical storms. Walking or driving down Riverside Drive afforded a view across the river to a dense forest of mangrove trees, shorter than the cypress found further inland, with branches of dense green leaves supported by a network of roots reaching down into the salty water.

They watched their luggage being placed on the platform after the train had pulled into the station. The platform had a shingled roof supported by white timber posts, which branched out into roof beams, allowing the shelter to be supported with only a single line of columns set back from the tracks. The open platform led to a small office and screened waiting room with wooden benches. Jerry stepped past the piled luggage and looked around. "Guess there aren't any taxis here. Let me see if I can get some help."

In the office he found an elderly man behind the ticket window. "Is there anyone here who can help us get our luggage to the hotel?"

"Are you Mr. MacDonald? That guy over there is waiting for you," the clerk said, pointing to a black man standing outside the waiting room.

Jerry turned and called to him. "Are you supposed to meet a Jerry MacDonald?"

"Yessir. The Turner Inn sent me. I'm the bellhop. I'll help you get your bags to the hotel."

"Thanks. This is my wife, Maria."

"Hello, ma'am," the bellhop said.

"Glad to meet you," Maria replied. "Thanks for helping us. What shall we call you?"

"Folks call me Rufe." He was careful not to look directly at her face.

Placing their bags in a wheelbarrow-like contrivance, Rufe led them down the sidewalk, saying, "Hope you don't mind walking, sir. It's only a couple of blocks."

"That will be fine," Jerry said with a smile. "We've been sitting on the train for the last twelve hours."

The Turner Inn was located on Riverside Drive, upstream from the Mangrove Lodge, on a corner lot. A large, white clapboard building, surrounded by a deep porch that blocked direct sunlight from coming through the high windows of the lobby, it was separated from the street by landscaped gardens and grass.

"Can't believe we're seeing green grass in February," Maria said. "Now I know we're in Florida."

A lobby with walls of dark cypress panels contained a desk and stuffed furniture. An open door displayed a barroom with polished glasses and bottles in front of a mirror, and beyond that a dining room with white table cloths.

A young woman greeted them. "Thanks, Rufe," she said to the bellhop. Turning to the couple she said, "Mr. and Mrs. MacDonald?"

"That's us," Jerry replied. "I see Pride Oil let you know we were coming."

"Yes, we have a room overlooking the river for you. I also have a telegram for you. We understand you will be staying for an indefinite period of time?"

"That's correct," Jerry said. "We're going to be drilling a well east of here. I'll be here until it's finished."

"We're glad to have you," the woman replied. "We don't usually have anyone stay for more than a few days. Please let me know if you need anything."

Rufe opened the door to their room on the second floor, placing the luggage on a stand and unlocking the shutters and a door to the second floor balcony. Most of the space was occupied by a double bed with a canopy, attached to netting descending to the mattress.

"What's the netting for?" Maria wondered aloud.

"Sometimes mosquitos get in through the screens or from upstairs. If they do, you can still sleep without being bitten," Rufe offered.

31

The room had a hardwood floor partially covered with rugs, a dark wood dresser and lamps flanking the bed, and an armchair in the corner. Although clean and well kept, Maria imagined it closing in on her after a few weeks. She watched Jerry give Rufe a quarter, putting it in his hand and thanking him for his help. The bellhop smiled and nodded, backing out of the room with a brief word of thanks.

His careful attitude, calculated not to offend them in any way possible, made her recall the last few days of her first trip to the South. More woods and open country than she had ever imagined. Miles of track with trees and brush only feet from the train, trimmed by the daily passage of the locomotive, dense woods laced with green vines that looked like a wall. Rivers, mostly muddy, but some that were amazingly clear had punctuated their passage. Open fields with shacks she could not believe were habitable lined the track, occupied by black and white families. Although both races were obviously living in poverty, the clothes of black families consisted of moldy cloth rotting into rags, and if wealth was measured by chickens, dogs, and an occasional mule, white people had a greater share.

Maria knew black Americans were lowly regarded and poorly treated everywhere, especially south of Washington, but she had had little contact with any black man or woman in her New York City life. The Italian immigrants who had surrounded her since birth were close-knit and inward looking, having no use for anyone, especially the Irish. Black people were everywhere, especially in Harlem, but rarely spoken to unless with an order. But their right to exist in the city was not challenged, and they uneasily commingled with the other races and nationalities in the polyglot community of 1930s New York City. So she had been unprepared for her first encounter with the rigid segregation of the post-Confederate south when the train paused for fuel and water at a stop in Virginia.

The station attendant had waved her toward the end of the waiting room in response to her inquiry, where she saw three doors labeled Men, Women, and Colored. The door to the bathroom marked Colored was open, hanging crookedly from a broken hinge. The sink hung from the wall, clearly not functional, and the toilet was stopped up. A black woman with a young boy pointed him inside, then stood in the broken doorway to shield him as he urinated into the brown stained toilet. Obviously no white person was ever going to clean the facility, and she supposed the black cleaning crew was usually given higher priorities, like waxing the waiting room floor. Maria entered the room marked Women, noticing it wasn't as well kept as one might expect in the subway, which wasn't much, but usable. The experience made a deep impression on her, the reality compared to the abstractions of newspaper reports causing her to feel disoriented, like when she had first seen two of her cousins beat a man in the street outside the bar. She was tough, not a bleeding heart, proud that she could take care of herself. But the rigid, legally enforced segregation of the South had depressed and upset her.

Returning her attention now to their new residence for the next three months, she said to Jerry, "Let's go down to the restaurant and get something to eat. It's late, and I'm hungry."

They sat at a table near the window and watched the cars, horses, mule-drawn wagons, and pedestrians push carts on Riverside Drive. The river water was cool in February and didn't appear to be flowing in either direction. A shrimp boat pulled into the seafood plant dock with nets suspended from vertical masts. Three deckhands relaxed as the captain maneuvered the boat parallel to the wooden pilings. No one seemed to be in a particular hurry, but the land and the water travelers appeared to have some purpose in their movements, a trait lacking in the men and women sitting on benches or front steps.

SUNNILAND

Jerry had promised Maria a trip to Fort Myers and a boat ride up the Withlacoochee River after they arrived, anticipating a few days of leisure before the rig arrived from Louisiana. The telegram handed to him at the desk on their arrival, however, communicated instructions to be at the harbor in Everglades City the next morning. He was to inspect the drilling location before the rig-carrying barge arrived. Evidently, the passage across the Gulf had gone well and they were ahead of schedule. The rig was contracted by the day, and idle time, as always, was to be absolutely avoided.

Dressed for the first time since they had stopped traveling in newly laundered clothes, Maria had been anxious to see something of the relatively large city of Fort Myers, the largest metropolis south of Tampa on the west coast of Florida.

"I'll find something else to do tomorrow, don't worry," she said, concealing her disappointment at having their outing canceled.

"You might go by the downtown square and see what kind of restaurants they have here. And find a bank where we can open an account. We'll need some local checks that people will cash. And see if there is a Catholic church."

"I'll do that. I can't believe we are in Florida. I've heard about it since I was four years old, but I never thought I'd be here. Tell me again why Edison and Ford moved here instead of to Palm Beach."

"Not sure. Edison came first and then convinced Ford to move in next door. Maybe they didn't like the people in Palm Beach. There is more of a Midwest flavor here—most of Palm Beach is from the northeast, you know, New York and New England neighborhoods, because that's the way Flagler built the railroad."

"I'm glad I'm here with you," she said. "Thanks for bringing me. We should be together at this point in our lives. There will be times when we can't be together, and we will wonder why we didn't do things when we could."

Jerry kissed her and then stared at the river as she excused herself and walked to the restroom. A newspaper article pinned to the back wall of the bar caught his attention. The article had been published in June 1942 and described the capture of eight German saboteurs. They had landed by rubber rafts from two German U-boats, the U-202 sending four ashore on Long Island, and the U-201 landing the other four at Ponte Vedra, Florida, just south of Jacksonville. All eight had lived in the United States for years, speaking impeccable English and appearing to be at home in America. After burying explosives and other gear in the sand, they departed for destinations around the country, planning to return and use the bombs to blow up rail yards, canals, and bridges. Their goal was to cripple the US transportation system and spread havoc and fear among the populace. Their leader had defected to the FBI and provided information to round up the others. Tried as spies and sentenced to death, six had been electrocuted in short order. The other two were imprisoned. The article had clearly caught the attention of one of the employees of the hotel. Jerry was familiar with the story, which had been extensively reported in the *New York Times* the year before. He wondered why it had seemed noteworthy to a bartender in Everglades City.

Chapter 4

The telegram from Mike Woods stated that someone named Eddie would meet Jerry in Everglades City and show him the way—there was no way he could find the well location on his own. He found Eddie the next morning by walking into the center of the small town. There wasn't much going on; a few men were sitting on the steps of a general store and not doing much of anything.

"Anybody here named Eddie?" Jerry asked as he approached the group.

"He's over at the dock working on his boat," said a deeply tanned man dressed in khaki work clothes and a straw hat.

"How do I find the dock?"

"Well, you might try over there by the water." This brought a series of soft chuckles from the group—damn tourist Yankees.

Looking west, he saw the wooden dock bordering the riverfront, the pilings rising to the height of a man's head above the decking to provide a place to secure lines from the boats tied alongside. There were a number of small wooden skiffs, a few with inboard engines and some with sails, but most with outboard motors. A man on board a larger skiff at the end tinkered with the fuel line of a single-cylinder inboard engine. He was thin and about thirty years old, six feet tall, with thick brown hair and sideburns. His appearance reflected the lives of those who were often called "poor white trash" in the South: two missing teeth, a scar running down his left arm, skin like that of an old man from being burned repeatedly by the subtropic sun, and bloodshot eyes. He did seem to know what he was doing with the motor, although Jerry wondered about the wisdom of the cigarette in the corner of his mouth, about a foot from the disconnected fuel line. The smell of gas was evident six feet away on the dock.

"You Eddie?"

"Who wants to know?"

"I'm Jerry. I understand you can show me the drilling location."

"Show you the what?"

"The drilling location. Where Pride Oil is going to drill the well."

"Never heard of that. "

"There would be a board road to it, and a set of pilings at the end."

"Oh. That's what that is for. We wondered why anyone would build a road to nowhere. Hold this fuel line while I get the water out, and we'll get started."

Handing Jerry one end of the rubber fuel line, Eddie put the fitting that attached to the motor in his mouth and blew hard. The effort dislodged a clog of what looked like tar, allowing the upstream gasoline and water to be ejected through the length of the hose and spray Jerry with the mixture. He quickly moved it away from his face, but not before it had thoroughly wet his shirt.

"That'll get it," Eddie stated with satisfaction, unperturbed by the sight of Jerry splashing water from a bucket on to his face and clothes, washing away most but not all of the gasoline.

Well, I guess that's one way to get a motor started, Jerry thought. Smelling of gasoline, he sat in the front of the skiff as Eddie steered it through the twisting channels of the mangrove forest. The water was amazing clear; he could see the bottom at fifteen feet.

As they went inland, the mangroves gave way to cypress trees, and the forest gave way to open grass. Entering a meandering bend, Eddie stopped the engine and let the skiff drift to a newly constructed wooden dock, covered with mud, and leading to a board road that stretched further into the swamp for about a half mile. Holding a line as he stepped onto the dock, he looped the rope around a piling. "Here we are," he said. "Now we have to walk."

The planks of the board road were wet, slimy, and covered with mud and weeds, a condition caused by an unseasonal tropical low that had produced a surge of two feet in the coastal Everglades. Rising higher than the cypress boards, the water had deposited a layer of debris as it receded to normal levels. The leaves of the marsh grass, usually a mixture of green and brown tones, appeared to be covered with gray paint. It gave the swamp a diseased look, as if everything had suddenly died of an unknown cause. A heavy rain would wash the sediment off the grass and the board road, but none had fallen since the high water, so the two men were forced to carefully move along the slippery planks, sliding their feet rather than walking in a normal manner. Jerry slipped and grabbed onto Eddie, who fell forward as his feet slipped, causing Jerry to bruise his hip as he also landed sideways on the hard surface.

"Sorry about that," Jerry said.

"S'okay. All the docks are like this right now."

"Let's get on to the location."

They trudged cautiously along, trying to stay upright, arriving at the cleared pad that marked the end of the road. Only a few months in the tropics had resulted in weeds that reached to mid-thigh, and Jerry saw an alligator sunning on the warm ground. He had seen a couple from the train window as it passed through the swampland, safely separated from him by iron metal and glass. This one was lying motionless, seemingly unaware of the presence of the two humans. About ten feet long, it had knobby scales along its back and tail, a blunt nose that exposed large teeth, and eyes that were covered with opaque lids. Unrestricted by any barriers, there was nothing to prevent it from attacking the two men.

Jerry had heard tales of the crocodiles of Africa and Australia, vicious and aggressive creatures that not only attacked large animals in the water, but would pursue them onto land. Attacks on humans were not unheard of, especially in shallow water. Some of the stories he had heard about alligators were that they were much less aggressive, and it was safe to be near them, even in the water. But some raconteurs who had boarded their train in Orlando, glad to have the chance to scare the living hell out of a Yankee, had told tales of alligators that got used to human flesh and preferred it to fish and small animals. They described the animals invading the cabins of swamp dwellers and sinking small boats with a swipe of a powerful tale. Not sure what to believe, Jerry backpedaled quickly at the sight of the creature, wondering if he could outrun it if it followed him onto the board road.

Eddie laughed. "That won't bother us. It's just sleeping in the sun. Just don't step on it."

"It won't attack us?"

"If you were in the water at night, it might. Or if you were hurt and couldn't move. Or if it felt you were going to hurt it. But it won't chase you on land in the middle of the day."

"Probably wouldn't have much trouble outrunning it anyhow," said Jerry. "It looks like it couldn't outrun a turtle with those short legs."

"An alligator can outrun a horse for the first forty yards," Eddie said as they walked around it. Disturbed by the sense of a nearby large animal, the reptile slithered off the dry land of the drill site into the neighboring canal.

Persuaded, Jerry walked forward, stepping off the end of the road and onto the boggy soil of the filled clearing. Looking around the future site of an oil well, located precisely where it was because of the map he had drawn, Jerry imagined the place during the Cretaceous period, when waves from the open Gulf had crashed on reefs built by giant clams. On dry land in other parts of the world, dinosaurs and giant ferns had lived and flourished until a meteor fell onto the Yucatan peninsula and brought on a catastrophic winter. The geology of the Florida peninsula was different than anywhere else on the Gulf Coast, resembling that of the nearby Bahamas. For millions of years, coral, clams, snails, worms, and shrimplike creatures had thrived in crystal clear water, living and dying, leaving crystalline shell material behind to accumulate in the shallow water. As the seafloor sank, a consequence of the perpetual movement of the earth's crust, new organisms took over, leaving more remains on the substrate formed by their predecessors. Sea water and then fresh water flowed through the layers of broken shell, dissolving and precipitating crystals of calcite, the mineral that formed the stalactites found in the caves of northern Florida. The result was a layer of the rock called limestone, thousands of feet in thickness, that resulted from shells and coral fragments transformed to hard rock. As the sediment was buried, higher temperatures resulted in the slimy remains of dead algae being cooked into crude oil. Ancient reefs, mounds rising above the sea floor and now buried miles below the surface, were especially attractive places for the crude to accumulate, searched for by the probing bits of the oil drillers.

Jerry had studied and mapped the rocks two miles deep in the earth, and recommended that the Pride Oil Company drill down to the reef, hoping they would find it full of oil. He had often thought about what the landscape above the reef would look like, but this patch of muddy, weedy, snake-infested grass was not what he had envisioned. It didn't make any difference what it looked like on the surface, but it would have to be cleared for the rig to move on and commence with drilling a well.

"Can you get some men to cut these weeds and stake out the outer edges of the location?" he asked Eddie.

"Of the what?"

"The dry part that has been filled in here. That's where the rig will set up. We call it the location. We need it cleared and marked when the barge gets here with the rig so they know what they are doing when they bring it onshore."

"I guess so. When do you need it?"

"The rig left Houma last Saturday. They should be here in two or three more days."

"OK. I'll see if I can find a couple of men and get it done tomorrow," Eddie replied.

Taking a final look around, Jerry started carefully walking back to the boat landing. He should have a couple of days to look around and get settled before the rig arrived.

Chapter 5

Two days later, a blunt-nosed steel barge edged up the channel of the Barron River, wider than the open water and knocking down vegetation on both banks. Pushed by an oceangoing tug larger than usually seen this far inland, the water turned a muddy brown behind the churning propeller, and sting rays, flounder, crabs, and shrimp floated to the surface as they were washed from the channel floor. Eddie stood on the open bridge of the tug next to Joe, who was looking suspiciously at the cypress dock now separated from the barge by a few feet of open water.

"How deep are the pilings on that thing?" he asked Eddie, lighting another Lucky Strike. The voyage across the Gulf had been uneventful but frightening. No weather or mechanical problems, but they had seen the distant fire of a burning tanker, the victim of a U-boat torpedo. Nothing to do but put on life preservers and proceed, hoping they would not be worth pursuing. With the derrick lowered, the barge resembled a hundred others that could have been carrying any kind of coastal merchandise. Either the U-boats were busy elsewhere or had better targets in mind. Now they were less than ten feet from the end of the journey, and Joe didn't want to unload the rig derrick on a collapsing dock.

"They go down about ten feet. We washed them down as far as they would go." Eddie had been glad to get a day's work guiding the barge from the open water of the Gulf into the swamp. The area between the Gulf and the mouth of the Barron River was known as the Ten Thousand Islands—winding channels through mangroves, all looking alike and few leading anywhere but to small lagoons. The barge was approaching the dock at dusk, and the greatest risk to survival in the Everglades was beginning to materialize as clouds of mosquitos descended on the crew. Joe's bare arm was black with feeding insects. Taking a breath with his open mouth was impossible. Quickly retreating to the pilothouse of the tug and slamming shut the steel doors, the men swatted the mosquitos that had invaded the space. Eddie had expected the onslaught and wore long sleeves and pants, coating his hands and face with mud and grease. It was impossible for a man to survive overnight without some means of avoiding or repelling the mosquitos.

The barge bumped the dock, and the deckhand, his face thoroughly coated with mud on Eddie's advice, tied off the forward cleats to the pilings. The engine noise ceased, and the only sounds were the cough of an alligator and the splash of some jumping mullet.

The tug captain relaxed in the helmsman's chair, ordering: "Let's wait until tomorrow to start unloading when we have some daylight and these damn bugs have gone away."

"That's half a day of rig time," Joe protested. "We can start unloading the mud tanks tonight."

"I said tomorrow. That's about ten hours from now. We'll get you off and be out of here by noon; you can start rigging up and I can get the hell out of here."

Joe acquiesced. He was tired too and was shaking a little as the adrenaline that had been with him across the Gulf subsided. Life on remote drill sites and the dangers of drilling wildcats had exposed him to situations where he had wondered if he was going to see Oklahoma again. But the burning tanker was his first exposure to the intentional killing and destruction of wartime. On a rig floor, there were actions he could take in dealing with an unexpected kick or a gang of local thieves who wanted a payoff: circulate out a gas bubble or wave a shotgun. But cruising across the Gulf, he felt helpless at the sight of the burning ship and imagined the men (and women?) floating in boats or only life jackets, surrounded by an oily slick they hoped was not set aflame.

Eddie saw a set of steel stairs leading aft to a galley, adjacent to a rectangular linoleum-covered table and benches bolted to the deck, occupied by seamen from the tug and roughnecks accompanying the rig. With doors and windows shut tight and the heat of the tug engine warming the metal decks, the air was stifling and hot. But it was preferable to the clouds of mosquitos—attracted to the lights in the windows—that hummed outside looking for food. Every man smoked, mostly Camels and Lucky Strikes. A couple smoked pipes. But no one seemed to be aware of the stifling heat or the noxious air.

Pulling out a deck of cards, Jacque asked Eddie hopefully, "Want to play Bourré?"

"Naw, never have," said Eddie. "But I'll play poker with you fellows—Five Card Draw or Stud."

"We'll teach you. It's what we play in Louisiana. Got any money with you?"

"No, but I can write an IOU. But not for much. No way a man can win when he's learning." Eddie had played some games of chance, but since he never had cash, his opportunities were limited. No one in Everglades City would have given him anything on an IOU. It took Jacque just thirty minutes to win back what he advanced Eddie.

Sleep came slowly and fitfully for the men, but eventually the night passed. Joe opened the door to dawn and fresh air to see Eddie standing on the end of the dock, relieving himself into the water.

Buttoning his pants, Eddie turned to see Joe and grinned. He had spent the night in a place with a soft mattress and no mosquitos, and he could smell bacon as the seaman who doubled as the cook started breakfast. Taking out a brown glass bottle from his overall pocket, he pulled the cork and swallowed hopefully, lowering it in disappointment.

"Don't suppose you have any liquor on this boat, do ya? I'm all out."

"No. Company rules. If I'd known you had it last night, I would have poured it out," Joe replied.

"I always bring a flask in my pocket. Made it myself. Hid it when I was playing Bourré, 'cause I didn't want to share."

"Well, if you want to keep working for Pride, you're gonna have to stay sober. Next time I see you drinking, you're gone."

Eddie nodded and changed the subject.

"Ever been down in the Glades before?"

"No, but they don't look that different from a lot of other swamps in the world. But the water is clearer. Less mud. You lived here long?"

"All my life. Tried to leave once but ran out of money and liquor by the time I got to Naples, so I came back. It's OK here, hot and mosquitos, but they tell me the fishing is better here than anywhere else."

"How'd you get that scar?" Joe asked. He usually didn't mind anyone else's business, but he enjoyed Eddie's cheerful manner and wanted to know more about him.

"Dog bit me. Took a while to heal. Doctor said I should have gone to the hospital, but I didn't have any money, so I just poured shine on it and it got better."

"What happened to the dog?"

"Nothing," Eddie replied. "Belonged to a fellow in town who likes the dog more than he likes me. If I had hurt the dog, he would have shot me. I try to avoid fights." He shook his head and chuckled, sounding unexpectedly shrill to Joe. "But sometimes they find me."

"We need some labor to get all this moved off the barge to the location and rig up. Do you know where any of the fellows who built the road are now?" Joe figured Eddie was probably not much of a labor contractor, but he had to start somewhere.

"How many do you want?"

"About ten. Same pay as before. And they better be sober. A rig-up is an easy place to lose an arm if you aren't careful."

"I'll see what I can do and be back in a few hours," Eddie said cheerfully. He would get a day's pay from each man he brought on. He stepped into his skiff, which had been towed upriver behind the barge, with the assurance of a man who has spent his life on small boats. Starting the small motor with a hand crank, he pushed off and headed downstream to Everglades City.

As Eddie passed from sight around the bend in the river, Joe rousted the rig crew and the tugboat hands, impatiently watching them eat breakfast and drink coffee. When they had finished, he began organizing the tasks of unlashing the equipment from the barge and moving it across the dock to the board road.

Later that afternoon, Jerry MacDonald climbed the ladder to the rig floor, careful to avoid a roughneck bolting together a section of steel floor. Seeing a man in coveralls impatiently watching the assembly, he asked, "Are you Joe?"

"That's me," the man replied. "You must be the geologist. I understand that for once they sent someone who understands something about field operations as well as rocks. How did that happen?"

Jerry had told the story many times. He was sure Joe didn't want to know everything that had led him to this place in the world at this particular time. His mind drifted back over the years of work and study, trying to come up with a brief answer to Joe's question.

Jerry's parents were both descendants of the Oklahoma land rush who had struggled to hang onto a small farm during the Dust Bowl of the 1930s. At sixteen, Jerry left the small schoolroom he had attended all his life and enrolled at the high school that served the surrounding county. The farm had provided shelter and food, but little cash for the clothes and movie tickets Jerry found essential for interacting with the girls he was delighted to find had also moved up from the isolated schoolhouses. To remedy this situation, Jerry found work during high school summers as a laborer for an oil-field contractor. The men he worked with were older, mostly in their thirties, their worn bodies showing the effects of years of brutal labor. They accepted Jerry without question, giving him the nickname "Jelly" and including him in the constant joking that made the days' work tolerable.

The company did the dirty, dangerous, and exhausting work the big oil company maintenance crews avoided. Cleaning up the oil-soaked ground after a flowline break, greasing the bearings and slides of the pump jacks, and chipping paint constituted a large part of his daily assignments. Baking in the Oklahoma sun, he counted the minutes until it was too dark to work and the crew would be dismissed and told where to report in the morning. But the pay was good, and his parents needed the help. The drought had killed not only the wheat crop but also the kitchen garden. Jerry knew hunger, and he didn't like it. He especially didn't like seeing his mother try to give him some of the little food she had. A chance to get some cash money was a gift from God.

The second summer, the foreman told him he was to clean out a separator tank that had sanded up. Looking at Jerry's puzzled face, the man explained that the rock formation from which the oil was produced had started to disintegrate, and sand was flowing up the well to the surface tanks. He pointed to a large vertical cylinder with an open manhole, bolts protruding from the circumference where the cover had been removed. Looking in, Jerry could see it was filled with oil-covered sand several feet deep. "How do I get it out?" he asked.

"You get in there with a shovel and shovel it out. That's the only way," replied the foreman. Reluctantly, Jerry stepped onto a wooden crate and entered the hatch. Able to stand up once he was inside, he started to shovel sand out the opening into a wheelbarrow positioned immediately below the opening. After filling the wheelbarrow, he exited the tank and pushed it over to an open pit, dumping the sand onto a cake of mud and oily slime. His clothes already soaked with crude oil, and feeling dizzy from the aromatic vapors, he reentered the tank and continued with his task. After a few minutes of shoveling, he passed out, falling onto the sand and out of sight of any passersby.

He awoke to someone vigorously shaking him and slapping his face. Extracted from the tank, he was lying in the shade of a small building, attended to by an unfamiliar man with a hard hat and clean clothes who was relieved to see Jerry breathing. His rescuer turned to the foreman who had sent him into the tank. "What the hell did you think you were doing?" he asked. "No ventilation, no one watching. He would have been dead in ten more minutes."

"I didn't think it was that bad," the foreman said defensively. "I couldn't smell anything when I stuck my head in."

"No one goes inside until you get a fan. And no one goes in without someone outside ready to help. Understand? Or we'll get someone else."

"I got it," said the foreman resentfully. "Jerry, take the rest of the day off. We'll get someone else to finish up here."

Jerry sat up, his head throbbing. The newcomer walked off.

"Who was that?" Jerry asked Al, an older laborer who had been on the crew when he started.

"That was the engineer. He's out here to supervise a pressure buildup."

"Oh. Looks like a pretty good job. Gets to walk around in a hard hat and doesn't have to clean tanks."

"It's OK. But you have to have a college degree. I think he went to OU," said Al.

His first semester paid for by the cash earned from two summers in the oilfield, Jerry enrolled at the University of Oklahoma in the fall, determined to obtain a degree in Petroleum Engineering. He expected to start learning how to do the jobs of the visiting field engineers he watched and occasionally helped, like making sure a string of tubing was in the specified condition, and calculating the pump size needed to make a stalled-out oil well flow again. Important work, using his mind instead of his back.

The end of the first day found him walking back to the dormitory room he shared with a somewhat wealthier roommate, a young man who had spent orientation week drinking all he could to celebrate his release from parental oversight. Jerry believed he could tolerate him, but he had little interest in getting to know him any better. The classes that day had been pretty boring. Calculus, chemistry, English lit. Topics that seemed to have little to do with engineering. A classmate had confided in him that it was only to weed out the dummies. The real engineering came later. No one ever did any calculus after they went to work. Maybe so, he thought, but it was going to be a long four years if his classes had nothing to do with the real world of the oilfield.

Managing to scrape together enough money to stay the spring semester, he enrolled in the physical geology course required of all would-be petroleum engineers. The subject fascinated him. The history of life on the earth, the processes that formed mountains and continents, the interpretation of layers of rock that had been deposited by ancient rivers, all struck something deep within him. The appeal of earth science was multiplied by the adventurous aspect of studying it. It was a field science, not a laboratory exercise. He wanted to travel the world and map the geology of the continents. It was also the basis for finding oil, which made it an avenue toward the material comforts he intended to have someday.

Six long years later, interrupted by the need to work in the oilfields to earn the wherewithal to continue his education, Jerry graduated from OU with a degree in geology. A few girlfriends, some parties, and a set of nicer clothes he painstakingly cleaned and saved for class were the only good things he would remember about college in later years. He was glad the days of eating a monotonous diet of Spam and bread while trying to stay awake to study after a four-hour shift at a Norman filling station were now in the past. College hadn't been fun most of the time. A lot more money than he had was required to enjoy the good times. But he went after the degree with determination and trusted it would lead to a brighter future, maybe with a car.

When he had finally completed all the classes, Jerry skipped the graduation ceremony. His mother was too ill to attend, and he didn't have money for a cap and gown in any case. Few of his classmates had jobs waiting for them, and most were discouraged about graduating into the depths of the Depression. Jerry had no prospects and went back to the oilfield, disillusioned about the benefits he had hoped to gain from higher education.

His coworkers welcomed him back, their attitude a mix of sympathy and derision. Used to spending the contents of a weekly pay envelope in forty-eight hours, they had admired his discipline to save all he could, using all of the money he put away over summers and Christmas breaks to finance another semester at OU. He had always turned down their invitations to stop by the dimly lit taverns after the day was finished. Their own boots were worn and torn, but the soles of Jerry's were patched with tarred canvas. Beaten down by the Depression and their encounters with the law, with women, and with poverty, they had shared in his dream of escaping the back-breaking labor. His return to the contract crew left them all discouraged, and instead of "Jelly" they now referred to him as "Graduate."

Greasing the rod on a pump jack one morning, Jerry was irritated to have his light blocked by someone standing next to him. He looked up to see a familiar figure dressed in coveralls with Pride Oil embroidered over the breast pocket.

"Hey, Larry," he said. "Get the hell out of my light. I'm a working man, not an engineer, and I like to see what I'm doing. What are you doing back today, anyhow?"

"Screw you," Larry replied. "Came back to supervise a work-over. Make sure that pulling unit crew is doing what they're supposed to. Got some news for you. We had a meeting in the district office yesterday, going over the year-end forecast. My boss was there, along with the chief geologist from New York. They're really interested in meeting a man who got a geology degree by cleaning tanks and chipping paint in the oilfield. Not too many geologists have a clue about oilfield operations. They want you to go to Tulsa tomorrow for lunch. I'm leaving in the morning, so you can ride with me. But you'll have to find your own way back."

The lunchtime visit to the district office in Tulsa resulted in a job offer, the terms printed on letterhead and delivered to the field a week later. The job was at Pride's office tower in Manhattan, a skyscraper built during the 1920s. Jerry had an inside office, windowless, with a drafting table that was always covered with several layers of paper maps. Another table had a glass top with a light bulb underneath it to allow several layers of map data to be viewed at one time. It wasn't the globetrotting field geology he had imagined when he began his studies, but instead an office job analyzing data from wells and seismic surveys, and constructing maps of the subsurface that indicated where oil might be found. But it was hard to find a job during the Depression, and his paycheck every month was more cash than his parents saw during a year.

Time passed, and Jerry learned the practice of petroleum geology. He also learned the subway stops, where to get good Chinese food, how to get tickets for the Yankees for half price, and where the young women of the city congregated after their workdays as secretaries, department store clerks, telephone operators, and bookkeepers. After growing to adulthood in the rural America of the 1930s, the world's largest, busiest, noisiest, and pushiest city fascinated him. His first paycheck, which had seemed like a fortune compared to his pay as a roustabout, was gone by the middle of the month. Admitted to a world in which he never expected to dwell, he drank too much, stayed out late, and had a string of girlfriends that ended when he met Maria.

Jerry's memories of his past were interrupted by Joe's impatient grunt, so he kept his reply to Joe's question brief: "I worked my way through college as an oil field roustabout. That's how I got the job with Pride."

Joe nodded. "We'll have the drill shack set up in an hour," he said. "You can use the other desk. Glad to have you here. There's only the two of us and the crew down here in the middle of nowhere."

Chapter 6

Jerry saw the skeleton of the derrick rising above the cypress trees as the boat motored slowly toward the dock. The staccato barking of a diesel engine was punctuated by the clanging noise of pipe being hoisted upward by thick steel cable. The industrial racket was accompanied by four men moving with an orchestrated dance-like motion, standing on a platform about twenty feet above the swamp, throwing a chain and connecting a huge device resembling a plumber's wrench to a vertical pipe. They stepped back and threw up their hands, and with a roar from the rig engine, the pipe was lowered through the center of the rig floor.

Disembarking and carrying his duffel bag and satchel to the far end of the board road, Jerry saw that the clearing had been filled with tanks and machinery. The platform where the roughnecks moved with coordinated precision was twenty feet above the ground, reached by a set of greasy stairs. Towering above the platform, the derrick was centered over a circular opening in the middle of a turntable device resembling a lazy Susan and turned by the power of the rig engine. A vertical pipe descended downward into the well through the spinning turntable. A small room with sheet-metal walls and roof extended from the rig floor, providing shelter from the elements when operations did not require the crew on the floor. It also housed the rig controls, including the power supply. About thirty feet from the rig, a prefabricated metal building resembling a travel trailer was located on blocks above the ground. This was the drill shack, containing Joe's office and a small desk occupied by Jerry. Large metal tanks containing a viscous mud churned to form a slurry of clay, chunks of heavy barite, and water. The tanks were connected by hoses to the top of the derrick. A lateral platform, sloping down from the rig floor, contained sections of drill pipe to be hoisted to the top of the derrick and then connected and lowered into the hole as the well progressed.

The well was already about six hundred feet deep, drilling into the bedrock below the marshy soil. The rotary table spun the drill pipe that passed through the hole in the center, allowing the bit screwed to the lower end to penetrate into the earth. Mud was pumped to the top of the pipe suspended in the derrick and flushed out of the drill pipe at the bottom of the hole. The mud lubricated the bit and washed the tiny particles of rock created by the grinding bit back up the hole between the drill pipe and the side of the borehole. The operation proceeded without interruption until a new section of pipe had to be attached at the top of the drill string.

It had taken two exhausting weeks, winching the machinery from the dock along the boards and onto the area raised with fill dirt that was the starting point for the wildcat well. The semi-dry land created by excavating the marshy soil consisted of a white, sticky mud, impossible to walk through without it sucking a boot off one's foot. At Joe's direction, the labor crew from Everglades City had cut and placed wooden boards to form crude sidewalks between the rig and the auxiliary machinery. The effort had assembled the seemingly haphazard collection of tanks, pumps, and hoses into a functioning drill rig, which was now driving the drill bit downward to the objective of the Sunniland reef. Jerry had not been to the wellsite since the rig had arrived, instead spending his time communicating with Mike Woods about the final permits and cost estimates. Now it was real—a group of men had arrived deep in the Everglades with more heavy machinery than had ever been found there. They were about to drill two miles into the earth, toward a location that had been specified by Jerry. A wave of anxiety passed over him—none of these people had any question about being in the right place. They had accepted his target without question, a circle two miles deep and five hundred feet in diameter. And they were expending a huge amount of treasure and human effort to eventually place the end of the drill pipe in the middle of it.

Watching the motion of the roustabouts, he wondered if gunners on a battleship felt the same way, inside a steel turret, unable to see what they're shooting at, just obeying orders and turning the knobs and levers as they're told. Hitting the target wasn't their responsibility, just performing the myriad of small tasks correctly that resulted in a projectile being launched across the open ocean. The gunnery officer on the bridge was responsible for translating the apparent position of the target into figures of elevation and azimuth that would crash the shell into an enemy warship. That was Joe's job, giving orders of rotation speed and pressure on the drill bit instead of elevation and azimuth. But he wasn't responsible for the position of the bottom hole target two miles below. That was totally up to Jerry. It was supposed to be the center of the Cretaceous reef in the Sunniland formation.

Jerry resolved to double-check the target location data when he returned to the hotel in a few days, although at that point it would be too late to change anything. If the rig crew hit the target, they had succeeded. If they hit the target and missed the reef, that was his fault.

The risk of making a mistake had seemed small when he had written down the coordinates in his New York office. He had determined the position on a map placed on his drafting table, painstakingly measuring the distance from the section lines with a triangular engineer's scale. Then he had asked Chris to come in and repeat the exercise to validate his results. He was sure of the answer, but seeing the magnitude of the effort in terms of sweat and huge moving pieces of iron made an error on his part untenable.

A sudden silence fell over the rig site. The throbbing of the pumps, the ratcheting of the pipe ascending to the derrick, and the background noise of the diesel engine all ceased instantaneously. The quiet of the swamp became evident as some ducks whistled overhead and were heard splashing down in a nearby pond.

"Goddammit!" he heard Joe swear.

"Sounds like the motor stopped getting fuel. Might have water in it again," said a thin man in greasy coveralls, peering suspiciously at the engine.

"Get it going, or I'll find someone who can," Joe snarled at him.

Frustrated, Joe turned his back on the man and noticed Jerry traversing a narrow walkway across the mud, careful to keep his boots dry. He regarded Jerry as a peer—not responsible for the workings of the rig, but someone he could confide in on matters he would not discuss with the roustabouts.

"J.B. sent this guy down from Ponca City as a motorman, but he doesn't know a damn thing about heavy machinery. I think he used to fix J.B.'s hot rod. I'm going to have to find someone else."

"I'll go over to Moorehaven if you want," Jerry offered. "That's in the middle of cattle-ranching country. Should be some men there who understand tractor engines. What are you willing to pay?"

"Find out what the going rate over there is and double it. We aren't making ten feet of hole a day the way we're going, and I've got five men just standing around. Tell the boat captain, whoever it is, to take you right back to town and find you a truck with a driver. Thanks. We'll just be sitting on our asses chipping paint until you get back."

Turning toward the mechanic, he said, "You're fired. Get on the boat. I'll have your last pay at the hotel tomorrow. I'd advise you to spend it getting back to Oklahoma."

"You can't do that. J.B. promised me three months' work for coming down here. He'll have your ass in a sling." The man approached Joe, who waited calmly.

"J.B. doesn't run things here. I do. I'm sure he will tell you the same thing. Now get on the boat, or you're going to have to swim back to Everglades City."

The mechanic hesitated, looking uncertainly toward Jerry for support. Finding none, he slumped and trudged down the board road toward the dock. A few minutes later, Jerry sat down on the bench next to him as the captain undid the figure-eight hitch on the forward cleat, put the board in hard reverse with the wheel hard over to port, then shifted to forward at dead slow as he spun the wheel to starboard. The maneuver caused the bow to head downstream, and the noise of the engine increased to full throttle. As the boat reached about ten miles per hour, a two-foot wake washed sediment from the mangrove roots into the dredged channel.

"Man thinks he's king here, doesn't he? I guess he'll learn something when I get back to Ponca City."

"He pretty much is," Jerry replied. "Yard managers like J.B. are easy to find. Tool pushers with Joe's experience are scarce. There's no contest. Why did you think you could do this anyhow, if you had never worked on heavy equipment?"

"Had to try. Needed a job, and thought I could figure it out." The man fell silent.

SUNNILAND

The main street of the town of Moorehaven, located on the south shore of the huge Lake Okeechobee, could have been found anywhere in America where the residents made a living farming and ranching. If a visitor didn't bother reading the sign advertising "Moorehaven Feed and Fertilizer" above the largest building, he could have mistaken the small town for Levelland, Texas; Blakely, Georgia; or any of a hundred rural villages. Feed stores, parked farm machinery, welding shops, a hardware store, and a small hotel housing a café lined the main street. The café, with windows overlooking the wooden sidewalk, had a counter with wooden stools and three booths. A griddle and refrigerator occupied the back wall behind the counter. A cigarette-smoking cook used the griddle to turn out fried eggs in the morning and hamburgers at lunchtime. There were seven men in the café, all wearing denim pants and boots. Five looked like they spent their days on horseback, and Jerry doubted they knew a fuel filter from an injector. But two looked like they had the greasy hands, broken fingernails, and oil-stained clothes that came from working with the tractors, generators, combines, and trucks essential to the operation of the ranches.

"I have a diesel engine on a drilling rig about fifty miles from here that isn't running. I have a job for anyone who can get it started and keep it going." Jerry announced, letting the door close behind him.

"Not sure what a drilling rig is, but I've never seen a machine I can't get to work," said a man who looked like he was part Indian. "And I need a job."

"Ever work on diesel engines?" asked Jerry.

"Some. Enough to know they don't run on gasoline."

"OK. Get in the truck outside and I'll take you to the rig, and you can give it a shot. What's your name?"

"Big Slough. I'm half Seminole. How much does this job pay?"

"We'll talk about that if you can get us going."

"I'll risk the trip," Big Slough said. He opened the door of the small truck, sat down, and relaxed. Soon he was fast asleep, lulled by the steady vibration as the truck passed over gravel roads.

The Pride Oil pickup truck drove south through farming country, the land divided into fields delineated by dirt roads and impromptu hedges of small green bushes, a trail of white dust from the limestone road rising behind them. The country gave way to swampland as they passed the northern boundary of the grass prairies and cypress swamps that occupied the southernmost part of Florida. Continuing south, they left the Tamiami Trail, taking the side road into the town of Everglades City. When the truck finally reached the dock on Riverside Drive, Jerry saw the boat captain standing by as instructed.

"Now we go by water," he told Big Slough. "There's a dock about two miles up the river. We'll take the boat; then we have to walk the last part on a board road across the swamp to the drilling rig."

"Pretty easy traveling so far," replied the aspiring mechanic. "You white men don't appear to take to dugout canoes or horses. Build yourself a nice dry road instead."

Joe was pacing the length of the board road, from the dock to the cleared drilling pad that supported the rig, impatient and irritable. The sight of the boat coasting into the dock and tying up gave him something to focus his anger on, and he walked quickly to the river. Three men were disembarking: the boat captain, Jerry, and a stranger who reminded Joe of the Indians he encountered everywhere in Oklahoma. "Who the hell is this?" he questioned Jerry sharply. "Not sure this guy looks like a mechanic to me."

"He said he knows diesels." Jerry replied. "Name's Big Slough. I told him that if he can get the engine started, he has a job. If not, he's on his own to get back to Moorehaven or wherever. Didn't talk pay. Said he can take that up with you if he can get us going again."

Walking quickly during the interchange, the three men arrived at the muddy grass of the drill site. Joe looked again at Big Slough, sizing up Jerry's new hire. "Can you get a diesel started?" he asked abruptly. "If you can, you've got a job. If not, the boat will take you back in the morning."

"I've worked on farm machinery since I was twelve," Big Slough replied. "Mostly gas, but some with diesel engines. Have to use a propane torch to get them going when it's cold, but that doesn't happen much in this part of the world. Other problem is almost always bad fuel. Give a diesel clean fuel and it will run forever. Gum up the fuel, and nothing will run. I'm assuming you got tools and some filters. Otherwise can't do anything. I'm not a magician."

Later than evening, sitting in the drill shack at a two-foot-square desk littered with papers, strips of annotated cardboard, bottles of chemicals and acid, UV lights, and a small microscope, Jerry heard the rig engine cough, sputter, then roar to life. After a few minutes, the driller engaged the clutch, and the next stand of pipe rose to the top of the derrick. Joe walked in the door, smiling.

"Not a bad hire. He found an air leak in the fuel line between the filter and the intake manifold. Patched it by overlaying a larger hose and two clamps. We'll order a new one from Oklahoma, but this will keep us going. Thanks. Not the kind of service I usually get from a geologist."

Joe walked out the door, leaving Jerry to continue setting up his workbench, preparing to start catching samples and log the formations as the hole was drilled to total depth. The plan was to spend several days on the rig, sleeping in the drill shack, then take the boat back to Everglades City for a couple of days and write up his results, transmitting them to New York by a telegraph summary and a mailed follow-up copy. He would miss Maria, but he was glad that after almost two weeks of travel the work that had brought him to Florida was finally getting started.

Chapter 7

The elderly couple, both thin with brown, wrinkled skin reflecting a lifetime of exposure to the arid climate and constant winds of West Texas, nervously entered the office building located at the end of a side street in Midland, Texas. The dead end marked where the edge of town gave way to a flat plain covered with mesquite and tumbleweeds. The building was one story, with a false front showing peeling paint, not one of the impressive stone monuments to wealth that had been constructed by wealthy wildcatters and landowners. It was occupied by individuals who scraped a living from the oilfields but never did very well—lawyers, landmen, drilling contractors, and surveyors living hand-to-mouth, shoving and pushing for the business on the periphery of the industry.

Doors with glazed windows opened off the lobby, which had no receptionist and no sign indicating the presence of those who leased space on a monthly basis. Seeing a door with a taped paper sign reading "Price Land," the couple knocked. Hearing a gruff "Come in," they entered a cluttered office with two desks. One desk was empty, the other occupied by a heavyset man smoking a cigar. He stared at them, not rising to greet them or offer them a seat.

"We're the Joneses," said the man. "There was a man surveying our property today. Said he worked for Tom Price. Is that you?"

"You're from down south by Monahans?" asked the seated man, removing the cigar from his mouth and blowing smoke at them.

"That's us. You have no call to be on our property. What are you doing there?"

"I bought the mineral rights from the bank. Have a copy right here. I leased them to Jack White, who's going to drill a well. The surveyor is staking out the location. You can't stop him from accessing his mineral rights. May need to tear down your barn to get the rig in."

"We have no business with the bank. Never have. Owned that property for thirty years and paid cash. That paper is a fraud."

Tom Price stood up, pushing back on the man's chest with two fingers. "I say it's good. And Jack White paid good money for the lease. Interfere, and there will be some people out to visit you and set things straight. Maybe if the well hits, they'll pay you something for setting up some facilities."

"You're trying to steal our land," the woman exclaimed. "That paper is worthless. And don't send anyone out to mess with us, or they won't come back."

"Get out of my office," said Tom Price. "And be careful if you go around saying I cheated you. I don't let things like that go by without getting back."

The couple turned and left, leaving the door open behind them. The landman looked at the paper he had waved at them, then threw it in the trash. It had been typed up by his partner, Pete, the week before, and looked sufficiently valid for Jack White to pay him a thousand dollars for the drilling rights. If Jack struck oil, he would have plenty of money to hire lawyers and get title to the land after the fact. If it was a dry hole, the thousand dollars was a cost of doing business for an independent wildcatter. Tom Price sat down at the desk again, looking at the property map near the Joneses' farm to see where else he might be able to put together a drilling location for Jack White. He scratched out a living in the oilfield towns of Texas and Oklahoma, forging documents and forcing signatures, sometimes with threats of violence. He was in Midland because he had recently served thirty days in Fort Stockton, after giving a worthless check to a rancher in return for the right to build a road into his property. He had hoped to leave town before the check bounced, but the landowner, skeptical of the handwritten draft on a bank in Houston, had quickly tried to deposit it at the local bank. An hour later, the sheriff had pushed Tom through the cell door, telling him that bond was one thousand dollars, or he would wait until the judge came around. The trial never happened, and needing the cell for a more recalcitrant offender, the sheriff had let him go without charges. Purchasing an old truck with another worthless check, Tom drove up to Midland and managed to persuade his new landlord to lease him space that would be paid for at the end of the month.

He wondered if he should leave Midland. That old couple looked unimpressed by his threat of what would happen if they interfered with Jack White's planned well. He remembered a scam he had run in Arkansas a few months ago. That time, he had told Pete to work over the man until his wife agreed to sign a lease agreement. Pete had been too enthusiastic, and the old man had been left unable to walk. He felt it was best to avoid violence when he could, but sometimes it was needed to close a deal. The thousand dollars from Jack White was the most cash money he had ever had at one time. If he could work something like that on about three more of these trashy farms, he would be able to set up a real office in Houston and make some serious money. He decided to stay. Distracted by the visit, he picked up a copy of the Midland newspaper and opened it to the business section, which was dominated by local oil and cotton news. But a short article on a different subject caught his attention.

Oil Well to Be Drilled in South Florida

Pride Oil Company has announced plans to drill a well in Collier County, ten miles from the coast in southwest Florida. The objective is the Sunniland Limestone of Cretaceous age. They hope to encounter Cretaceous reefs similar to those in the Edwards Formation of Texas. The drilling contractor is LT Drilling of Ponca City. The well is planned to spud in February.

Interested, he circled the article with a pencil. When Pete came back, he would show it to him. Florida sounded like a good place to go next, if things got too uncomfortable around Midland. A place where no one was familiar with the details of leasing land for oil wells meant there would be plenty of suckers who would believe anything they were told. Relaxing after the departure of Mr. and Mrs. Jones, he opened the side drawer of his desk and took out a flask of whiskey, pouring a double shot into a dirty glass on the desk and swallowing half of it in one gulp. Feeling the rush of alcohol to his head, both calming him but enhancing the animosity he felt toward anyone who interfered with him, he was not in a mood for bad news when the door opened to admit Jack White. The independent oilman was dressed in cowboy clothes, a Stetson hat on his head, and expensive riding boots on his feet. He was short, and his belly hung over a large silver and turquoise belt buckle. His chin pointed toward Tom Price.

"That Jones fellow just shot at my surveyor and told him he wouldn't miss again if he didn't get off the property. I thought you said you had bought those rights and things were set to go."

"That old clodhopper," said Tom Price. "Don't worry; I'll take care of it. Tell your surveyor to go back tomorrow, and I'll fix it before then."

"You'd better. Or give me back my thousand dollars," said Jack heatedly. He wasn't too particular about how the leases he bought had been obtained by the seller, but he did expect no interference with his operations. He suspected that Tom didn't have any kind of legal title to those mineral rights, but it was a promising location and he wanted to drill, so he had ignored his apprehensions. But now Jones was holding up a rig that Jack was paying good money for every day, and Tom Price would have to get the old couple out of the way. Jack left the office, slamming the door and stepping onto the cracked sidewalk.

Tom poured another glass of bourbon. That old man had screwed up any possibility of more deals around here, he thought. Enough commotion, and the sheriff would be out there, and Tom's phony title to the mineral rights would be apparent. The likely result was another thirty days at least. But before he left town with Jack White's thousand dollars in his briefcase, he would take care of the Joneses for blowing up a good thing for him.

The door slammed as Pete entered the room, looking at the bottle and asking," What's going on? Got another glass?" Dressed in a cheap suit with a light brown hat, he looked rougher than Tom. Not because of scars or missing fingers, but because of the aggressive stare and unyielding appearance of a man who had no problem causing pain. They had been partners for two years now. Tom set up the deals and took care of the paperwork, while Pete checked out the land. If there was a problem convincing someone to sign a lease document or the need to quiet a complaint from a cheated landowner, Pete handled it. The men looked for small pieces of property, often isolated from roads, that had an impoverished appearance.

People who needed money and didn't have any way to cause a stink if they didn't like what they ended up getting.

"The Pearsall property looks pretty good for us," Pete continued, helping himself to a half glass of whisky. "Ninety acres on the edge of the Roberts's field. A new rig is drilling about a quarter mile from their house. Two miles to Highway 33, and no phone line. Want to pay them a visit tomorrow?"

Tom was tempted but replied, "We're going to have to leave tonight. Old Jones shot at Jack White's surveyor. He didn't scare. If Jack sends the guy back out tomorrow and Jones shoots him, the sheriff will be there, and it will be obvious we don't have a lease. So let's get going with Jack's money while we can."

"Where do you plan on going?" asked Pete. "We've been run out of half of Texas. And I still have an assault charge against me in Arkansas for breaking that fellow's arm. Should have signed where you told him."

"Look at this," said Tom, tossing the newspaper with the circled article to Pete. "Let's go to Florida. If this well hits, there's a lot of money to be made. The place will be crawling with landmen the day after they log. If we get there first, we can likely sew up some loose property. And the farmers won't know what they're signing; no one has ever drilled around there."

Pete looked at the article and then said, "I'll go, but first I want my half of that thousand dollars."

"I'll give it to you, but we split all expenses till we make a strike. It's going to take some cash to get to Florida and get set up."

"When do you want to leave?" asked Pete.

"After we get something to eat. We need to stop by the junkyard and get a new plate for this old truck. But on the way out I want to stop at the Joneses' place and leave them a farewell card for screwing up our deal."

The old truck drove slowly down the dark gravel road, lights off, and coasted to a stop in the dry, dusty yard of the farmhouse, located within a fenced enclosure. Within the fence perimeter they could see a barn, several sheds, and a chicken coop. A dark brown mongrel, thick-shouldered with the look of a pit bull, jumped from the porch and charged the truck. It didn't bark, but growled in a low, menacing tone as it rushed the cab door. Pete cranked down the window on the passenger side and threw out an object that looked like a lump of clay, then hastily raised the window again as the dog's paws scratched the glass. The animal paused, then leaped at the ball of ground meat, devouring it in a second. A minute passed and the watchdog began to wobble, then collapsed on the ground, twitching violently. Another minute and it lay motionless, spittle drooling from its open mouth. Pete assumed it was dead and stepped out of the truck cab.

"What was in that?" asked Tom.

"Not sure. Some kind of rat poison, I guess. It said extremely poisonous to livestock on the bag. I got it at the hardware store. Sure worked quick." Pete replied. He opened the cab door and stepped onto the porch with a length of chain, starting to wrap it around the doorknob and fasten it to a mailbox nailed to the siding. It would effectively lock the door on the outside, making the house a jail cell.

"Don't do that," said Tom. "The sheriff will find it, and they'll be looking for two murderers. Maybe they'll get out; maybe they won't. But if it we don't make it look like arson, they'll just think it's a fire."

Pete grunted assent, and removed the chain and threw it into the yard toward the body of the watchdog. He watched Tom pour gasoline on the corner of the porch, then threw a match onto the soaked wood. Baked by the West Texas sun for fifty years, the wood caught instantly. The two men slammed the cab doors shut, Tom grinding the starter and shouting, "C'mon, c'mon!" as the worn motor failed to catch. Hearing an encouraging cough from one cylinder, followed by a steady "vroom," he threw the truck into gear and accelerated toward the highway, both of the men looking back at the roof of the Joneses' house collapsing in a huge orange flame.

They drove east on Highway 90 through the Texas hill country, then followed the Gulf Coast past the smoke rising from the refinery stacks on the Houston Ship Channel. Crossing the Sabine River into Louisiana, the road took them southeast through Lafayette and into the cypress swamps of the Atchafalaya Basin. Stopping for the second night at a motor court in the small town of Houma, they saw a drilling rig being loaded onto an ocean-going barge, the logo of the LT drilling company painted on the side.

"Where's that going?" Tom asked one of the laborers carrying sacks to a growing pile situated at the end of the barge deck.

"Won't tell us. Say they don't want to let the German U-boats know."

"I'll bet that's the rig that's going to drill the Florida well," Tom said. "Paper said LT was the drilling contractor."

"Don't know nothing about any Florida well," said the man, bent over by a hundred pound bag. "But they're leaving soon. There's the tug."

A large tug, with a sign that read "Mr. John" fastened to the front of the pilothouse, was moving into position behind the barge. A man dressed in red coveralls and wearing an aluminum hard hat with a sticker that said "LT" on the front watched it slide back and forth in the water, the eddies from the huge prop making the heavy barge shift. Two deckhands began to attach the barge to the tugboat bow using heavy steel cable, ratcheting it tight with a lever. On the deck of the barge, a welder was securing the horizontal derrick to the deck. Machinery, tanks, pipe, and sacks of cement completely filled the remaining open space.

Well, if they're leaving now, we should be in Florida at least a week ahead of them, thought Tom. Shoving Pete, he told him to get back in the truck. They would get some dinner and sleep tonight at the motor court, then drive straight through to Everglades City.

Chapter 8

Jerry arrived at the hotel in Everglades City, a satchel full of wet, dirty papers and small bags containing mud with fragments of rock slung over his shoulder. The rig engine had responded to the ministrations of Big Slough, and drilling had progressed without incident for several days, the crew settling into a familiar routine. They had drilled down to about a thousand feet, then pulled out the drill pipe and run into the hole with twelve-inch casing, cementing it in place by pumping cement down the pipe to the bottom, then allowing it to flow upward outside between the pipe and the cylindrical rock face of the wellbore. It would take a couple of days for the cement to cure before the rig could commence drilling again, so Jerry had taken advantage of the break and returned to Everglades City.

There had been intermittent groups of visitors to the board road, attracted by the sight of the derrick rising above the grass and the ever-present clatter of the machinery. The visitors included Seminole Indians in dugout canoes, with implacable faces and colored shirts. Jerry understood that the United States was still technically at war with the Seminoles, a peace treaty never having been signed after the Seminole War, but no one seemed anxious to do anything about it on either side. Onlookers also included trappers and moonshiners in skiffs, rough-looking men, most of them living in the swamp for a reason. Tourists came from the Mangrove Lodge, brought by fishing guides on their way to catch the snook and red drum in the mangrove islands. A newspaperman from the Tampa Tribune arrived, as well as a few black men, dressed in rags, carefully moving to the side of the board road when whites walked past. The onlookers docked their boats, walked to the rope stretched across the board road to keep casual visitors safely away from the machinery of the rig, and gawked at the pipe being hoisted to the derrick, connected to the drill string in the well, and turned by the rotating table in the rig floor. The machinery of the rig appeared to toss around heavy sections of steel pipe like matchsticks. The constant engine noise and slamming metal made Jerry feel on edge, ready to duck in an instant from a flying piece of broken chain. He was looking forward to a few quiet days in Everglades City.

Jerry opened the door to the hotel room, smiling at the sight of Maria sitting in a chair by the open window, reading a book she had brought from New York. Hearing him push back the door with his foot as he carried in an armful of luggage, she looked up and waved. "Hi, stranger. What's the matter? Did the gators run you off?"

Hugging her, he said, "The gators were OK, but I got tired of the tourists. How were things while I was gone? Did you find the Catholic church?"

"That didn't work out too well," she replied. "I went down to the courthouse and asked a man at the counter where I might find a Catholic church. He said there wasn't one—not many Catholics in this part of the world. He asked why I might want to find it, and I told him I was Catholic and wanted to go to church, and maybe help in their altar guild or something."

"And?"

"He said that not telling anyone I was Catholic was probably a good idea. There were people here who didn't like Catholics any more than blacks, Jews, and Indians."

"Well, we're in the old Confederacy now," Jerry replied. "The country that lost the war seventy-eight years ago. The East Coast of Florida is pretty cosmopolitan, with the rich people coming to Miami from New York and Boston every winter. But that isn't the case over here."

"Well, there isn't anything to do. "

"Want to go home? I'll be back in about three months. I'll miss you, but I can understand."

"No, there are lots of people in worse places than this hotel in 1943. I said I wanted to come, and I'll stay. I'll find something. I think I'll ask the hotel owner if he needs some help in the bar. I can make a better Manhattan than anyone in Florida. "

"Good. I want you here. I'll do the best I can to get back here every three days," Jerry replied, and started to unpack the satchel. "I've got a couple of days work logging these samples and sending a report to Mike Woods. But let's go find something to eat first. And I could use a drink—no alcohol on the rig. At least there's not supposed to be."

They strolled down the street, holding hands and squinting against the setting sun, to a pier built out into the river. Constructed of planks set wide enough apart to catch a careless toe, the pier was about four feet above the water and served as dockage for a fleet of dilapidated-looking small craft engaged in shrimping, crabbing, oystering, and gill-netting mullet and seatrout. A restaurant at the end served fresh seafood and cold beer, and offered seats at wooden tables outside under a tin roof. The tables were full, but the bar was only half occupied. Jerry and Maria sat on two empty stools and ordered Schlitz beers while they waited for a group to vacate a table.

Finishing another beer when supper was over, Maria asked, "What kind of fish was that? Snooker?"

"No, snook. It's a local fish. How did you like it?

"Best fish I ever had. Better than the bluefish we get in the city. Not as oily."

"Everything tastes great when it's fresh. Hard to get fish when gasoline is rationed and a lot of the men are gone. But there are so many fish in these waters that the restaurants always have something that was caught today. Your snook probably came from a guide, one left over after the customer took what he wanted."

"So how are things going with the well?" she inquired.

"So far we're right on track with what I predicted, as far as the subsurface. Had some engine trouble a few days ago, and I volunteered to drive over to Moorehaven. It's a farm and ranch town on the south shore of the lake about fifty miles north of here. Found a mechanic named Big Slough. He's part Seminole Indian, and Joe hired him. He got things going. The whole operation seems to be leveling out pretty well. The crew that came from Houma knows what they are doing, and they're breaking in the new men."

"So you going to be pretty busy tomorrow?"

"I have some work to do on the well file. But we should have some time together."

"Good. We haven't been married for a year yet. I have some ideas," Maria said in a conspiratorial tone. "Don't plan to get started early on that paperwork."

Jerry happily accepted a late start the next morning. Drawing symbols on linen paper unrolled from a wooden box, he carefully drafted a record of the progress of the well to date, marking the type of rocks drilled and the rate of penetration of the drill bit in a column annotated by depth. Comparing his work to similar records from a well drilled in 1938 to the north near Arcadia, he was able to compare the depths at which the LT rig was finding changes in the rock formations to the Arcadia well. The results were about what was expected, and he saw no reason to change his prediction of when they would encounter the Sunniland Limestone. He summarized his results in a telegram to Mike Woods, ending with "So far, so good." In New York, he had been confident of the Sunniland prospect to the point of arrogance. The arrival of the rig and the actual operation drilling the well had made him question the confident prediction he had made of encountering a reef. Correlating his predictions with the Arcadia well restored his optimism. *This well will hit a reef, he thought, unless something totally unexpected interferes.*

Maria and Jerry found a diner two blocks back from the river where they sometimes had breakfast together. The place was a converted railroad car at the end of the block, with a red neon sign that read, appropriately, "DINER." The interior had a Formica counter with ten stools and two booths that could each seat four people. The breakfast menu was bacon, eggs, toast, grits, and good coffee. And it cost about half the price of a morning meal in the hotel dining room.

The diner hosted a group of regular customers, mostly men, who made a habit of stopping in before making their way to the bank, stores, and the courthouse located in the small downtown. What they knew about oil wells was largely based on movies about Texas, and blowouts—unimaginable riches and forests of closely spaced derricks—were what they expected. The arrival of the Pride rig had sustained their breakfast conversation for a couple of weeks. They expected a Spindletop gusher to dwarf the ninety-foot derrick at any time, and they were not sure whether that would be a good thing or a bad thing for their businesses. Smoking cigarettes to finish their morning ritual, the men glanced sideways at the young couple talking quietly at the back table. Acting like newlyweds, they had been eating breakfast in the diner every few days, and the regulars had made inquiries as they did for any new arrival in Everglades City. The Turner Inn clerk had told the regulars that Jerry was the man in charge of the well operation, and that Pride Oil was paying whatever it took to keep him in Everglades City. *He sure has a pretty wife,* they thought. And seems young to be in charge. *And doesn't seem in a hurry to get back out to the well.*

They politely waited for Jerry and Maria to finish breakfast, impatient for information but not wanting to irritate them by interrupting their meal. Seeing the plates cleared and the couple finishing their coffee, a delegation of three ambled over, one of them saying, "Good morning. Welcome to Everglades City. I'm Howe, and this is Richard and Jeff. "

"Hi. I'm Jerry, and this is my wife Maria," Jerry replied. Aware of their attention during breakfast, Jerry was anticipating some questions and was happy to answer them. He enjoyed talking about his work. "Have a seat," he offered.

"Thanks," Howe replied. He sat down next to Jerry, and Richard squeezed in next to Maria, while Jeff pulled a chair to the end of the table. They nodded to Maria, who had also noticed them watching the progress of their meal. She wanted her time with Jerry before he left to spend several days on the rig but was impressed by the attention he was receiving.

"We understand you're in charge of that well drilling east of town," Howe said. "How are things going with it?"

"I'm not in charge. There's a man called Joe who's the tool pusher, and he's responsible for the operation. But to answer your question, it's on schedule."

"If you find oil, is there going to be a gusher like in those newsreels from Oklahoma?" asked Richard, a short, middle-aged man, bald and wearing a suit and tie. Jerry later learned he was the bank president. "Make a hell of a mess in that swamp."

"No, the drilling mud will keep the oil in the ground until we complete the well," Jerry replied. "Those old pictures showed an operation that wasn't controlled. We won't be doing that."

"Why are you drilling here, of all places? Be a lot easier to drill up near Ocala," Howe said.

"We think there are some ancient reefs two miles down, like the ones you see in the Keys. That's our target."

"What are you going to do with the oil if you find it? Not much use for it here," commented Jeff, a thin man with a red face, clothed in a khaki shirt and trousers.

"We'll build a tank to hold a few days' production, then barge it. Probably take it across the lake to the East Coast, then up the waterway to the refineries in New Jersey. But we might ship it by rail. Hasn't been decided yet. But either way, the U-boats won't have a shot at it," Jerry replied.

"How much longer do you have to go?" asked the bank president. "We're glad to have the business. Lot of equipment going through town, and the hotel business is up."

"This well will take about three months. If it's a discovery, we could be drilling for years. If it's a dry hole, we'll be done." Jerry replied. He enjoyed the conversation, educating people on the business of drilling an oil well. A complex operation, but one that was well understood by its practitioners in 1943. Not as complicated as manufacturing and flying an airplane, but then building a plane didn't have to be done two miles underground.

"What happens if the oil gets away and spills in the swamp?" asked another member of the impromptu audience who had wondered over to join the group, standing behind Jeff. A younger man than the others, with glasses and red suspenders, he had an air of curiosity. Jerry later learned he was the editor of the local newspaper. "The oil that drifts in when those U-boats sink a tanker is bad enough. Stays in the swamp for days, and some looks like it will never go away."

"Well," Jerry said carefully, "you don't have to worry about this well spilling any oil. Joe, the man in charge, knows what he's doing, and Pride spends enough money on equipment and men to make sure everything works. But I won't kid you. If we find oil, and there are another twenty wells and tanks and pipelines and pumps around here, it will change the countryside around here. It's like putting a phosphate plant on a river flowing into Tampa Bay. Provides jobs and money, but things won't be the same."

"We'll take the jobs and the money," said the bank president. "Don't have enough of either here."

"I guess so," said the newspaper editor. "But it's beautiful here. I hate to see it changed."

"If we find oil, it will, for better or worse depending on your perspective," Jerry replied. "If it's a dry hole, the board road will make a good fishing spot. This is a beautiful place, even with the oil washing in from those tankers. I understand both sides. But I work for an oil company, so this is what I do."

Howe shook hands and said, "Thanks for the update, hope to see you here tomorrow." The three men seated at the table, accompanied by the crowd listening in from behind them, left for work. Jerry looked at Maria, sighed, and nibbled at the last piece of toast left in the basket.

A young woman carrying a pot of coffee accidentally brushed against Jerry as she cleared the table. Jerry and Maria recognized her from their last few visits.

"Y'all need a cook out there? I can do coffee, grits, beef, and chicken if you got it, fish and crabs if you don't. I can get out there when you want, and be out of the way and gone when you want that, too."

"Why would you want to work out in the swamp with some roughnecks when you got a nice job waitressing here in town?" Jerry asked.

"I'm tired of getting grabbed and hustled by all these so-called successes you seen in here, and they don't tip worth a damn. I've had a hard life, and they all know about it and think they can say anything to me. I just want to work and make enough to pay my way. Your roughnecks can't be any worse than this crowd."

"We run two twelve-hour shifts, twenty-four hours a day, and the men eat breakfast before they show up and have supper when they get back to town. They bring lunch, but we might want to have a hot lunch for them. Save time and keep them from quitting to go fishing. I'll talk to Joe, the tool pusher. What's your name?

"Eileen. I can start any time."

"OK. I'll let you know next time I'm back in town. You'd have to ride a boat out in the morning and back in the afternoon."

"I can do that. Grew up on boats. Let me know, and thanks," she replied.

The next morning, Jerry sat by himself at the counter in the diner. Feeling poorly, Maria had told him to go on down by himself.

"Are you OK?" he had asked Maria.

"Yes, it just feels like a cold. Maybe I'm allergic to all this tropical stuff down here. I'll get over it, but I don't feel like breakfast. You go ahead."

"OK. I'll bring you back some toast and coffee." Closing the door quietly, he descended the staircase and found his way to the diner alone.

The cook behind the counter nodded hello to Jerry as he pulled a tray of biscuits from the oven. Jerry had found out a few days before that he used to work for the Ringling Brothers Circus, traveling with them every summer on the circus trains as one of the many cooks needed to feed the hundreds of entertainers and other workers needed to set up, put on a circus, strike everything down, and pack up in one day. In the off-season, he lived in Gibsonton, a small town north of the Sarasota headquarters. With the circus on hold until the end of the war, he had found work in Everglades City.

"Hi, Al," Jerry replied. "The usual, please. Maria won't be here—she's not feeling well." He took a seat on one of the counter stools, noticing that two men he didn't know occupied the booth closest to the door.

"Adam and Eve on a raft," Al nodded. He cracked two eggs onto the cast iron griddle, and put a slice of white bread in the toaster. As the eggs sizzled, he put bacon strips and a spoonful of grits on a plate, then buttered the toast and set it next to the bacon. The eggs were sunny-side up, the white edges bubbling and starting to curl. Sliding a steel spatula under them, careful not to break the yolks, Al placed them on the toast. "There you are. Want more coffee?"

"Yes. I'm going to sit here and write a telegram I need to send later."

As Jerry broke the eggs so they would soak into the toast, one of the men sitting in the booth sat down two stools away. He was an overweight white man, about fifty, dressed like a farmer or fishing boat captain in town for business in a straw hat and khakis.

"Morning," he said. "My name's Tom Price. That's my friend Pete over there." He pointed to a rough-looking individual who nodded at Jerry.

Jerry suppressed some irritation. He usually didn't want to talk while he ate his breakfast, but he replied courteously. "Glad to meet you. I'm Jerry."

"Thought so. Heard about you. Understand you're with that oil well they're drilling west of town."

"That's right," Jerry replied. "I'm a geologist with Pride. They're drilling the well."

"We're landmen, from Midland, Texas. A friend of ours sent us over here to see what was going on, and maybe to lease some acreage."

His statement clarified a lot for Jerry. A company couldn't drill a well without acquiring the mineral rights from the landowner, and landmen, a wandering part of the oilfield community, negotiated with farmers, searched courthouse records, and wrote the contracts. Those who were the most successful were a combination of salesman, lawyer, and storytellers, some becoming wealthy by acquiring their own rights to future oil fields.

"Well, Pride has leased all the rights close to the well," Jerry said. "I expect if it hits, there will be a hundred landmen here in a day. But not much activity yet."

"We're trying to get ahead of the crowd." Tom looked around to see if anyone was listening. Al's back was turned as he scraped the griddle. "We'd like to put you on a retainer, let us know first what's happening. Be a lot more if the well hits and we've already got some good leases."

"No." Jerry turned his back on Tom, not wanting further conversation. He had been approached before with bribes for inside information. A good way to lose the job he had worked so hard to get, and perhaps go to jail. Tom looked at him for a moment, hoping for an opening to continue talking and perhaps convince him that this was too good a deal to miss, but Jerry focused on his breakfast, paid Al, and left. Time to return to the rig. He was sorry to leave Maria not feeling well, but he packed his duffel and kissed her forehead, leaving to meet Eddie at the pier.

Happily aware that the rig was back to drilling and that the morning sun was burning off a low mist over the river, Jerry hummed as he picked up his duffel bag and walked through town to the dock. Eddie was at the boat, the engine idling as they prepared for the short trip back to the board road dock. He grabbed Jerry's duffel bag and placed it under the small foredeck, next to a box of bolts and other hardware.

The boat ride back to the rig had become familiar, but the variation in weather and the wildlife of the swamp often provided a new experience. Nearing the dock, Jerry could see Jacque, a small figure in the derrick at that distance, pushing ninety-foot stands of pipe to be connected as the bit continued its descent into the earth. Suddenly hesitating and pointing out into the marsh, Jacque returned his attention to the drill pipe being rapidly hoisted to the top of the derrick. When Jerry reached the rig, Jacque had returned to the derrick floor as the connected pipe slowly rotated, turning the drill bit thousands of feet below.

"What were you pointing at up there?" Jerry asked.

"There's a guy sitting in a boat out there, about two hundred yards from the edge of the pad. He's set up some binoculars on a tripod and is watching every move we make. "

Looking east into the swamp, Jerry could see the boat, anchored where the river meandered near the rig location upstream from the board road dock. He recognized one of the men from the diner, not Tom but his companion, watching him through a set of binoculars. Jerry waved, but the observer did not respond.

Joe wasn't surprised by the surveillance.

"That river is public property, and anyone can go upstream in a boat. I've seen this on a lot of wildcats. They can get an indication of how deep we are by counting the sections of pipe as we run in the hole, and get some idea of what kind of rock we are drilling through by our penetration rate. And if we start to flare a lot, they can guess that we've found oil. Nothing we can do about it but ignore him."

Unnerved at first, the crew became accustomed to being watched and seeing the boat arrive after daylight. The man they nicknamed

Peeping Tom brought his lunch and could be seen writing in a note-book when not searching through the binoculars. One afternoon a sudden thunderstorm caused him to lie flat in the bottom of the small craft, helpless in the event of a lightning strike. The observer re-turned to Everglades City at the end of each day while there was still light to navigate the river.

Joe had spoken up the first day, telling the men, "Pride wants this to be a tight hole. That means no one talks about what we are doing. Especially to those guys who are watching us. Understand?"

The drilling crew from Louisiana understood, not surprised by the order for secrecy. They had been told to keep their mouths shut on about half the wells they had drilled. The new men looked up, wondering what was so special about drilling a hole in the ground, but nodded.

"Anyone I find out that talked is fired," Joe concluded.

A week later, Jerry saw Eddie pushing a wooden cart up the road, accompanied by Eileen. The cart was loaded with a chest and bags of groceries, and the steel wheels clacked as they crossed the gaps between the cypress planks. Stepping off into the muddy weeds of the drilling location, Eileen looked around, happy to recognize Jerry.

"Glad you've been hired," Jerry said, nodding to Eileen. "We can use something better than bread and spam for lunch. What's in the bag?"

"Chickens. I'm going to roast them. Along with some corn and potatoes."

"Sounds great. We don't have a kitchen, though. Thought about that?"

"We'll build a fire for today. I'll talk to what's his name, Joe? About something
better."

"If you can cook chickens over a fire, I'm sure you're going to be Joe's kind of cook. He'll have you fixed up in no time. "

Eileen looked at Eddie, who was holding the chest he had removed from the cart. "Take it over to that corner. Can you help me with a fire?"

"Sure," he replied. "There's some dried cypress over there left over from when the clearing was done. Should burn pretty good."

Picking up an ax from a tool chest, Eddie brought over a pile of limbs, most several inches in diameter.

"You're going to need some kindling," Eileen advised.

"Don't need it. Plenty of diesel oil around here." Making a pile of the dried wood, he doused it from a metal can, then soaked a stick with the oil. A match held to the end instantly ignited the oil and then the wood burned with a yellow flame. Eddie tossed it onto the pile of cypress limbs.

"That should be down to coals in about twenty minutes."

Eileen smiled, her nervousness about whether she could actually cook dinner evaporating with the lighting of the fire. She noticed a man in red overalls coming over to where she stood, looking at the flames.

"Hi, I'm Joe. You must be Eileen. Glad you can come cook for us," he said, extending his hand.

"Thanks for the job. I'm going to roast some chickens and make a potato salad."

"Sound good to me. The men will be happy. Need anything?"

"Some small rods I can skewer these chickens on. Got anything around?"

"Eddie, get some of those stakes we used to mark where the mud tanks were to go. They're over there," Joe ordered. He made sure Eddie picked up the right stakes, then returned his attention to the derrick.

The stakes were metal rods, four feet long. At Eileen's direction, Eddie cleaned off the mud and sharpened one end to a point using a file from the tool chest. She opened her chest and took out a jar of oil and another jar of spices, premixed salt, pepper, and garlic powder. She rubbed oil and spices onto the chickens, skewered them onto the rods, and placed them across the coals, resting on sections of pipe brought over by Eddie.

"Any water around here?" she asked Eddie.

"There's drinking water at that tap over there. We bring it out in drums on the barge. Don't mix it up with the fire hose; that's swamp water."

"Get me a couple of buckets, if you will," she requested.

She tilted one bucket and rinsed her hands, then brought potatoes from her grocery bag, placing them in the second bucket and adding more spices. "Can you get me some pieces of small pipe?" she asked.

"One thing we got plenty of here is pipe," Eddie said. He brought over lengths of small pipe, placing them over the fire to form a crude grill. Eileen placed the bucket of potatoes on it, then relaxed. She noticed Joe had returned, silently watching her work.

"It will take a couple of hours for the chickens to cook, and I'll make some potato salad after they boil," Eileen told him.

"Well, if you can cook like that over a fire, I can imagine what you can do when we build you a kitchen. That's starting to smell pretty good," he said, making her blush with the compliment. He turned and walked back to the stairs leading to the rig floor with a purposeful stride, yelling some instruction that Eileen couldn't understand to a roughneck using a chain hoist to pick up what looked like a wrench the size of an automobile.

Chapter 9

The captain of the German U-boat 167 sat with his wife in the sitting room of the apartment. The unit had been occupied by a French family of four before being commandeered by the Germans to house U-boat officers from the new base at Lorient. They had been forced to leave their furniture, which showed the wear and tear of a working-class couple raising children in a two-bedroom apartment. It was dark outside, but the blackout curtains prevented any hint of the time of day or night. The U-167 was due to sail the next evening, and Gunter wanted to give his wife some advice and direction before he departed for the American Gulf of Mexico.

"I think you should take the children and go stay with Emily. There was another air raid last night. And there will be more. The British are sending over more planes every day." Gunter had spoken firmly, intending to be obeyed by his wife as he was by the men he commanded.

"They are bombing the U-boat sheds here," she protested. "We live ten miles away from here. They aren't bombing apartment buildings. And there is nothing to do in Hanau with Emily. I would go crazy."

"What are you going to do if you stay here?" he asked. He knew the answer. Emma had fit immediately into the social life of a junior officer's wife, probably the main reason she had married him. Gunter had met her at a party in 1935, taken her home and spent the night, and stayed a week with her until his U-boat had sailed. They married when he returned to port. As Gunter rose in the ranks of the pre-war U-boat service, Emma had accepted with pleasure the increased status that came with being the wife of an executive officer, then a commander. Part of the reason she didn't want to go to Hanau, he knew, was that Emily was married to a sergeant in the Wehrmacht. Living with a sergeant's family was not consistent with the position of a U-boat captain's wife.

"At least I'll have some friends to see," she replied in a whining voice. Gunter had heard rumors of her life when he was at sea. He knew she was a mainstay of the social network at every naval port where they had been stationed. Men came back from patrols that lasted months and made up for as much lost pleasure as possible during the brief time they were in port. Parties were attended by the commanders and lieutenants who happened to be ashore and the wives and girlfriends of those at sea. He had overheard some accounts of Emma staying late and being taken home by some of his friends, not wanting to believe she could be unfaithful, but unable to stop wondering what she was doing. He had never brought it up, adapting to a life of half-trusting her.

"They might not bomb an apartment house on purpose, but if it is foggy and they can't see the boatyards, they aren't going to carry the bombs back to England. They'll drop them wherever they think there might be a target, and that could be you and the kids."

"I can't believe the Navy hasn't set up something for the wives of captains in some safe place. We deserve it. They leave us on our own to find a place to go away from here, when they should have set up something nice in a hotel where we could all be together. "

As Gunter had moved up the ranks, Emma's criticism of the way the Navy treated them had increased. Expectations of luxurious housing, servants, and rations had not been met, and it had made her petulant and whiny. Gunter had not come from a naval family, the son of a butcher who had never lived near the water or been on a boat. The life the Navy had provided was far better than he had experienced as a child, and he was aware that he was treated the same as every other U-boat commander. Not an admirer of Hitler, but willing to accept that he had brought Germany back from the disarray of the Weimar Republic, Gunter's allegiance was to the Navy and the U-boat service. He had proven resourceful and aggressive, resulting in having been given command of the U-167 last year.

The conversation ended without a commitment from Emma to go to Hanau, just a promise to consider it if things got worse. Gunter said goodbye to her and his two boys, hoping he would see them again. He walked outside and got into the waiting staff car, which drove through the dark streets to the submarine pen, a slip inside a concrete bunker with a sloping roof. Illuminated by bright floodlights, Gunter could see the final loading of diesel fuel and the last of the torpedoes taking place on the U-167. Another U-boat, the U-213, was docking in the adjacent slip, returning from two months at sea. The crew stood on deck, looking filthy, wearing ragged uniforms, and grinning broadly at the prospect of shore leave. Wearing a sweater and overcoat against the winter European weather, Gunter boarded the submarine, climbed the ladder to the top of the conning tower, and descended through the hatch to the control room. He nodded to Franz, his executive officer.

"How do we look for a departure at eighteen hundred?" he asked. They would leave at night, giving them hours to reach water depths sufficient to submerge during the daylight hours when the British airplanes would be scouring the French coast.

"The supplies are almost all onboard. It looks like a kindergarten playroom down there now, but we can get it sorted out after we leave. That half-assed dock crew says they repaired the rudder stuffing box. They finished welding it, but we'll have to watch it. The crack from our grounding is a weak spot."

During their last cruise, they had been depth-charged by an American destroyer off of Florida. The violent explosions, the loss of light as the main circuits shut down, and the ever-present claustrophobia had pushed Gunter close to panic, fighting down his fear to present a face of calm to the crew. They had drifted slowly to the bottom, silencing every noise possible. As the vessel reached the seafloor, the rudder struck a rock, turning it sideways and cracking the bearing that allowed it to turn without water flowing into the boat. It was a slow leak, which they managed with the pumps when they were able to return to the surface, and the rudder functioned well enough to get home. Gunter and the XO both knew that another similar incident could sink them, but there was nothing else to do at this point.

"What's the forecast?"

"West at fifteen knots, seas four to six feet. Foggy, which is good. Good weather to get started."

"How about the crew?"

"About half of them are back. The rest should be on board by twelve hundred."

"I want to see anyone who shows up after twelve hundred in my cabin. And give a list of anyone who misses departure to the provost marshal when we leave." Gunter did not expect anyone to miss the beginning of the voyage. The crew was all volunteers, who had signed up for the U-boat service for one reason or another. Conscripts had no place in a steel tube for four months at a time.

The U-167 left France with orders to proceed into the Gulf of Mexico and attack shipping from the Gulf Coast headed through the Straits of Florida. Its voyage was part of a larger offensive that lit the skies of the eastern seaboard and Gulf Coast with the fires of sinking ships, and soiled the beaches with oil. The American public was unaware of the intensity of the campaign, purposely downplayed by Washington. But they could hear the explosions and see the fires, and they found the debris and bodies of the crew on the beaches. The primary target was the oil tankers that carried crude from the fields of Texas and Louisiana to the refineries in the Delaware Valley. The planes, tanks, and trucks of modern warfare consumed fuel voraciously, and the war effort on both sides would grind to a halt without gasoline and diesel fuel. Interrupting this supply for the Americans was why the U-167 and other U-boats had been dispatched to the western side of the Atlantic Ocean and into the Gulf of Mexico.

The cruise proceeded routinely. The submarine, one of the latest IXB models, was capable of managing the swells and storms of the Atlantic crossing with ease. The gray seas and storm-tossed breakers of the French coast gave way to tropical temperatures and marine life as they passed Bermuda, cruising southwest at a steady ten knots on the surface. They were spotted twice by airplanes as they neared the coastline, diving to evade strafing and a potential depth charge. They sank a small coastal freighter off Miami. The supply of fresh food was depleted by the time they reached the Bahamas, and the crew began to smell pretty bad. Fortunately, they were numb to the shared odor, and plenty of canned goods remained for what was planned to be a two-month voyage. The submarine passed south of the Keys and cruised eastward through the Florida Straits.

Seated on a stool in the control room, Gunter focused his attention on the nautical chart taped to a table. The position of the boat based on their last noon sight was marked with a crayon on the transparent overlay. The noon sight, a measurement of the highest elevation of the sun measured with a sextant, was a navigational technique dating from the days of Columbus. Gunter and Franz had both measured the angle of the midday sun when they surfaced two days ago, which provided a precise value for the submarine's latitude and the local time. After consulting the chronometers that had been set to Greenwich time before they left Lorient, Gunter had been able to quickly calculate their longitude. Their position could also be found with a three-star fix at night, but the chronometers and a good noon sight made that complicated procedure unnecessary.

They had established their location as ninety miles southwest of the uninhabited islands of the Dry Tortugas, a coralline complex of land due west of Key West. Since then, they had motored due north for twenty-four hours at ten knots, which put them about a hundred miles west of Naples, Florida, an ideal position to intercept shipping that emerged from the Straits of Florida between Cuba and Key West, headed to and from the mouth of the Mississippi River. Tankers carrying crude oil loaded in New Orleans and Galveston would be forced to pass nearby as they approached the Straits of Florida. Moving in the other direction, passengers and freight were being transported to ports along the Gulf Coast where they would disperse to the Midwest on the web of rail lines, untouchable by the Axis. The cargo was only vulnerable at sea, and disrupting this shipping before it reached safe harbor was the goal of the U-boat blitz. Gunter had sufficient torpedoes, fuel, and supplies to remain on this station for several weeks. He would rendezvous with the U-459 to refuel before returning to Lorient.

His attention to the chart was disrupted by the sound of an approaching aircraft's rise in volume and pitch, an inverse Doppler affect as the Coast Guard plane came closer to the frantic men atop the conning tower of the U-boat. It was dawn in the Florida Straits, and the plane came from the direction of Cay Sal, the rising sun rendering it invisible to the lookouts. Cruising due west on the surface, the submarine was recharging batteries and pumping fresh air into the steel hull. The distinctive roar of a radial engine resulted in a cascade of men through the hatch to the deck below, reminding Gunter of firemen descending from their sleeping quarters to board a waiting truck, but without a pole. As soon as the last man plummeted through the hatch, he slammed it shut and spun the dog wheel.

"Dive!" he shouted, the hoarseness in his voice betraying his excitement in spite of his efforts to appear calm. He wanted the crew to think this was a routine event that could be handled without any problem. But he knew that if they had closed the hatch two seconds later, a lucky bomb launched from the airplane might have blown the U-boat apart.

The submarine nosed downward and was about twenty feet below the surface in the crystal-clear Gulf Stream when the plane flew overhead, firing a burst of fifty-caliber machine gun bullets to no effect. The pilot reported the position and circled the still visible U-boat until it faded from view. With no armament to attack a submerged submarine, the plane resumed patrolling the azure waters between Cuba and the Florida Keys.

Heartbeat slowing, Gunter sat in the tiny cabin allotted to the captain of the vessel, a curtained-off space barely large enough for a bunk, a small chest, and a fold-down writing table. A photograph of Emma and his two children was taped to the bulkhead above the desk. It was a miniscule space to live and work in, but luxury compared to the cramped crew quarters, where men slept in layers of three bunks surrounded by pipes, electrical conduits, machinery, and the implements of a fighting ship.

Gunter picked up the logbook and started to document the attack by the American plane and the subsequent dive to escape, careful to note the names of the lookouts and the XO, Franz, who had calmly and efficiently secured the submarine and started the dive. The logbook was the basis for any later recognition and promotion, and he was careful to credit his crew for exemplary performance. They knew it, and his reputation for fairness and success made the U-167 a vessel that never lacked for volunteers.

Two days later the submarine surfaced next to a Pride Oil tanker, shining a spotlight on the bridge located aft of the long, flat deck over the oil tanks. Helpless, the tanker proceeded slowly to the southeast. It had been running alone, unescorted, hoping it could make the turn into the Florida Straits without being detected. They had been protected until this morning by foul weather, traveling with a cold front moving toward Cuba from Texas. But the front had stalled, forcing the ship to emerge from the protective cover of thunderstorms and heavy clouds into hazy sunlight. The daylight had passed, giving the mariners a sense that darkness might again protect them from their enemy. The sudden emergence of the conning tower of the U-boat, rising from an empty sea, was terrifying in itself. But it also foretold the end of the defenseless ship, and the lives of most if not all of the crew. As the ship slowly cruised on a straight course, the helm now lashed with a cord, the crew scrambled to find whatever shelter they could behind the steel bulkheads. Several had started to prepare one of the two lifeboats for launch, stripping away the cover and unlashing the straps that secured it to a cradle.

It would be an easy sinking with a torpedo, Gunter thought, but he wanted to save the submersible guided bombs for when a submerged attack was unavoidable. The ship could easily be sunk with the cannon mounted on the foredeck of the submarine. Turning to his gunnery officer, Fritz, he said: "Set fire to it with incendiary shells."

"Yes, Captain," replied Fritz, a young officer who had been both fatter and smelled better when they left Lorient. The cruise had not been what he expected. Slaughtering civilians in merchant ships did not seem to be what should be expected of a naval officer. He had enlisted in the Navy, expecting to serve on the Bismarck or the Tirpitz, envisioning a repeat of the battle of Jutland. But with the sinking of the huge battleships by the British, he had been reassigned to the submarine service. Still hoping for an encounter with enemy warships, sending them to the bottom of the ocean with a combination of torpedoes followed by surface gunfire, he was disgusted with his experience of sinking Allied freighters and tankers with the powerful weapons. But he followed orders.

Shouting to the seamen manning the cannon forward, he pointed to the side of the tanker, illuminated by the spotlight. Fritz yelled "Incendiary, to the tanks!" to the cannon crew, an order they had been expecting. They opened the breach and loaded a shell containing high explosive accompanied by a chemical that would ignite on impact. Adjusting the aim of the cannon barrel by turning geared wheels, they fired at the side of the ship, where they knew tanks containing the crude oil would be located. The first shell failed to ignite—months at sea had dampened the contents.

Following up quickly with a fusillade of three more, the crew saw the tanks ignite in an explosion that blew the deck off of the tanker, killing the men who had been standing by deciding whether to jump overboard. A man on fire leapt from the bridge to the deck below, but no one else appeared to be alive on the bridge. Seamen appeared from the tower at the aft end of the ship, exiting onto the deck of the tanker through steel doors. The ship was an inferno in seconds, remaining afloat for perhaps twenty minutes, before sinking in an expanding oil slick. The weight of the engines at the stern of the ship caused the bow to rise almost vertically, resembling the wick of a giant candle surrounded by an orange flame. None of the ship's complement of men escaped the initial conflagration, all of them covered with burning crude oil and dying too quickly to jump into the sea.

Gunter ordered the submarine to sail north on the surface at idle speed, charging the electric batteries that allowed them to live and maneuver submerged. Sinking the vessel with the cannon, approaching at close range on the surface, made the killing of the tanker officers and seamen more personal. Sending torpedoes while submerged, watching the destruction of an American ship through the eyepieces of the periscope, had been like watching a newsreel. The human figures were small caricatures of real people, and not lives he was deliberately ending. This was more like an execution of helpless men. He thought of his two sons and hoped that they would never have to go to war.

"Two ships sunk. Not a bad cruise so far, sir," Franz said to Gunter when the captain descended to the bridge deck within the conning tower, after watching the flames of burning oil diminish to the south.

"No, that's pretty good. We're about halfway there." Gunter brought his thoughts back to the present situation. "We can stay on station about two weeks, then we'll have to head home. Any word on refueling?"

"Yes, sir, the U-459 is supposed to meet us east of Cuba in two weeks. We'll be pretty low by then, but they can give us enough to get back to Lorient. But right now we have enough to continue cruising and sinking the Americans."

The U-459 was a support vessel, a U-boat referred to as a milk cow, carrying diesel and groceries to the U-boats on patrol off the American coast. It allowed them to stay out for months at a time. Its presence was unknown to the Americans, who suspected local fishermen and other sympathizers of supplying the submarines. The Coast Guard off Galveston actually checked the tanks of the shrimpers daily, making sure there was no unaccounted-for consumption of diesel fuel.

"Good. This boat won't sail very well. We could rig up a mast, but it would make a lot of leeway."

Franz snickered. "We need some food and water now, though. There's a little town called Marco Island due east of us. Let's send a boat in and see if we can find something."

"We'll stay out another few days," Gunter said, "and see if we can find another tanker or two. Then we'll send another landing party ashore."

Four weeks before, the submarine had sent three men in a rubber boat into a small village on the Florida Keys. The raiders had been successful in intercepting a small coastal cruiser, carrying mail, groceries, and sundry hardware south to Key West. They had killed the crew of two and motored the boat out into the deep water of the Florida Straits, rendezvousing with the U-boat and transferring the cargo. One small anti-aircraft shell had been sufficient to set it on fire. As the wooden hull burned, the machinery of the engine and steering gear broke away and sank, leaving only a few charred pieces of lumber to mark the destruction of the boat. The vessel would be missed, but there would be no reason to suspect it was the result of a German attack. Gunter considered the expedition a great success, and he saw no reason not to repeat it. Living off the local population had been a custom of war for thousands of years. No reason the Americans shouldn't make a contribution.

Chapter 10

The drill bit, a device with steel teeth on rollers invented by Howard Hughes, father of the legendary movie producer and millionaire, had worn out. The rig was pulling drill pipe out of the hole to replace it. Ninety feet of pipe at a time would be lifted to the top of the derrick, suspended above the rig floor. The roughnecks on the floor clamped five-foot tongs onto the suspended pipe, then signaled the driller to unscrew the pipe hung in the derrick from the section still remaining in the well. The disconnect resulted in a shower of mud, and the crew was covered in a gray mess from steel hats to rubber boots. Standing on a small platform near the top of the derrick, Jacque stacked the disconnected upright stands of pipe. The operation consisted of violent, fast movement of steel, inches from arms and fingers protected only by overalls and gloves. But it was a routine job for the crew and was being executed smoothly.

Jerry and Joe stood side-by-side in the door of the drill shack, watching an oncoming thunderstorm. The storms appeared every afternoon in southern Florida, and usually passed over without incident. Rain was not sufficient reason to stop work. This one was still a couple of miles away, blackening the horizon to the east and causing a cool wind to blow toward the Gulf as cold air sank from the anvil-shaped thunderhead and outflowed near the earth's surface. It was moving toward them, and in a few minutes they could expect a heavy downpour, then clear skies as it moved on towards Everglades City. The storms fascinated Jerry. Growing up in Oklahoma, he was used to the violent, tornado-spawning spring thunderstorms that blackened the sky. New York City had thunderstorms, but they were noticeable only by the darkening sky, thunder, and sudden rain. Seeing one form up over the Everglades, the tall clouds turning black and reaching upward, marked by lightning and an occasional waterspout, appealed to his interest in all natural processes. He learned to predict the formation of storms by the areas where the puffy white clouds expanded vertically, creating updrafts that fueled the formation of the thunderheads at thirty thousand feet. The storm coming toward them was increasing in intensity, turning the sky a greenish black.

Jerry suddenly heard the radio antennae humming, reacting to some strange phenomena in the atmosphere. The hair on his arms rose, and his scalp tingled. A sudden flash of white light blinded him momentarily, accompanied simultaneously by a sound resembling the dynamite charges that had been used to clear the cypress stumps in the channel.

Lightning is never predictable, and the bolt that struck the drilling rig was no exception. Created by a difference in electrical potential between clouds six miles in the sky and the ground, an electric charge with the energy of a nuclear bomb travels to the earth at the speed of light. Small precautions taken by men in the final feet of its journey become insignificant asterisks in the physics driving the huge force into the ground. The bolt missed the derrick, leaving Jacque deafened but otherwise unharmed, and struck the pipe rack adjacent to the rig floor. It then flashed to the metal tongs, killing the roughneck grasping them with gloved hands.

The rig floor was quiet, then the sound of heavy rain landing on the steel surface made it difficult to hear the sound of every man yelling at once.

"Rack this stand and shut down!" Joe shouted. The driller nodded and raised the top of the pipe to the derrick man. Joe took the place of the dead floor hand, and the stand of pipe was disconnected and racked in the derrick. The pipe remaining in the hole was suspended by slips, metal fingers at the rig floor that kept it from moving downward. The well was stable, and operations could be halted while Joe looked around and assessed the damage.

"Anyone else hurt?" he asked. He had seen lightning strike rigs before. The derrick had a steel rod extended above it, grounded to a heavy cable connected to a steel stake in the ground. This should act as a lightning rod, and although a man in the derrick at the time of a strike was still at risk, it usually protected the crew on the rig floor. But it didn't work this time.

Receiving headshakes from the crew and Jerry, Joe knelt over the slumped body of the floor hand who was dressed in muddy coveralls and old, worn boots. The lightning had blackened his face and burned his hands, and his shirt sleeves were still smoldering. Joe picked up a bucket, filled it with mud, and dumped it on the smoking arms. The rain continued, and another lightning flash showed a scene of dirty and shaken men peering at their electrocuted comrade.

"Get inside the drill shack," Joe said. "We'll start again when the rain stops. Jerry, take the boat and this man back to Everglades City. I don't know anything about his family—he only started two weeks ago. See if you can find Eddy when you get to town and see what he knows."

Jerry looked at the body and thought about the ride back in the rig supply boat.

"OK," he replied, feeling ashamed at his nervousness about being near the newly dead for the first time. If he was on Guadalcanal, he would have had plenty of time to get used to it by now.

"Help me get him in the wagon," he told Jacque. Lifting the body by the hands and boots, they placed their dead coworker in the small wagon that Eileen used to bring supplies for the meal she cooked at noon. The steel wheels clanged on the road as they pushed the cart a half mile to the dock. As usual during daylight hours, the boat was moored to the dock, ready to transport people or materials. About thirty feet long, with a small wheelhouse and an open deck, it had been contracted by Joe to ferry people and food, tools and lubricating oil, and any supplies that could be loaded by hand. Larger equipment, pipe, bags of drilling mud, and fuel arrived in the weekly barge and required a crane to be lifted onto a steel trolley for the final movement to the rig. The boat was also on standby for unplanned errands or an emergency evacuation, in case of an uncontrolled fire or gas release from the well. The captain and owner, who made a scarce living netting mullet, was happy to spend his days sitting on the aft deck and waiting for orders. He looked up at the sound of the approaching wagon.

"What do we have here?" he asked Jerry, seeing two booted feet sticking up above the front of the vehicle.

"New hand. Got killed by that lightning strike that just hit. We have to take him back to town. Where do you want to put him?"

"Jesus Christ. I thought that might have hurt someone. Never been so close. Let's put him on the after deck. I've got a blanket we can cover him with on the way back."

The three men picked up the body of the roughneck, Jerry holding his armpits and the boat captain and Jacque each supporting a leg. Jerry stepped across the open space between the dock and the boat, cursing as the boat moved away, but successfully putting both feet on the deck. After a couple of clumsy moves, the dead man was successfully lowered onto the aft deck, hidden from view by a dark green ragged blanket.

Not expecting or receiving any assistance, the captain started the engine, untied the bow and stern lines, and pushed the bow into the canal. Returning to the wheelhouse, he turned the wheel hard right and motored ahead a few feet. Spinning the wheel to the left, he reversed course as the prop turned the boat, allowing him to head down the river. The small pilothouse had a glass windshield and side windows, the back open to the rain. The three men crowded close to the wheel, flinching at the sound of continuing thunder. The storm had moved toward Everglades City, and the boat proceeded slowly, the captain allowing time for it to move into the Gulf before they arrived at the dock.

"What are we supposed to do when we get to Everglades City?" the captain asked Jerry. Take him to the hospital?"

"I don't think there is any rush at this point, but since we're not doctors, I guess that's the thing to do. Let's tie up, and I'll go to the sheriff's office and ask for help. And I want to find Eddie and see if he can take me to see this man's family. Damn it, I don't even know his name. Maybe Eddie will."

Jerry found Eddie, half a bottle down of some moonshine he had traded for egret plumes, but still awake.

"I need your help. Do you know the new man you sent out to us a couple of weeks ago? Well, he's dead. Struck by lightning."

"Willy? Son of a bitch. Dead? Yeah, I know him. What do you want from me? I'm not the coroner," Eddie replied in a needling, defensive whine, reflecting the beginning of a hangover.

"I need you to take me to see his family and tell them what happened. Now."

"They live further up the river from the rig. House on a small island. Need to take my boat."

"OK. Let's get going." Jerry was not familiar with sudden death, but he knew how to behave in the aftermath of a life's end. This seemed familiar, helping a family. He had done this before. Following Eddie, he sat in the bow as the boat motored up the river past the drilling rig, following the meandering path of the channel through the marsh. I wonder why they live out here in the middle of nowhere, he thought.

Eddie's skiff drifted slowly toward a stake driven into the river bottom, in front of a cabin built of weathered cypress on an acre of dry land. The island was a shell midden, the result of discarded oyster shells and other debris left by generations of prehistoric inhabitants. Periodic flooding had deposited a layer of thin soil on top of the shell fragments. Cypress trees grew in a wooded area at the back of the island, away from the river. There was a small patch of vegetables, a few chickens, and a rack of drying nets and traps. A small boy with a shirt and shorts, both with holes, was gnawing on a bone that looked like a squirrel leg. Two other children, both girls, watched them approach the house, ducking inside as they stopped just below the sloping porch. A young woman, once pretty but worn down by life, wearing a yellow dress and lace-up boots, walked down to the bank.

"Maggie, this is Mr. McDonald from Pride Oil. He has something to say to you." Eddie introduced Jerry and stepped back, wanting no part of the blame for Willy's death. Willy had been hired as a laborer to move bags of drilling mud and carry pipe, but when Jim had been called to report to the Army induction center last week, Joe had given Willy a chance on the floor. Uneducated but quick-witted and eager to learn the workings of the rig, he had been accepted by the crew after a week of shoves, insults, and the intentional showers of mud given to every new recruit.

"Hello, Maggie. I am sorry to have to tell you that Willy was killed by lightning this morning, during that thunderstorm that just passed over. He was on the rig floor when it hit. I don't know what else I can say about how it happened. I'm very sorry."

"Dead? Wheah is he?" she asked in a high thin voice, her speech reflecting the isolated rural southern existence that was all she knew. Her face trembled as the realization that Willy would not be coming back took hold. They had hacked out a life together in the wilderness, never in love, but at times affectionate. He had been mostly good to her, drinking only occasionally when he had a dollar in cash, and never hitting her.

"In town. We brought him back. I'm not sure if he is at the hospital or not. Are you his wife?"

"Common law. Them two girls are mine, the boy is ours." Her face froze, and she looked around furtively, as if seeking help. The shock of Willy's death caused her mind to flitter, searching for something, anything, else to think on while she processed the news. Looking around the small farm, she let worry about the future share her consciousness with the grief of losing Willy.

"Don't know how ah'm goin' to make it now," she continued. A sudden panic overwhelmed her as she thought about the almost complete lack of food in the cabin. They had been scratching out an existence, and Willy's chance to work for LT Drilling, arising from a conversation with Eddie on a trip to town, had given them a rush of excitement and joy. They sent hungry children to bed at night, counting the days until his first pay envelope. It would be due on Friday. She would mourn Willy in due time, but shocked by the news of his death, she quickly became obsessed with how she could possibly provide for her children.

"There will be some money coming." Jerry didn't know what the company would do. Willy would get back pay for the time worked. Lightning was not an accident caused by the rig, but Willy had died working for Pride Oil. He didn't know what Mike Woods would approve, but there would be some money. Maggie would be better off than if Willy had died on his boat, harvesting mullet with a gillnet.

She yelled to the children, "Get on ovah heah!" They shuffled slowly, looking at Eddie and not meeting Jerry's gaze.

"This man says that yoah Daddy's daid and not comin' back," Maggie told the three of them. "Kilt by lightning."

They looked uncertainly at Jerry, the bearer of ill news, then turned and ran to the cabin. Jerry could hear the boy crying. He pulled out his wallet, finding only ten dollars when he opened it, and handed her the money. "Take this and get them something to eat," he said. "Do you want to go back to town with us?"

"Not now. Ah'll have to comfort them some. Ah'll bring them in later today in the boat. Should have enough gas to make it." Maggie looked intimidated at the prospect of getting through seeing Willy and a funeral. "When do I get the money?"

"Let me work on that," Jerry said. "I'll have at least a part answer for you later today when you get to town. And I am sorry."

Eddie was talkative on the ride back to Everglades City. "Only seen one other man kilt by lightning," he said. "Offshore shrimping. I was in the next boat when a bolt hit the outrigger and flashed right through him. Sank the boat, too. Me, I always try and lay low when I see one of them storms a-coming. But sometimes you're not in a place to do that. "

"We have lightning in the city, but it never seems to hurt anyone. You can see it hitting the tower on top of the Empire State Building. Doesn't seem to do any damage. But once it set a neighbor's house on fire in Oklahoma," Jerry said after a few minutes, thinking about the small family they had just left.

The wind shifted to the northeast as the storms passed, and cool dry air blew from the inland prairies. The one-cylinder motor propelling the boat didn't buzz or hum, but made a series of bangs that could be heard separately. Eddie steered with a tiller, avoiding invisible snags and sandbars, quiet now. Pulling into the dock on Riverside Drive across from the Turner Inn, he waved goodbye as Jerry stepped off, turning back upstream without a word.

"I don't see how she can survive," Maria said after listening to the story. "A woman alone living in the woods with three kids. Do you think she'll get much money?"

"I talked to Mike Woods today when I got back. Willy worked for LT Drilling, not Pride, so it's really up to them. But Mike promised a hundred dollars from Pride anyway. I told her that and she sounded pretty happy. It should last her for a while if someone doesn't get ahold of it."

"Does she own that property where she's living?" Maria asked.

"Don't know. Could be squatting, or renting, or sharecropping. If it's renting, probably paying with shrimp or oyster. But maybe they own it. I'll check at the courthouse tomorrow before I go back out."

A thought struck him, too good to happen, too unlikely to say anything about it to Maria right now. But the next morning, after their breakfast cooked to order by Al at the diner, he wandered over to the Collier County Courthouse, an impressive building for the town, designating the community as the county seat. Pushing open the front door and entering the lobby, he saw a desk facing outward to greet visitors, occupied by a bored-looking woman stamping mail.

"Morning," he said. "I'm Jerry MacDonald. Are you in charge here?"

"As much as anyone," the gatekeeper replied. "I'm Katie. Work for the Clerk of Court. What can I do for you?"

Responding to his request for the location of the property records, she pointed to a hallway leading toward the back of the building.

"Back there," she said. "If you want to look at them, you need to sign in here. There's a table back there you can use."

Signing in the ledger after showing a New York driver's license, Jerry followed the hallway to a room with tall windows and several tables. He saw a row of file cabinets, recording the title to all property in Collier County not owned by the federal government or the Seminole tribe. A map crisscrossed with lines dividing the county into small squares was posted on the wall, and after some searching he found the island he had visited yesterday.

Township 34, Range 29, NW of the NW quarter of section 16 he wrote on a page in his notebook. Turning to the file cabinets, he saw that the draw containing section 16 had been recently searched, the folders stuffed back in apparent haste.

"Anybody else been in here?" he asked Katie, who had followed him into the room, glad for a break in the monotony of the job. It was fair pay for not doing much of anything, but most of her days were spent alone. She seized on any opportunity for conversation.

"A couple of guys from Oklahoma yesterday. I didn't have time to straighten the files after they left. They made some notes and took off without saying thanks. Kind of rude." Maintaining the files was evidently part of her job, and she didn't appreciate the lack of respect for orderly records displayed by the visitors.

Jerry sorted through the file drawer and located a record concerning the NW of the NW quarter of section 16. It had apparently been homesteaded in 1916 by William Eversby. No record of a change of ownership was in the file drawer. Maggie had described herself as a common-law wife and was apparently using Willy's last name. Willy had died at about thirty years old, too young to have homesteaded the property in 1916, so it must have been his father. Backwoods folk couldn't afford attorneys and wills, so the property had apparently just passed to Willy from his father without a recorded change in the deed. Willy had continued to live where he had been raised, later bringing Maggie to share his home.

"You know anything about William Eversby?" Jerry asked Katie, who was now paying some attention to him. Calls by good-looking young men who wanted to see the records were not a common occurrence.

Wonder what this is all about, she thought. "The dad? Sure. Died in 1938. Caught some kind of fever and was dead in two days."

"Was he married?" Jerry asked.

"Had been. His wife ran off a few years earlier, leaving him with Willy. Got tired of living in the swamps and just left one day. He never saw her again."

"Thanks," Jerry told her. "I may be back, but I got what I need for now."

"OK. Glad to see you any time. I'll be here Mondays through Fridays from nine to four. And I take an hour for dinner; the door will be locked then. But if you're already here and signed in, you can stay while I go eat."

Back at his desk in the Turner Inn room, he stared at the map he had drawn months earlier of the South Florida Basin, a sagging bowl of limestone and anhydrite thousands of feet thick. The location of the hoped-for Sunniland reef was at the edge of shallow bay waters during the Cretaceous period, where the ocean floor had dropped off rapidly to abysmal depths. Jerry knew that the modern reef south of the Florida Keys was similarly situated, where the mud flats of Florida Bay transitioned in a short distance to the depths of the Florida Straits. Reefs are built by stationary organisms that filter microscopic food from the water and require constant wave action to bring them a continuous supply of nutrients. The giant rudist clams that lived during Sunniland time, accompanied by a variety of corals and sea fans, had built reefs from Florida to Texas that grew in the breaking waves at the edge of a shelf of shallow water.

Jerry's map showed the Cretaceous shelf edge on a sheet also marked with property boundaries and the township, range, and section numbers that divided all of Florida into one-mile squares. It had been used to identify the property owners so that Pride Oil landmen could make deals and lease the mineral rights. They had managed to sew up most of the land within a mile of the well, and were still visiting farmers and ranchers. Normally, Pride would have not started drilling without more of the land being leased, but the wartime pressure from Washington had led them to show their hand by bringing in the rig without having finished acquiring all the mineral rights. If the well struck oil, the price of poker would go up overnight.

The sharp break in water depths during Sunniland time, when the reefs grew in the surf that rolled in and crashed on the wall of coral and shell, crossed the center of the island that constituted the Eversby property. It hadn't been leased. Jerry thought for a minute, then went downstairs to the lobby.

The pay phone was at the end of the downstairs hallway, on the wall next to the laundry room. It was a party line, so Jerry hadn't used it much, relying on telegrams and the mail to relay information on the drilling progress to Mike Woods. Looking around, he picked up the receiver.

"I'd like to make a collect person-to-person call, please."

"Who to?" the operator asked.

"Franklin 20659 in New York City, please. For Mike Woods."

"Who should I say is calling?"

"Jerry MacDonald."

Mike Woods' familiar voice said, "Jerry?" after three rings. "What the hell is going on? I thought we were going to use Western Union."

"I want to find one of the landmen down here, right away. The woman I talked to you about yesterday, Maggie Eversby, owns some good acreage. I think she's got title. The well is looking good, and I know we're trying to get a better land position, so this would do two things. Help someone whose husband died working on the well, and it's a potential reef location. And I know we have some competition. There's two landmen from Oklahoma down here."

"OK. Sounds like it's worth pursuing. Roger is up in Naples; I think he got there yesterday and is staying at the Broom Hotel. I'll switch you over to Ellen and she can give you the number there. Should be able to find him tonight." Without further words, he abruptly ended the conversation, and Jerry heard Ellen's voice on the phone.

"Hi, Jerry. How's sunny Florida?"

"Kind of slow down here, but we're enjoying ourselves. Staying at a rustic little hotel in a rustic little city. Never saw so many people excited about fishing, which is about all there is to get excited about here. Except drilling an oil well."

"What can I do for you?"

" I need a number for Roger. Mike says he's supposed to be staying at the Broom Hotel in Naples. Do you have a number?"

"Yes, he sent a telegram yesterday. It's Pearson 37214. Hope you find him."

"Thanks, and I should see you in about a month. Take care," he said, hanging up the phone.

Jerry needed a payphone that wasn't a party line, so later that evening, he walked to the train station. The waiting room was dimly lit, a black pay phone visible on the back wall. Picking it up, he dialed "O" and heard the operator respond.

"Long Distance, Pearson 37214," he said.

"Please deposit seventy-five cents for five minutes."

Taking three quarters from a roll wrapped in paper, not expecting Roger to be able to put a collect call on his hotel bill, Jerry placed them one at a time in the circular slot at the top of the phone. Hearing them clang into the coin box, the operator made the connection.

"Hello," said a voice Jerry didn't recognize, but then he didn't know Roger at all.

"Is this Roger Sanders?" he asked.

"Who wants to know?"

"I'm Jerry MacDonald. I'm the geologist sitting the Sunniland well. I talked to Mike Woods this afternoon, and he said to call you about a property. But can you verify you are Roger Sanders?"

"Yes, I've heard of you," Roger said. "We're chasing all over the swamps leasing acreage based on your maps. I have one here. It shows the northwest corner of the reef we're drilling to be in Section 13."

"That sounds like you're working for Pride," said Jerry. Maggie's personal situation, property description, and ownership status took him more than five minutes to describe, interrupted twice by the operator's request for more money to continue talking.

"This sounds good," Roger said. I'll go down and do a search tomorrow. If she's been a common-law wife for more than two years, she should have title. Then I'll go out and see her. We've been working further north near Immokalee, but this makes sense. How's the well going?"

"So far the tops are coming in right where we predicted. So that basin edge location hasn't changed."

"Even more reason to go see Maggie. I'll check the records and let you know. If you're on good terms with her, it might help if you came along."

"Glad to. Keep in touch." Jerry hung up the phone and went upstairs.

Chapter 11

Eileen ground the coffee beans into small chunks, putting them in a battered gray pitcher with two gallons of water, and lit a fire on the oil stove using a kitchen match. The coffee would be ready after boiling for a few minutes, decanted off the coarse ground residue. It was a simple process that didn't require percolators or a drip pot. That was important, because although the rig crew had built the kitchen and installed an oil stove and an icebox, she was forced to buy cookware and utensils from the money in the can hidden above the beams in her bedroom. Joe had hired her to cook a midday meal for the crew, reimbursing her for groceries, but expected her to bring whatever she needed to cook the meal.

The butcher shop in town had not had any meat worth buying today, so she had purchased a barrel of fresh mullet from one of the gillnetters at the dock. While the coffee boiled, Eileen rolled up the sleeves on her red-and-white-checked dress and started cleaning and scaling the small fish. They would be dusted in flour and fried whole. The crew liked them well enough, but they were craving calories and fat after hours of hard physical labor. So she started some bacon to provide grease for frying okra from one of the small farms near Immokalee. That and some bread would suffice for dinner today.

The cookhouse Joe had constructed for her at the edge of the manmade island in the Everglades was cool before noon, with an overhanging roof, waist-high wood walls, and screen on all four sides above the walls. It was elevated on cypress piers, above the occasional floodwaters and incessant varmints. There was a wooden table, flanked by benches, where the crew gathered when the operation allowed at least most of them to take their lunch break. Eileen had supervised the building of the cookhouse for two days while cooking over an open fire. She had asked Joe about a stove, worried about costing too much too early but wanting to cook in a real kitchen. The recipes that lent themselves to an open fire were limited.

"Draw a picture of what you need, and I'll have it by tomorrow."

"It will take longer than that to get the order to Fort Myers," she replied.

"Who said anything about Fort Myers?" Joe had laughed. "If it's metal and burns oil, we can make it better here."

"Got a pencil?" she asked.

Handing her a pad from the pocket of his overalls and a wooden pencil that had been sharpened by his pocketknife, Joe watched her sketch a drawing of a stove, six burners on top and an oven below.

"That will let me bake pies while I'm frying fish. I don't know how to draw an oil burner. I know that furnaces have them, but I never looked inside one."

"We can handle that. We use them to heat water to mix the mud in the winter. Haven't needed them down here, but they came with the rig from Oklahoma. Not a problem to weld up some more, along with the piping."

Walking away from the cookhouse, Joe motioned to one of the roughnecks. It was the fellow who had welded the rig to the barge deck weeks before. "I want you to use some of the plate from that water tank we're not using and make a stove for Eileen," he said. How long will it take?"

Two days later, after several loud arguments and advice from the rig crew about the best way to construct a stove, a newly welded steel stove with oil burners piped to a large tank occupied a corner of the cookhouse. Eileen smiled as she remembered how fast it had been constructed, by men both wanting to impress her and hungry for a hot meal. They had also welded together a sink, piped to a water tank resting on stilts above the roof of the cookhouse, which provided running water. A wooden icebox, lined with tin, completed her kitchen. Delighted with the setup, Eileen was able to prepare a hot meal for the rig crew at noon, with leftovers saved for the night shift in the icebox.

"Is it ready yet?" Joe walked into the cookhouse, twenty minutes after she arrived as always.

"One more minute and you can have the first cup."

It had become a morning ritual with them. Eileen served Joe a cup of hot coffee as he sat down at the table. The surface was rough-hewn boards cut from the cypress that had been used to build the board road. Not fancy, but serviceable. *Like everything else at the drill site,* she thought. Money wasn't spent if it wasn't needed to get the job done.

"Thanks," said Joe. "How are things going? Any trouble getting here this morning?"

"No, I was at the dock when your boat pulled in. Only problem is that the boat from Naples was late, and no fresh meat. That's why I bought the mullet."

"Well, the men from around here like it fine, and the ones from Oklahoma think it's bass. So we can get by fine for a day or two. They sure like it better than bringing a sack lunch." Joe sipped the coffee, drinking it black from the metal cup. "Any more trouble from anyone?" he continued.

"No, I hit Jimmy with a hot spatula after he grabbed me the last time, and told him I would put it where the sun don't shine if he touched me again. He knows me from a long time and thought that gave him some special privileges." Eileen had gone through a period when she had freely slept with the men she happened to like in Everglades City, and some of them thought she was still available when they wanted her. A few years ago she had decided to change her life, but not all of them had gotten the word.

"Jacque and Bobby slammed him up against the shale shaker, and banged his head against it pretty good. They told him they didn't want to go back to sack lunches, and that if you quit, they were going to make him drink some mud." Joe chuckled at the story. If he had witnessed it, he would have had to stop the lesson, but hearing about it secondhand made him pretty happy. "Let me know if he bothers you again, and I'll let him go," he said. "A good cook is harder to find out here than a new roughneck. Besides, I don't like him."

Joe had hired a few new hands from Everglades City, most of whom knew nothing about drilling but were willing to work hard to learn. Jimmy knew nothing and didn't seem too interested in learning. But he did provide muscles when required.

"Let me know when you're ready, and we'll stop and circulate for thirty minutes. I'll send in everyone but Jimmy—he can wait until the others eat."

"OK," she replied. "Be about an hour."

About ninety minutes later, the drill pipe stopped rotating and a group of men in dirty coveralls walked over to the firehose to rinse off. She had gotten to know them all: Jacque, Bobby, a driller from Oklahoma sent down by the LT company, Big Slough, and a new man hired to replace the roughneck killed by lightning. Eddie, delivering some paperwork to Joe, seemed to time his errands so as never to miss a free meal. Jimmy remained on the rig floor, with orders to yell if anything stopped working. They cleaned their hands and boots as best they could, and trooped into the cookhouse to sit at the wooden table. Eileen stood at the stove, bantering with them as they sat down.

"Got some fresh bass from Lake Okeechobee today, boys," she said.

"What happened? You spend all the grocery money LT gave you on that new dress?"

"They sure look like mullet to me."

"Got any ketchup? Or did you pour it all into the coffee?"

The chance to sit down and have a meal in the company of a pretty woman was something none of them were used to. And to have a hot meal that actually tasted good was even more of a rarity in their lives. The daily ceremony kept a constant supply of men looking to get on with the rig, and let Joe choose who he wanted working for him. And it kept those who were already employed happy enough so that the free life they enjoyed in the swamp didn't pull them away.

The men shoveled the mullet and okra into their mouths, wiping their faces with some cotton waste that Eileen had put on the table. Drinking coffee and water, they finished eating and returned to the rig floor. Eileen started to clean up and put the remaining food in the icebox for the night shift.

Later that afternoon, she heard the whistle announcing the arrival of the supply boat at the board dock, her ride back to town.

Picking up the empty canvas bags she used to bring groceries, she walked past the rig, waving to Jacque in the derrick, her shoes sliding in the mud until she reached the board road. Elevated three feet above the marsh, the road gave her a perspective of the swamp that she always enjoyed, safe and dry but able to see the life beneath her. Small fish schooled in the little pools created by gaps in the marsh grass, and blue claw crabs scurried across the bottom. An alligator gar, a fish about four feet long with lethal looking teeth, floated silently in a larger pool, waiting for prey.

She spotted the tail of a redfish, as it rooted on the bottom of the shallow brackish water, feeding on small shellfish. The board road gave her the freedom to stop and watch the creatures in the water. She felt like a bird flying over the swamp, looking down on the life beneath it, searching for food. The sun was low when she arrived in the morning, but was high above when she returned to the boat dock in the afternoon. The light passing through the clear, shallow water made the bottom appear as a finely wrought tapestry in constant motion.

Eddie joined her on the boat, sitting on the transom seat as the barking sound of the unmuffled engine increased, and the boat gained speed.

"That was a good lunch," he said. He had known who Eileen was all his life but had never eaten a meal with her or even had a conversation, until the rig had arrived. They had gotten to be friends as they traveled the river together, and she welcomed his help to set up the kitchen and carry the heavy sacks of groceries.

"Thanks. I'm sure you know it was mullet and not bass."

"Fine with me. I always like fried mullet."

Falling silent for a moment, watching the mangrove banks pass by, he suddenly asked, "You think they're going to find oil? We sure could use some more wells like that around here. I don't want to go back to fishing and trapping."

"Joe doesn't know," she replied. "He says it's just his job to get the well drilled where they told him. The geologist, that Jerry guy, seems pretty confident, though."

"I've sunk pilings for a dock before, and it's hard enough to keep them straight. I don't see how they can keep that pipe straight for two miles," Eddie said.

"Don't know either, but Joe does. What are you doing when we get back?"

"I'm supposed to pick up the mail and bring it back in the morning. Have the rest of the day off except for that. Think I'll go check on my cabin."

"You mean your still? If you have any extra shine, I could use a bottle." Eileen liked a drink or two at night, and although now she could afford a store-bought bottle of liquor, she was still partial to the moonshine she had drunk since she was fifteen.

"I got some. Will bring it by later. I sure am getting used to having some money," Eddie said wistfully.

The boat docked, and Eileen returned to the room she rented in a small house where she had lived since moving south from Naples after the death of her mother. A single bed, a washbasin, a chair, and a small dresser contained all she had in the world after thirty years. She changed her clothes and went out to sit on the front porch with the elderly woman who rented her the room.

Chapter 12

Maggie smoked a corncob pipe as she sat on the front steps of the cypress cabin, watching the unknown man walk confidently up the path from the river bank, carrying an expensive-looking briefcase. Tanned and well-dressed, a paunch overlying his belt, he looked like someone who lived in town but was used to the outdoors. He had arrived in a motorboat driven by another man who appeared to know him, from the way they were talking before he stepped ashore. The second man had a rough, impatient look. She wondered why they had bothered to make the trip from town to her isolated patch of the swamp.

She looked much better than the day Jerry had visited to tell her of Willy's untimely demise. Some of the hundred dollars she had received from Pride Oil had been spent on new clothes, a few chickens, and some Prince Edward tobacco. The children had new shoes on their feet, something that had never been purchased for all three of them at the same time in their lives. Right now they were all barefoot, however, proudly saving the shoes for visits to town. Jerry had come out a few days ago and told her she should get something more from LT Drilling. So she felt like things were looking up. She stilled missed Willy, but maybe now she would be able to move to town, get a job in a store, and be done with the shack in the swamp.

The visitor stopped a few steps short of the porch. "Maggie Eversby?"

"That's who Ah am. Who are you?" she replied.

"I'm Tom Price. With Willy's death, I now own this property. He signed it over to me a year ago when I lent him some money. I agreed to let him keep living here, but now's he gone and it's mine."

"Ah never heard anything about that," Maggie said, suddenly defensive. "Willy didn't gamble."

"Doesn't matter. Fact is he took the money, and I own the property. I'm going to let you keep living here like I did Willy, but I need you to sign this paper."

"What does it say?" she asked, peering at the document. "Willy did all the readin' and writin'."

"It just says you get to keep living here. Now write your X by the line, and I'll be gone. You'll be fine."

Suddenly suspicious, Maggie said, "Ah'm going to have to think about this. Can you come back tomorrow?"

"Deal's off tomorrow. You sign now, or you have to move off my property. Now." Tom moved closer, his face only inches from hers, and pushed the paper at her with a sharpened pencil. She reluctantly drew an X on the line he indicated at the bottom of the page. Reading and writing had been a childhood dream she'd never realized, her chance to spend time with someone who would teach her the mysteries of the strange symbols disappearing with the birth of her first child. After that, her days had been filled with nursing, cooking, mending, and tending the vegetable garden.

"OK. Stay as long as you want." He retraced his steps to the boat pushed up onto the riverbank, and sat down as his companion started the motor and turned downstream toward Everglades City.

Roger Sanders sat at a wooden table in the courthouse, the room cooled by overhead fans drawing in fresh but warm air from the open windows, thumbing his way through files of property records. Hearing the front door open, he looked down the hallway to see a heavyset man, unusually well-dressed for the South Florida climate, enter the courthouse lobby. The new arrival approached the woman behind the gatekeeper's desk, producing a sheet of paper.

"I want to record this oil lease in the property records."

Taking the paper, the woman read it briefly and looked up at Tom Price.

"Maggie Eversby made her mark here?"

"Yes, that's right. She signed over the mineral rights to me. That's her X."

"You have to have a mark notarized. I can't enter this unless she comes in and makes her mark or you go to the bank and get a notary to witness it." Katie returned the man's stare, confident of the authority that came with her position, until he looked away with disgust.

"Well, she signed it. I'll go get her and bring her in person to-morrow," Tom said, irritation evident in his voice. He grabbed the paper back, placing it in a leather briefcase with a brass lock, and strode angrily out the door.

Roger waited a minute until he was a block down the street, then left the courthouse and walked to the Turner Inn. Maria was reading on the front porch, enjoying a free afternoon until her shift at the bar started at five.

"Hi, Maria. I need to talk to Jerry right away. Is he in town, or at the rig?"

"He left an hour ago on the supply boat. Plans to spend a couple of days logging samples."

"Damn. Let me see if I can find a boat. I need to talk to him. See you later." Roger turned and walked to the river, sighting a skiff with an outboard motor tied to the landing. Ten minutes later, a boatman happy to make an unexpected dollar untied the lines and headed upstream.

The following morning found Maggie Eversby collecting eggs from her new chickens, a mist rising from the marsh and creating a light gray fog before the sun burned it off. She saw Tom Price, accompanied by the boat driver from yesterday, walking purposefully up the path from the bank. The second man, like Tom, was somewhat city-dressed for the southern swamp he found himself in, but tanned and acting at home in the outdoors. Tom smiled as he approached.

"Good morning, Maggie. Sorry to bother you, but I need you to go to the courthouse with me and make your mark. They won't take your mark on the paper without seeing you. Let's go and get this done so you can stay on my property."

Straightening up, her hands behind her on her lower back, Maggie looked at Tom.

"Ah thought about it some more last night. Ah'm going to talk to a friend of mine who can read before Ah sign that. So Ah won't be goin' anywhere."

His smile vanishing, Tom said, "You don't understand. You made a deal. Now you have to go through with the paperwork. No backing out."

"Ah said Ah won't go. Ah am going to talk to my friend."

Tom stepped aside as the second man approached her, moving close enough to force her to step backwards. He slapped her hard on the cheek, reddening her skin. Her eyes watered as the resistance went out of her. She had been slapped before, but never by Willy. Afraid of a further beating, her shoulders slumped and she nodded sadly.

"You're going to go, Maggie. Pete here will stay with these brats and watch them. Make sure nothing happens to them while you're gone with me. Let's go."

Tom grabbed her arm above the elbow and quick marched her down to the landing, while his companion sat on the front steps, lighting a cigarette. The three children looked out the open doorway, watching their mother leave, not receiving a glance from the man named Pete. The sound of the rope pulling on the outboard motor reached the cabin, followed by an increase in the puttering of the engine as the boat followed the meandering bayou towards the town of Everglades City.

Jerry sat with Roger at the wooden table in the courthouse that Roger had occupied all week, perusing files of land ownership, looking for the odd homestead tract that wasn't included in the large leases acquired by Pride Oil. A small gap in the lease map could allow a competitor to drill in a discovered field, potentially draining oil that Pride had spent millions discovering. They were really just killing time, waiting for the sequel to the discussion that Roger had overheard yesterday. Hearing the front door open, they watched Maggie Eversby, her face bruised and her walk unsteady, enter the lobby with Tom Price.

Jerry stood up and walked quickly to the lobby, approaching Maggie as Tom tried to march her toward the clerk at the lobby desk. Blocking their path toward Katie, he ignored Tom Price and said, "Hello, Maggie. How are you doing? Did you fall on your cheek?"

The last time Maggie had seen Jerry, he had brought her one hundred dollars in cash and played with her children. With the exception of men looking for casual sex when she was younger, she had met few people in life that had any interest in her. But her gut told her this was someone who might help her. Tom Price had told her on the boat ride what Pete would do to her children if she didn't follow his exact instructions, but maybe Jerry would do something to stop him. Taking a breath, she decided to risk the threatened retribution.

"He told me I had to come in and make my mark in front of the desk, or he would hurt my kids," she said gesturing toward Tom.

Jerry glared at Tom and said, "Is that true?"

"No, she's just going to finish the paperwork on a deal we made yesterday. No problem. I wouldn't hurt those kids."

"You left them alone?" Jerry asked Maggie.

"No, he left them with a man name Pete, who will hurt them if I don't make my mark," Maggie said. "Please help me."

"Maggie, if you haven't made your mark in front of the clerk, the deal isn't final. You own that land, not Tom Price. I'd like to talk to you about leasing your land to Pride Oil. We will pay you some money upfront, and part of what we sell the oil for if we discover any," Jerry said.

"I'll take it. I trust you after what you've done for me. But what about that man with my kids?" she looked at Tom as she spoke, fear and anger in her expression.

"I'll go back to your house with you. Nothing had better happened to your children," Jerry said quietly, staring at Tom Price.

"Damn you and your New York lies," Tom swore. "I won't forget this."

He left the building quickly, throwing his briefcase onto the seat of an old truck and starting the engine, throwing it into reverse. Slamming on the brakes, he shifted to first gear and drove rapidly north toward Naples. He thought about Pete left in the swamp, and remembered that Pete had left his bag in the motor court room they were sharing. No way for Pete to leave Maggie's place until a boat got there, and the boat would probably have the sheriff on board.

Pete was likely do some time in jail for messing with the kids and didn't need his half of the thousand dollars they had brought from Texas. Tom swerved into the parking lot of the motor court, deciding to pick up the money. He would need it to get wherever he was going next. Maybe Canada. There was oil up there.

"He's probably scared that something did happen to those kids," Jerry whispered to Roger as the truck drove away. "You go tell the sheriff what happened. I'll get Eddie to take me and Maggie back to her place as fast as we can get there."

The boat edged up to the landing at Maggie's homestead, Eddie looping a line around a tree stump, Jerry and Maggie stepping onto the wooden plank that had been placed on the shoreline to form a crude landing. They looked around for Pete and the children, seeing no one, but they heard a whimpering sound from behind the cabin. Maggie ran, skirt flying and arms pumping, as the noise increased in volume. Turning the corner of the cabin, they saw Pete lying in the cleared area behind the house, flopping and moaning, and the three children running toward them from the woods.

"That man hit us. We ran away and put some beaver traps in the grass, then yelled at him and told him he was chickenshit, and he chased us over the trap, and it caught his foot, and he's been layin' there cryin' since," the boy said.

Maggie walked over to Pete and looked down at the steel jaws clamped down on a misshapen foot, obviously broken by the force of the trap closing. The mechanism was secured to a cypress root by a steel chain, which Pete had been unable to loosen.

"I didn't hurt them. Just told them to be quiet and stay put and they ran away. I'm getting out of this place as soon as I get back to Everglades City. Just undo the trap and take me to town in the boat, and I'll give you a hundred dollars," Pete whimpered, twisting as far as he could away from her.

She kicked his broken foot hard, making him scream in pain. Then kicked it again. "Got you, you son of a bitch. Ah'm going to shoot you. Let me get my shotgun. Ah'll shoot your other leg first." She spit out the words, her tone leaving no doubt in Pete's mind that she meant it. He cried out again in fear and pain, his voice shaking. Looking at the rage on her face, Jerry understood the stories he had heard in West Texas about how the Comanche captives dreaded being turned over to the women. There was no doubt in his mind that she would kill Pete for hurting her children.

"No, Roger's bringing the sheriff. Things are going too well for you to spend time on a murder charge," Jerry said. "Let the sheriff take care of this scumbag. He'll have plenty of time in jail to heal that foot, but he probably won't ever be able to walk on it again. Just leave him here for now. "

Maggie hesitated, slowly gaining control over the impulse to painfully end the life of the man who had beaten her and her children. She took a deep breath, then another, then nodded. The satisfaction of blowing a hole in the man who had threatened her children didn't outweigh a chance to leave this miserable swamp and start a new life. Wrapping her arms around her children, she turned and walked toward the house.

Roger looked up at Jerry from a plate of fried snapper. "So we gave her a bonus of one hundred dollars, which includes the right to shoot seismic, and a one-eighth royalty. That's standard around here, at least until we get a discovery. She has one hundred and sixty acres, which would be enough for four wells. But we'll probably combine her acreage with some of the other leases and form a unit if we get enough encouragement to drill."

Roger had moved into the Turner Inn and was spending his days at the courthouse, trying to sew up the lease situation as much as possible before the well was completed. Jerry had wandered over to the courthouse after breakfast that morning, startling Roger as he bent over a file drawer, and suggested lunch.

"I saw her yesterday," Jerry said. "She looks like a new person. Got some new clothes and a haircut. Says she's going to learn how to read from a teacher after school hours. Wanted to rent a house on the back side of town and get out of the swamp. Found something she's living in with her kids."

"Well, a hundred dollars won't last her forever, but it should be enough if she can land a job here in town." Roger looked up at a strange vehicle rolling down the street, unloaded from a rail car. It had four huge tires with a small platform, including a driver seat, suspended several feet above the ground.

"Looks like the seismic crew has arrived," he said. "They use those swamp buggies in Louisiana. Can carry the jugs out where you can't walk."

"I've never seen a seismic shoot in a swamp," said Jerry. "Watched them one time in Texas, near Midland. A lot easier out there, I imagine. They can drive a truck to lay out the jugs and bring in the equipment to drill the shot holes."

"Well, they're going to start at the rig and then shoot a line southeast, including Maggie's island. Will take a couple of weeks. They'll be looking for some men to lay out the jugs; do you think your man Eddie can find them some?"

"I'm sure he can," replied Jerry. "He seems to have a waiting list of guys who want to work for us. Pretty easy pay compared to shrimping and trapping. Let me talk to the geophysicist managing this operation, and I'll see what he needs."

Chapter 13

Eddie poled the skiff through the shallow water between the mangrove trees, a car headlight at the bow illuminating the bottom courtesy of a boat battery he had stolen from the Mangrove Lodge dock. A newcomer to the mangrove forest would have expected brown, muddy water, the result of silt and clay carried downstream by distant eroding mountains, ending in a plume of brown water draining into the crystalline waters of the Gulf. But the mangroves were organisms of the tropical, salty seawater and lived at the edge of a shoreline where there was not enough wave energy to wash them away. Such an environment prevailed along the Gulf Coast of Florida south of Naples, where the freshwater Everglades met the Gulf of Mexico and the mangrove forest thrived. The bottom sediment was composed of fragmented seashells and rotting leaves from the mangroves, bound together by seagrass and algae. The result was crystal-clear water, washed in by the tides, flowing in the channels between the clumps of trees, and at night the bottom was clearly visible fifteen feet down. The light showed a strange world, with creatures only seen during daytime at the end of a hook and line. Stingrays, crabs, and small sharks rested on the bottom, with an occasional sawfish carrying a toothed bill, reminiscent of a prehistoric monster from the Cretaceous period.

The channels Eddie poled were not created by water draining from highlands to the sea, but by the creation of mangrove islands, with one tree spreading seeds and enabling the sprouting of new seedlings nearby. As the trees grew in clusters, they filled in the open water, with twisting bayous of open water between them. The channels were erratic, many with no outlets and ending in small ponds surrounded by the trees. Eddie knew the waterscape by heart, but a newcomer had little chance of making his way through the labyrinth without a local guide.

Eddie sighted flounder at reliable intervals, gigging them with a spear fashioned from a bamboo pole and a point made from an old arrow. Right now he had about twenty in the box, about half of what he hoped to get by morning. Eileen would buy them for cash in the morning, planning to grill them on the oil stove in the rig cookhouse later that day. Flounder yielded firm white meat, unexpected for such an unattractive creature. It was delicious when cooked fresh and served with lemon and pepper.

Moving ahead slowly, he saw a doormat-sized flounder resting on the bottom, resembling a stingray without the tail. It was an odd-looking fish, flat and white on the bottom, spotted brown on top. Both eyes were located on top of the triangular head behind a mouth filled with small, sharp teeth. The fish would rest on the bottom, waiting for minnows or shrimp to drift by, then accelerate with amazing speed to grab a meal. Its habit of remaining motionless on the bottom, not disturbed by the light from the boat, made gigging a productive way to harvest the fish. Eddie knew where they congregated, lying in ambush where small fish and crustaceans would likely drift past.

Exchanging the pole for the flounder gig made him turn to his left, noticing that the light illuminated a weird object in a mangrove tree at the edge of the channel. It was brown with a flat black bottom and black fuzzy material on one edge. The mangrove limbs immediately above the arching roots formed a triangle that trapped whatever it was in spite of the moving tide.

Eddie thrust the gig downward, forcing the barbed spear through the flesh of the fish and into the soft bottom. Lifting the struggling and flapping creature free of the water, he could tell it would probably weigh more than five pounds, worth fifty cents from Eileen. Placing the flounder in a wooden locker, he looked again at the brown shape, poling closer to the tree so that his light now shone directly on the strange object. Drawing nearer, he recognized a man's shoe, still attached to a leg, which was part of a body deeper in the tree. Wearing the dungarees and t-shirt of a merchant seaman, with a life jacket covering the torso, the corpse was stained with oil and showed the predations of crabs and fish on its journey from the torpedoed ship to the mangroves. Eddie checked to see if there was a purse, and finding one in the dungaree pocket, removed three dollars and replaced the merchant seaman's union card. The explosion had rocked the town two nights earlier, and the flames had lit the Gulf west of Everglades City. He wondered how many more of the crew would drift ashore. In the meantime, he continued his search for flounder. He would tell the sheriff when he got to town in the morning.

The sun was nearly overhead when Eddie guided the sheriff's boat, propelled by a putting outboard motor and carrying the two deputies, to where he had gigged the large flounder the night before. He pointed at the shoe in the mangrove island, then let the boat glide closer.

"There he is. Stuck in that tree there." Eddie pointed to the life jacket.

"What were you doing out here? Thought you liked to stay in away from the mosquitos at night." The deputy speaking was about forty-five. He wore his uniform but with white rubber boots on his feet instead of the usual black leather shoes. He had known Eddie since he had been brought to Everglades City as a boy from the island midden. Like all of the small police force, he had grown up in the Everglades, fishing and shrimping before he got on with the sheriff's department.

"Gigging flounder. Got a buyer. Eileen cooks them for the rig crew."

"Things seem to be going pretty good for you now," the deputy replied. People called him PT. He had arrested Eddie a few times for drunkenness, thievery, and once for shooting at a trespasser, but had nothing against him. Eddie was good company when he didn't have an official reason to go see him.

"Pretty good, but still hard times." Eddie didn't want to brag about the money he was making finding labor, running errands, and occasionally carrying passengers in his small boat. If word got out, there were a lot of locals looking for money who would be some competition.

The boat bumped against a branch at the edge of the mangrove. PT secured it with a length of gray cotton rope. It was a sunny day, the slight offshore breeze evident in town blocked by the mangroves this far inland. As soon as the boat's motion stopped, mosquitos swarmed from the mangrove swamp. Anticipating this, the three men rolled down long sleeved shirts and smeared mud on their exposed hands and necks. Their heads protected by billed caps, they brushed the mosquitos from their cheeks and foreheads.

"What are we supposed to do now?" asked the younger deputy, trying not to gag at the odor of the decomposing body.

"I guess we have to put him in the boat and take him back to town. He is a casualty of the war. Killed by those German bastards in a U-boat. Wish one of them would wash ashore. We only seem to see bodies from whatever they sank." PT started to cut away the mangrove branches with a saw, surprised at how securely the dead man had been wedged into the foliage.

Two hours later, the boat pulled up to the town dock in Everglades City with a tarp covering the dead mariner. A curious crowd had gathered, alerted by a prisoner who had been arrested for drunkenness the night before. Freed in the morning after a night in jail to sleep it off, the inmate had heard Eddie loudly inform the deputy of what he had found in the swamp. The crowd watched as the body was loaded into a wagon and taken to the Seal Funeral Parlor, then dispersed quietly, muttering curses against the Germans.

Standing behind the bar in the Turner Inn, Maria served a martini to the Tampa Tribune reporter who had come down to cover the story of the torpedoed tanker. It was late afternoon, and she was alone in town. Jerry had been gone for two days, and she was glad to have the bartending job to occupy her time. After her futile attempt to find a Catholic church where she could help out, she had approached the hotel owner and suggested he hire her as a bartender. Nonplused at first, he listened to her story of bartending in New York City from the age of fifteen and agreed to let her try the job.

Aside from a quiet drunk occupying the end stool, the room was empty, a quiet time after the watermen and townspeople had stopped by for a beer or whiskey. Her shift started at four and ended at nine, giving Sam, the regular bartender, a chance to get dinner with his family while still getting her out the door before any serious rowdiness occurred. Reluctant to leave her alone at first, Sam had become convinced that she could handle the clientele that Everglades City might send her way without getting insulted or assaulted. He had watched her reaction the first week when the assistant manager of the five and dime had patted her behind as she was clearing a table. She twirled quickly, throwing half a glass of beer on his suit, and smiled, saying: "You must have thought I was your wife. Do that again and the next time I'll toss it in your eyes. But it would be better to not do it again and enjoy a drink. I like to give people the benefit of the doubt."

The man looked around, seeing the group he was about to join smirking and enjoying the encounter, waiting for his reaction. He shrugged and sat down, calling to Maria, "How about an Old Milwaukee and a towel?"

"Coming up," Maria answered, drawing from a keg and putting the glass on the table and a towel on his chest.

He patted his wet shirt, soaked from the glass she had thrown on him, then put the towel down. "I guess it will dry out before I go home. I'll tell Sally someone bumped me."

Sam watched the incident and decided Maria could handle herself. Since then, they had fallen into the routine of Maria managing the happy hour shift alone, mixing drinks and relishing the chance to converse with the hotel guests and the local regulars. Her uncle's bar in Queens had been a place of constant talking, arguing, quarreling, and an occasional fistfight. She hadn't realized how much she missed it. The locals had become protective, reacting quickly and forcefully to slights or insults from newcomers. *Just like my cousins,* she often thought. But they were not capable of her relatives' casual brutality when confronted.

The bar was dark and cool, the screened windows open to the breeze from the Gulf. The young reporter wore glasses and was dressed in a short-sleeved shirt and a brown tie, a brimmed hat on his reddish hair. He had met Maria on a prior visit when he traveled out to the rig location for a story titled "Oil in Florida?" It had made the lower half of the front page, the best he had done since joining the paper. Staying in the hotel on his return to Everglades City for the tanker story, he had quickly gravitated to the bar, hoping to see her again.

"Does anyone know who he was?" she asked, aware of his attraction to her. He knew she was married and didn't cross the line, and it felt nice to be appreciated. He was an interesting and different kind of guest in the hotel. She was glad to see him back in the bar.

"He had a merchant seaman union card in his purse. His name was Richard Oliver, from New Jersey. He joined the Merchant Marine last year, after being rejected by the draft board because of his eyesight, like me. Twenty years old, no real interest in the sea, but doing what he could during the war."

"Would have been safer in the Navy. At least he could have shot back," said John, the owner of the hotel, Maria's employer and landlord. Finished with the work of the hotel for the day, he occupied his usual place at the end of the bar, watching the river traffic and listening to the conversation.

"That's true. These guys don't get credit for the risks they take. Just targets, and right now they are sitting ducks."

"How much of this is going on?" asked Maria quietly.

"A lot," replied the reporter as he finished the martini. "This guy was on a tanker carrying crude oil from the Louisiana fields near the mouth of the river, planning to go around the Keys and up to Wilmington. There aren't any oil fields up there, so the refineries will shut down without the tankers. That's why the U-boats want to stop it. This was the only body recovered— the rest must have been trapped inside when the ship sunk or were eaten by sharks. The government hasn't given us any facts. They want to keep it quiet. But you can see what's happening from just watching the night sky off the coast. They must be sinking a ship a night."

"I heard that in Galveston they're checking fuel in the shrimp boats every day, to make sure they're not transferring it to a U-boat," said the hotel owner. "Think we should be doing that here? Don't know of any turncoats, but you never know what some of these backwoods guys from the swamps would do for some hard cash, if the Germans could pay for fuel."

"I don't think so this far south," the reporter said, coughing as he put down a cigarette. It's shallow a long way out; the shrimpers would have a hard time getting out to water deep enough for a U-boat to meet them and back the same day. And they don't stay out at night these days."

"Well, the Navy doesn't seem to be doing anything useful if we're losing a ship every night. Maybe we ought to start some patrols ourselves," the owner said, imagining the glory that would come to a fishing boat captain who sank a U-boat.

"That won't work," replied the reporter. "Some charter boat captains tried that on the East Coast. These are steel warships with machine guns and cannons. They could just ram a fishing boat without it slowing them down, not even bother shooting."

"I guess so. Night, Maria." With that, the hotel owner held onto the bar as he put his feet on the floor under the barstool, steadied himself, and walked out the door. The sun was setting over the Gulf in the west, an orange ball visible above the mangroves that separated the town from the open water. It illuminated the interior of the bar like a searchlight for a few minutes before it dropped below the trees and Maria turned on the overhead lights.

She saw Eddie walking onto the porch, waving at her. He walked in and sat on a barstool.

"Want a drink?" she asked.

"No, can't afford it. Even with the cash Joe's paying me, I can't afford to drink in a bar. Just wanted to tell you Jerry said he would be out a day longer than he thought."

"Thanks. How's it going out there?"

"Joe seems happy. I guess the drilling's going OK. Jerry says he's seeing what he expected so far, but too early to tell."

"Where are you headed?" she asked.

"Back to my shack. Just wanted to give you the message. Got some traps I have to fix in the morning."

"Do you ever get lonely out there by yourself?"

"Sometimes. But that's just the way it is. Nobody would live out there with me, and I don't have any way to live somewhere else."

"What happens when you get sick, or hurt?" she asked, wondering how anyone could survive in a shack without running water or electricity.

"I heal. Only thing I'm afraid of is spiders. There's some big ones that always want to live in a cabin. Tarantulas. I hate them, kill all the ones I see, but sometimes I wake up and see one sitting on the ceiling, looking down at me." Eddie shuddered, remembering the time one had dropped onto him.

"I don't like them either. But I'd be more afraid of animals than spiders." Maria wasn't used to any animal that wasn't a pet or in a zoo. The thought of anything that weighed more than five pounds and wasn't constrained gave her nightmares. She hadn't told Jerry, not wanting to be told she needed to go home to Queens, but it was a fact of life in Florida that she hadn't anticipated when they had come down. But fortunately there weren't too many wild animals in Everglades City, just the occasional gator warming itself on the side of the river or a possum meandering down the main street after dark.

"I don't worry about that," Eddie said. "If I don't like it, I shoot it. And I've got some dogs that chase away anything that tries to get close. Including people."

Walking around to stretch her legs after closing time, Maria looked down a side street and saw lights in the small gray house that Maggie Eversby now occupied. Unpainted, resting on concrete blocks three feet off the ground and surrounded by an unkempt dirt yard, the owner had rented it to Maggie for ten dollars a month. At first not willing to have an illiterate tenant who had spent her life in the wilderness, he had been convinced after a deposit of thirty dollars that Jerry had handed him under the condition that Maggie not find out. She had a little money now, which had made her too proud to take charity. Maria turned and approached the front porch, seeing Maggie talking to a child through the uncurtained screen windows. The step sagged and creaked as she put her weight on it, causing her to trip and catch herself. Maggie turned from the little girl and saw Maria standing outside the screen door, looking tired but cheerful.

"Hi, Maggie. I was just walking a little after standing at the bar for four hours. Saw your light on and thought I'd stop and see how things are going."

"Oh, hello, Maria. Thought it might be you. We doin' OK. Electric lights and running water in the sink. Never had that before in my life."

The money from Pride Oil and the chance to leave the swamp had transformed Maggie. She had scrubbed herself clean and obviously cut her own hair in a mirror, crudely but at least showing some attention to how it looked. The purchase of a cheap blue-and-white checked dress, some shoes to replace the boots she had worn on the homestead, and a red belt made her look like someone who cared about her appearance. Her hair was fixed with a ribbon, and she had a confident demeanor that was lacking when Jerry introduced her to Maria the week before. She was a pretty girl, slim and straight-backed. She had already started to adopt the accent of the town dwellers, shifting from the slurred drawl she had learned in the backwoods. Maria had heard her practicing the other day on the sidewalk, saying, "Eye, Eye, Eye" over and over, trying to engrain the sound in her speech when she referred to herself in the first person.

"Want to come in and set awhile?" she asked Maria. "There's a table and two chairs in here that came with the house."

They sat on metal folding chairs at a table with a scratched linoleum top that rested on chromed steel legs. "It ain't much," Maggie said. "Sorry Ah can't offer you nothing to drink. The water is rusty and smells bad; you wouldn't want it."

"That's fine. You'll make this place look good in no time. Looks like you're getting to be a town girl," Maria said. "How do you like it?"

"Ah never wanted to live in that swamp in the first place. Ah was raised near Chokoloskee, living in a stilt house with nine other kids. A friend of my mother's came by one day, and I left to live with him, and had these two girls. It wasn't much better with him; he was mostly gone fishing and came home to drink and chase me. I learned to clean fish, raise chickens and vegetables, and hunt squirrels with a twenty-two. But I never did learn no reading. I want to now."

"Any chance of a job here in Everglades City?" Maria asked.

"Ah went by that old hotel down the street from the Turner today. They said they might need a housekeeper; one just quit. I never cleaned no houses, but they said if I was willing to work hard and learn, they would show me. Doesn't look too hard."

"Any more trouble from that Tom Price guy?"

"No, I understand he left town when Jerry met me at the courthouse, when he left that man on the island with my kids. Haven't heard from him. The one that hit me, Pete, is doing thirty days for assault. Jerry said the sheriff promised to run him out of town as soon as he does the thirty. So Ah don't expect to ever see either one of them again."

"I'm sorry about Willy," Maria said. "But it looks like your life is taking a turn for the better."

"It is," Maggie replied. "Willy came along one day when these girls' father was gone fishing, and Ah left with him and the girls. He had his own land and was good to me. But it was still living in the swamp. I miss him, and I'm sorry he's gone, but I don't miss that life I had living out there on that island."

"What did the girls' father do when he found out you were gone?" asked Maria, curious.

"He came to Willy's homestead and said he wanted us back. Willy stood up to him and said we had decided to come live with him, and that was that. I thought there might be trouble, but after I gave back a twenty-two rifle I had taken with me, I never saw the man again. I think he was glad to be rid of us."

There was a tough intelligence in Maggie, Maria thought. All she had been asked to do in life so far was bear children and take care of a garden. Freed from her exile in the backwoods of the Everglades, she concentrated intensely on the smallest details of her life in town, watching how people talked, walked, dressed, ate, and moved around others. Cleaning beds in a hotel might not be that great a life after a few years, but right now it was a hell of a lot better than where she had come from. Maggie would never be rich, Maria guessed, but she might be happy. At least she was going to try.

Chapter **14**

The rotating bit was encountering small pockets of natural gas as it pulverized the layers of porous limestone. Like a microscopic sponge filled with ammonia, the calcareous matrix of the rock emitted gas when crushed and turned into tiny crystals of clear calcite. The gas formed tiny bubbles in the drilling mud, and then escaped to the atmosphere when the mud was circulated to a steel tank called a gas buster at the surface, resembling carbon dioxide bubbles breaking out of a soda bottle. The escaping gas created a vapor of methane that was collected by powerful fans and sent on a path to the flare tower. The tower was a vertical pipe located off to the side of the clearing, the tip designed to burn off gas like a huge Bunsen burner in a chemistry laboratory. A routine operation, as long as the equipment worked as expected.

Jerry stood by the shale shaker, watching the cuttings being separated from the circulating mud by the horizontal motion of the machine. Mud returning from the bottom of the well was flushed from a hose onto the shaking screens, then washed down into the mud tanks. The broken shards were retained on the screen, and the cleansed mud was ready to be pumped down the drill string again. Small pieces of rock broken loose by the rotating teeth of the bit, the cuttings were flat chips about the size of a flake of coarse pepper. To Jerry they looked like dolomite and anhydrite, which he expected at this depth. Scratching an ant bite, he looked toward the flare tip at the edge of the drilling location. The flare was out. Evidently the pilot light had malfunctioned again, and unburnt gas flowing from the flare tip was escaping into the marsh. Not according to protocol, but not unheard of.

A raccoon walking through the grass underneath the flare tip suddenly began to shake in quick, erratic twitches. It took a few more steps, then fell flat and rested motionless on the ground. A bird perched on the unlit flare tip suddenly fell to the mud. Jerry noticed several more birds in the mud nearby, lying in unnatural positions. Disturbed by the unexplained paralysis of the birds and animals, he ran to the drill shack. Pushing open the door, he saw Joe sitting at his desk, eating a leftover piece of pie from Eileen's noon meal. Jerry spoke calmly but very rapidly, "Why are those dead birds on the ground underneath the flare tip?"

Joe looked out the window and yelled to a roughneck: "Light the goddam flare. We must have some sour gas."

The man went into the control room and pushed a button, intending to create a spark at the flare tip and ignite the vapors. Nothing happened. Lighting a small torch at the end of a pole, he set off toward the flare, intending to use the torch like a kitchen match held to a stove. Halfway out, he collapsed on the ground. Joe took a deep breath, ran down the path and picked up the torch. Without breathing, he rushed to the flare tip and held up the torch. A large woosh and a fireball of igniting gas nearly set his hair on fire, but he knew to stay low and keep his face away. Still not breathing, he moved back to the prostrate roughneck and dragged him back to the drilling trailer. Kneeling over him, he started the process of artificial respiration, raising the man's arms and pressing on his back to change the air in his lungs.

An hour later, Joe sat in the drill shack with Jerry. The roughneck had regained consciousness and been sent to the small hospital in Everglades City by wagon and boat.

"There was more hydrogen sulfide in that gas than we thought. It's more dangerous than cyanide, and you can't smell it or know it's there until it kills you," Joe said.

"Is it unusual?" asked Jerry.

"Not in West Texas. Where you have anhydrite, you find it. The sulfur comes from the anhydrite. I should have expected it."

"Can we keep drilling?"

"Sure. It happens all the time in West Texas and Arabia. But we'll have to make some changes, keep the flare lit and get some masks in case we have a major release from a kick. But it can be handled."

Jerry nodded and went outside, cautiously sniffing the air even though Joe had told him the poison gas had no odor. Feeling fine, he looked out at the Everglades swamp surrounding him in every direction. It was undisturbed by the unexpected flow of a deadly chemical, trapped miles below ground until today, that had resulted from human endeavor. Drilling the well had perturbed the balance created by geologic processes that had been occurring for twenty million years. It was like poking a stick into a sleeping cougar. Joe seemed to know what to do in every situation, but there was still one dead man from the lightning, and almost one today. Jerry resolved to look out for himself and pulled out the gas mask he had placed under his small desk in the drill shack. It was intact and functional. Covering his face, and connected to a small bottle of compressed air, it would give him about five minutes to get away from the poison gas. He resolved to practice donning it and turning on the fresh air when he returned to the rig. But right now he was intent on packing and taking the boat back to the Everglades City hotel. He wanted to see Maria and spend a couple of days in a quiet room with a real bed.

Eddie shuffled up the board road, looking more ragged and dirty than usual. Arriving from Everglades City, he was unaware of the deadly gas release that all of the crew had just narrowly escaped. He looked at Jerry. "You ready to go?"

"On my way. I've had enough of this place for a while."

After the boat trip back to Everglades City and a shower and dinner in the hotel restaurant, Jerry was relaxing on the veranda of the Turner Inn, seated in a wicker chair next to Maria and finishing a glass of wine produced from some new vineyards in North Florida. It wasn't very good, but it was a welcome change from beer and Cuban rum.

"I have to go up to Fort Myers tomorrow. I need some more sample bags, and I told Joe I'd go by the hardware store and get some cable and wire. I'm going to take that Pride truck we have parked in the lot here. Want to come along? We can spend the night and do some sightseeing."

"Of course. What time do we leave?"

"Let's go right after breakfast. It's about an hour-and-a-half drive. I can run my errands, and then we can look around. Maybe you'll get at least a day of a real Florida vacation."

The next morning was cool and dry, unusual for March in Florida, the result of one of the few cold fronts that make it that far south. Announced by thunder and flashes of lightning the night before, the line of storms had cleared the air of the humidity and spring pollen that had created a gray haze over the marshes. The top of the derrick was clearly visible three miles away, a spire rising above the mangrove forest at the edge of town.

Maria wore a black dress with yellow flowers, her bare arms covered with a light sweater she had not unpacked since leaving New York City. Sitting happily on the bench seat of the pickup truck, which Jerry had covered with a clean towel, she hummed a rhyme from her girlhood, something about the road to Mandalay.

The road changed from shell to pavement, and the ride became smoother as they approached the city. Fort Myers is located on the Caloosahatchee River, a wide, deep stream originating inland at Lake Okeechobee that empties into Pine Island Sound behind Sanibel Island. They saw downtown bordering the river, a natural harbor with docks occupied by fishing craft, small freighters, and barges. A bridge crossed to the northern bank, rising over fifty feet above the river to allow boat traffic to go upstream to central Florida and Lake Okeechobee.

Pulling in to a parking space near the hardware store, Jerry switched off the ignition. "Come on in with me while I get this stuff; then we'll walk around."

The interior of the store was dark with wooden floors worn down by foot traffic and sliding heavy pallets over the years, the windows blocked by shelves containing small bins filled with items to be weighed and bagged. A counter with a locked glass case contained firearms, pistols, shotguns, and rifles, Winchester Model 12 pump guns being the most popular. Maria smelled fertilizer, mildew, pine soap, burlap, and grease—not a bad smell but strong—and one that would last in her memory. She followed Jerry to the counter where an older man was opening cardboard boxes.

"Hi," Jerry said. "I'm from Pride Oil. I called you about some canvas bags, one-inch steel cable, and some other stuff."

"Good to see you. I'm Bill. We've got what you wanted together. Need anything else?"

"Yes, Joe asked me to pick up some twelve-gauge buckshot shells and some 30/30 rounds. There's been some wild hogs rooting around the rig, and he wants to get rid of them. Can you hold on to all of it until tomorrow while we do some sightseeing?"

"Sure. It'll be here. Where are you from?"

"New York City. Our first trip down here."

Maria was at the front door, looking out across the wooden porch to the street, the unseasonal coolness and the urban setting making her suddenly homesick. The days of travel, followed by the time alone in Everglades while Jerry worked several days at a time at the drill site and she spent nights alone, suddenly caught up with her. Turning toward Jerry, she blinked back tears.

"What's the matter? I thought we were here to have fun."

"I don't know. It just seems strange all of a sudden."

"Let's go have some lunch," he said impatiently, wondering why everything had to be complicated.

"OK."

Maria tried to summon some enthusiasm as they sat down by the window in a small diner overlooking the river. They ordered fried chicken, a southern dish Maria had learned to like more and more. Jerry was puzzled and unhappy, unsure of what had caused the sudden change in her mood.

"Let's walk around after we eat. Looks like a lot of shops I want to see. Maybe I can find some shoes for my job in Everglades City. These aren't very comfortable for standing in."

Maria felt better as they moved from store to store, and the bags in Jerry's arms multiplied to all he could carry without dropping something. Shoes, a dress, a blouse, and some stockings were all Jerry could remember her buying, but from the weight he was carrying he knew there was a lot more.

"I want to have some things to take home that I can say I bought in Florida," she said. "No one in my neighborhood has ever been to Fort Myers. When they say, 'Where did you get that?' I'll just say, 'On the river in Fort Myers.'"

"If they look at the label, they might see it was made in Ohio," Jerry replied. But he didn't argue, glad to see her smiling again.

"Let's go find the hotel and leave this stuff in the room. Then we can go have some dinner. Or supper."

The hotel was a brick, two-story building situated on a street two blocks back from the waterfront. There were about five varieties of palm trees around the property, some with coconuts suspended from the clusters of leaves near the top. Carrying their single suitcase up the three steps to the front door, Jerry stepped inside and held the door for Maria. The lobby had high ceilings from which spinning fans were suspended, with light filtering through twelve-foot-high windows set back from the porch.

Maria rang the bell on the counter at the front desk. "We're the MacDonald's," she said when a young woman came from the back room.

"Glad to see you. We have your room ready. And we have a telegraph for Mr. MacDonald."

Sitting on the bed later, Jerry looked up from the telegram. "I have good news and bad news."

"Now what?"

"I got a raise. And Mike Woods wants me to go to Venezuela after this well is finished. I'm supposed to be the new district manager there."

"What's the bad news?"

"I thought you were homesick for Queens. If you think Florida is nothing like the city, I doubt Venezuela is even close. Do you speak any Spanish?"

"Molto bene, grazie."

"You can't fool me; that's Italian. What do you think?"

"I want to go. I'm sorry I had a little meltdown today. Sometimes I do that and don't know why; things just seem like too much. But I'm glad they think you can handle it, and I want to be with you. I'll get a Spanish dictionary tomorrow and start practicing. Don't want to hear about you and any of those pretty senoritas down there."

Later that afternoon, they boarded a net boat Jerry had hired to take them down the river. The Caloosahatchee widened west of the town, flowing through marsh lowlands near the entrance to Pine Island Sound. As the boat entered the sound, the flat water of the river changed to a choppy head sea driven by a stiff southwest breeze, spraying them with salt mist. A boarding wave soaked them a few minutes out from the mouth of the river.

"How far before it calms down?" Jerry asked the captain of the small craft.

"No shelter for the next mile," the boatman said. "It's wide open from the south until we get to other end of Sanibel. Then it will flatten out when we get behind the southern tip of the island. "

"Let's turn around and go back up the river past Fort Myers, then," Jerry said. "We don't need to get drenched, and there's not much to see out here but sand and water. We're on a pleasure cruise, not a fishing trip."

"Got it," said the boatman, the boat yawing as it turned north and then wallowing again in the swell as it headed back into the river. Thirty minutes later, they passed the estates of Thomas Edison and Henry Ford, marveling that two men with the money to live anywhere in the world had built these winter retreats here in southwest Florida instead of the French Riviera or the Greek Isles. But in 1943, their decision looked to be clairvoyant. Couldn't get much use out of a villa in Italy this year, thought Maria.

They cruised slowly upriver, enjoying sandwiches and potato salad from a picnic lunch prepared by the hotel and drinking a bottle of white wine. The landscape changed as they penetrated further east into the low-lying country, the trees giving way to grass and palmetto bushes. Wanting to get back before dinner, they asked the boatman to turn and head back for Fort Myers, enjoying not having anything to do but watch the river shoreline slide past. Docked once again at the city pier, a boardwalk paralleling the muddy bank, Maria stepped onto the gunwale, holding Jerry's hand, then onto the pier. Enjoying the day, she laughed as Jerry fell on one knee when the boat pushed out from the dock.

An older black man carrying a sack of oysters over his shoulder walked slowly down the pier, transporting the muddy load from an ancient oyster boat to the seafood market. He shuffled with a stoop, bent over from the weight of the shells. A burly white man, about twenty years old, pushed his shoulder into him, forcing the oyster carrier off the dock and into the mud. The black man looked up at Maria, then immediately down at the ground, twitching but intent on not making eye contact with anyone. Florida had never been part of the cotton belt with the huge plantations dependent on a workforce of industrial slavery. The poor limestone soil found south of Georgia supported smaller farms and different crops, with citrus trees eventually becoming the moneymaker for the state. But in 1943, its heritage was still that of the Deep South. Every small town population included some white men who would whip, shoot, or hang a black man accused of any untoward behavior toward a white woman. The oyster carrier knew that a simple glance, eye-to-eye contact, could be interpreted as an insult and result in a nighttime visit from hooded strangers. So he focused his eyes on the muddy ground, shouldering his load and walking through the shallow water toward the seafood plant.

The bully rolled his shoulders, walking briskly down the center of the dock, aware that his action had upset Maria. "Hey. Why did you do that?" she called out to him as Jerry grabbed her arm to prevent her from pursuing him and making her point.

"'Cause I can. He should've gotten out of the way. What's it to you? You some damn Yankees?" The man stopped and turned around, facing the MacDonalds.

"He's trying to make a living. Didn't bother you. Think you're tough? Wouldn't last ten minutes in my neighborhood."

The man walked up to them, ignored her, and looked at Jerry. Then he pushed her hard on the shoulder, causing her to fall to the dock, watching Jerry's reaction but expecting none. She fell sideways on her hip, skirt flying to mid-thigh, her hand scraping the rough boards.

Jerry felt the relaxed atmosphere of the sunny day disappear, replaced with hatred and aggression as he hit the man's face, punching through the plane of his opponent's body as he had been taught. The nose broke in three places, forcing a shower of blood onto Jerry's clean shirt, as the man turned sideways to shield himself. He held one hand to his face, then turned and tried to strike Jerry's chin with the other. The blow hit only air as Jerry lowered his head and hit the man three times in succession on the left eye, avoiding the broken nose, afraid of driving fragments up into the brain. Following with a straight right to the ear, then another left to the jaw took him about half a second. The onslaught of pain destroying his balance, his opponent dropped to the dock, looking up in pain and surprise and waving his hand in the universal gesture of surrender. Jerry stared down at him, breathing in and out but not winded, waiting to see if there would be a second round.

"No one touches my wife. Understand?" he said.

The man nodded, not moving. Holding Maria's hand, Jerry led her toward the hotel.

Later that night, Maria said, "My cousins said you wouldn't be able to take care of me. I knew you would fight for me if you had to."

"I just lost it when he pushed you. I didn't care what happened next. I just went after him without thinking."

"Where'd you learn to fight like that?"

"When I was at OU, we all had to take three semesters of phys ed, they called it. The first semester I looked at what was available. Since I was a freshman there wasn't much, since the upperclassmen got first choice. There was a boxing course I thought might be interesting, so I signed up. "

He remembered the first day in the gym. A slim man in his fifties walked in to greet the young men sitting on the floor in shorts and t-shirts, introducing himself as Coach Reisling. A whispered conversation had been taking place among the students, passing along the rumor that the coach had boxed in the Navy.

Coach Reisling stood in an open space and said, "I suspect a few of you took this because you're tough guys and thought it would be easy. There's a science to boxing, just like in any sport. The guys you see on Friday nights have learned it, and that's what I'm going to show you. You won't learn how to box in one semester, but you'll know why the pros do what they do. Now I need a volunteer for a little demonstration."

There was a pause, and then a guy with slicked-down black hair, a thin face, and the look of the streets stood up.

"I'll do it," he said.

"Come on up, and thanks. I won't hurt you," said Coach Reisling. "What do they call you?"

"Ricky. And I don't think you can," replied the volunteer.

The coach tossed a pair of gloves to Ricky and then pulled on a pair, instructing Ricky to stand in front of him.

"Try and hit me," the coach said. "I won't punch back, but I will tap you."

Ricky smiled, then attacked in a flurry of fists, blows directed at the coach's face. Effortlessly blocking and slipping the punches, the coach tapped him twice on the face with his left hand, once on the right ear, and then slipped around and hit him twice in the kidneys. Mad now, Ricky tried to land a roundhouse blow to the coach's mid-section, who brushed it aside and then tapped him three times in the stomach, his fists moving faster than the eye could follow.

"That's enough. Thanks," said Coach Reisling. "You're a pretty good street fighter, and if you learn some boxing, you could do well in the ring if you want to follow up."

Impressed, the group spent the next sixteen weeks learning how to form a fist that was a straight line from the knuckles to the wrist, how to put their weight on their left foot, how to watch the muscles of their opponent's midsection telegraph a punch, and how to deliver jabs and hooks. Jerry enjoyed it more than he thought he was going to and signed up for the class the following semester. At the end of his freshman year, the coach pulled him aside.

"I see you enjoy this. You can't take the class any more—there's a limit of two semesters, so you'll have to take lacrosse or something next fall. But we do have an intramural boxing club. Try it."

Jerry hadn't won often, but he'd enjoyed the sparring, the atmosphere of the gym on a cold winter afternoon, and the respect earned from the other would-be pugilists. He hadn't hit anyone since leaving college, but he was glad to see the muscle memory was still there. He hadn't even had to think about what to do when he went after the scumbag who pushed down Maria.

The next morning, as Jerry was gathering his supplies from the hardware store, Maria saw her assailant from the day before, his nose bandaged and eye blackened, walking near the riverfront. He looked at her and then turned his head away. She reached into her purse and wrapped her fingers around the small switchblade one of her cousins had given her, along with the advice to never take any crap from anyone. If the man crossed the street toward her, he would not push her down again. But he turned and walked away, and she relaxed, smiling at Jerry when he came out bent under a coil of steel cable.

Chapter 15

The freighter had been hit on the starboard bow before dawn, taking over two hours to sink while successfully launching the small white lifeboats from both sides. The boats had floated aimlessly since in the spreading oil slick after the ship vanished below the surface. Each was equipped with two sets of oars, enough to pull away from a vessel that had caught fire, but not sufficient to propel the boats more than a mile. Packed with over twenty people each, and with a scant freeboard of about two feet, they were in danger of swamping with any building sea. The wind was freshening, blowing about fifteen knots out of the southeast, and the two-foot swell threatened to double within hours. There were six boats in all, the last refuge for eleven women, three infants, and ninety-seven men. Routed from Key West to the mouth of the Mississippi River by the shipping line, they had expected to reach the safety of the river in another day, and had been looking forward to relaxing for the ten hours it would take to travel upstream to the city of New Orleans.

SUNNILAND

They rocked on the azure blue water, drifting with a line of orange Sargasso weed, small orange berries entangled with small clumps of tiny leaves. The weedline had coalesced where there was a change in the water density and hue, creating an invisible wall that collected any floating objects, including the Sargasso. Pallets from freighters, either washed overboard or set free from a torpedoed ship, were interspersed at regular intervals in the patches of seaweed. A few empty lifejackets with the name of their vessel, the ROBERT E LEE, had also collected where the water changed color. The weedline attracted small fish, which in turn brought in the smaller predators, dolphin fish, wahoo, and small tuna. Distracted by the view of the aquarium beneath them, visible for one hundred feet down into the depths of the Gulf, the passengers were startled as the water thrashed violently a few yards to the west. A spear-like bill broke the surface, followed by the skyward leap of a huge marlin, crashing downward into the school of bonito. The resulting spray showered the boat, scaring the passengers who had never seen or imagined such a fearsome creature in the ocean. Wondering what would happen if their boat had been beneath the descending fish, they were happily distracted by a smudge where the blue sea met the sky.

A thin column of smoke showed on the northern horizon, indicating an approaching vessel. The gray vapor rose almost vertically, then drifted to the northwest as the prevailing wind scattered the ash particles. Terrified that the U-boat was returning, the passengers shouted at the men resting on the oars, encouraging, ordering, pleading with them to turn south. But exhausted from trying to keep station after the sinking of the ROBERT E LEE, and realizing they would make no more than a half mile before the approaching ship reached their location, those responsible for maneuvering the boats declined to go anywhere. Maybe it was not a U-boat, and if so, maybe it would not sink the lifeboats.

As the vessel approached, it took the shape of a small ship, the hull painted gray with a red stripe on the bow, the markings of a US Coast Guard cutter. It slowed and circled about three miles from the drifting lifeboats, then commenced to rapidly retrace its course to the north. The abandoned passengers heard a series of three explosions, sounding like muffled thunder and causing fountains of water higher than the radar mast of the cutter. The ship commenced to travel back and forth in a small area, evidently searching for evidence that the depth charges had damaged the submerged U-boat.

"Why don't they come over and get us?" asked Jill, a middle-aged woman sitting between two sailors on the lifeboat bench seat. She was wedged tightly, burned by the sun, and thirsty beyond anything she had ever experienced. Leaving Key West, she had vomited continuously for the first hours underway, then had become accustomed to the rolling motion of the freighter. Now, the rocky motion of the small open boat in which she found herself had brought on a new case of mal de mer. She wanted to get out of the lifeboat and onto something that had shade and didn't rock, more than she wanted to live. If she could leave the ocean behind, she would settle for whatever fate brought her.

"I guess they want to see if they sank the U-boat. If they didn't, and they start loading us on board and it surfaces, it could sink them pretty easily." The sailor holding the tiller of the boat, keeping the bow into the waves, shaded his eyes while peering toward the cutter. *It was a good thing the Coast Guard had shown up,* he thought. The freighter's radio had functioned for only a few minutes after the torpedo hit, but it must have been enough time for the SOS and position to be picked up by the antenna high above the beach at Sanibel Island. The lifeboats had a few jerry cans of water and cans of pork and beans that were always stored aboard. But the panic to get the boats loaded with passengers and in the water before the freighter sank meant that little additional water was now on board, and packed to the gunnels with people, they could only survive about two days in the tropical sun. But unless the U-boat won the duel with the cutter and gave them some company in the lifeboats, they should soon be out of here.

Two hundred feet below the surface, the depth charges rang through the steel tube of the U-boat, tossing the packed crew against pipes, valves, torpedoes, and steel bulkheads. Gunter sat in the control room, covering his ears to preserve his hearing, and flinching when the sonar pinged on the hull, revealing their location to the ship trying to blow them apart. Anticipating another explosion, he wrapped an arm around a pipe and lowered his head. If they survived this, there would be broken bones and concussions to deal with, as well a badly damaged U-boat.

The depth charge was a steel barrel, launched from the stern of the cutter when the pinging sonar indicated the U-boat was directly below. It plummeted downward like a ballast stone, the pressure switch igniting an explosion twenty feet above the U-boat, causing a vacuum in the water and a pressure wave sufficient to cave in steel plate. The U-boat had descended on hearing the sonar ping, avoiding a disastrous explosion directly adjacent to the vessel, which would have ruptured the hull. But the shock wave bent the forward deck plates downward into a bowl, twisting pipes and causing the fuel in the starboard bunker to be released to the sea. Eight thousand gallons of diesel fuel, less dense than seawater, rose to the surface and created a spreading slick, quickly growing in size and including the lifeboats in the iridescent sheen.

Gunter looked at the crew in the conning tower bridge deck, apparently all alive but shaken and bruised. He ordered, "Keep us at this depth, and stop the motors. Fritz, go down and tell the crew we have total silence discipline until I say otherwise. Maybe they will think they got us."

"Aye, sir," whispered the helmsman. The other seaman went silently through the hatch to the lower deck, softly passing the order for silence to the crew. The last time they had been depth charged, in shallower water off Tampa, they had rested on the bottom for a day, hoping the steel hull could not be distinguished from the sea floor by the sonar pinging. Surfacing after sunset, they had found an empty ocean illuminated by a full moon, tracing a path of light across the waves and validating that they were still alive. This time, Gunter knew they were in deep water and could not reach bottom without the hull collapsing from the pressure of a thousand feet of seawater, and he hoped the damaged vessel could stay at this depth without sinking or porpoising to the surface. It required some noise from running the electric motors to control the ballast, but that was unavoidable. Maybe the cutter would not search too long.

Jill watched the cutter approach them slowly through the oil slick, evidently convinced by the spreading oil that the submarine, if not sunk, was not an imminent danger. The ship showed the strain of constant patrolling during wartime, rust-stained, with peeling paint and missing rivets from the hull plates. The engines smoked and vibrated, and the crew was wearing ragged denims. Approaching the boat on the downwind side, the Coast Guard crew allowed the smaller vessel to drift alongside, halfway down the length of the cutter, where a ladder allowed access to the mid deck near the depth charge racks. Jill grabbed a rung of the ladder and tried to step out of the lifeboat, but the rocking of the small boat and her exhaustion prevented any further progress. A Coast Guardsman grabbed her wrist, and one of the sailors from the freighter pushed on her bottom, hoisting her unceremoniously to the deck. Collapsing on the deck, she was pushed out of the way to get the next passenger onto the cutter as quickly as possible. Fifteen minutes later, she had shade, and a bottle of slightly salty water to drink. Heaven. The sound of the engines of the cutter increased, and an occasional wave crashed over the side, soaking the passengers seated on the deck. But as the ship headed toward the entrance to Tampa Bay at twenty knots, those who had survived the torpedo and the lifeboats felt for the first time that they would live.

Hearing the noise of the cutter's propellers diminishing, Gunter realized they would have to surface, regardless of the American presence. The air in the U-boat was getting bad, and without running the CO_2 absorbers, they were in danger of suffocating. Two seamen were gravely injured, both by puncture wounds in the chest caused by being tossed against machinery. About ten others had slammed against the cramped maze of pipes and bulkheads with sufficient force to break bones or result in coughing up blood. They needed fresh air, and the commander needed a damage assessment that could not be done without an inspection on the surface. Gunter ordered the ballast tanks blown, and called for a party of four seamen to prepare to inspect the outer hull. The two divers were also ordered to prepare to survey the bottom and running gear for damage.

The U-boat breached the surface and started rolling in the swell, which had increased since they submerged the day before. Opening the hatch and starting the diesel engines resulted in fresh air being pumped through the boat, rapidly enough to blow papers on desks and the wardroom table to the deck. Gunter rushed up the ladder to the deck atop the conning tower, ahead of the lookouts, to scan the horizon. A faint plume of smoke to the east indicated the presence of a vessel in the direction of the Florida coast, but no airplanes or other craft were in sight. Relaxing, he watched the damage-control crew move to the bow to begin their inspection, as the two divers screwed tight helmets and started into the water. He knew there would be damage, but hopefully things could be fixed by the meager supply of spares and tools on board.

"How does it look?" he asked the divers an hour later, looking down at the two men standing on deck below the conning tower, helmets held in their arms, bracing against the rocking of the submarine.

"Running gear is OK. There is a large caved-in area on the fore-deck, but it doesn't appear to have breached the pressure hull. The starboard fuel tank looks OK—it must have drained through the vent line. Didn't rupture. Everything else is OK to go." The diver looked exhausted, worn out from maneuvering in the heavy suit following the hours of submerged terror.

"We lost the gun and blew away the radio mast, so we can't communicate until we get a new one. But mechanically things seem under control for now," Gunter told the XO standing next to him on the conning tower. Let's get underway and start charging batteries and see what we can do for casualties."

"We're supposed to meet the U-459 next week to refuel, but I don't think we have enough fuel left to get to the rendezvous point after losing what we had in the starboard tank, and we can't contact them until we fix the radio," Gunter continued. "I'm going to go below and take a look at the chart, and see what we can do."

The U-459 was a specialized craft, designed to bring diesel fuel and supplies to the U-boats on distant patrol on the American coast. It allowed them to stay on station for months. But if they couldn't meet it, the engines would go silent. That would mean opening the hatches in deep water and taking to the rubber boats, hoping to be rescued by patrolling Navy or Coast Guard ships and then imprisoned. Their orders were not to allow the U-boat to be captured intact. Admiral Donitz, the head of the U Boat service, was fearful that a close examination by American naval architects and engineers would enable the Americans and British to further refine their sonar, depth charges, and tactics.

Almost succeeding in keeping an impassive face in front of the crew, Gunter descended to the main deck and passed through the curious crewmembers to his tiny cabin, entering and closing the curtain behind him. Alone, the emotions of fear, excitement, and uncertainty made him hold his face in his hands. Dying in a sinking vessel was not what he dreaded most. He had prepared himself for that since the beginning of the first cruise of the U-167. He accepted the fact that he was likely to suffocate or drown in the depths of the oceans, trapped in the submarine after attack by depth charges or surface cannons. But now the most likely outcome was that he would die of exposure in a rubber boat, after being forced to scuttle his ship because he ran out of petrol, like a motorist on the autobahn. Standing on the top of the conning tower while they ran on the surface in these tropical waters, he knew that a man could not survive more than a few days in the scorching sun, even with adequate water. And the boats could not hold enough water to keep everyone alive. He resolved that if it came time to scuttle the ship, he would go in as close to shore as he dared, let the crew off in the boats, and take the submarine out to be sunk in deep water with only one or two volunteers. Once it was set on a course, it didn't need the complement of over fifty men to run it. He would open the valves and go down with the U-boat, ending his life quickly, not dying slowly in the tropic sun.

But first he needed to do what could be done to save the ship. Gunter unrolled a paper chart he had brought from the navigators' station, depicting contour lines of depth and the outline of the Florida Gulf Coast from Apalachicola to Key West. There was no use trying to steal diesel from one of the larger ports—they were heavily guarded against just such an event, the result of widespread suspicion that the U-boats were somehow obtaining supplies from the mainland that allowed them to continue their attacks. From Clearwater to Naples was out of the question. But north of Tarpon Springs, and south of Naples, the coastal geography appeared to be marshes extending miles inland, with a few small towns to be found on rivers and streams flowing to the Gulf. There would be fishing vessels in these towns, and perhaps capturing one might supply them with sufficient fuel to make their rendezvous.

To the north, the village of Cedar Key, occupying a small island in the Gulf and west of a large area that appeared to be unoccupied forest, looked attractive. The notes Gunter had made on the chart indicated it was a fishing village, the local economy supplemented by a factory that made pencils. He didn't need a pencil, but he could use a recently topped-off fishing boat. The alternative was the town of Everglades City, south of Naples. It was similarly isolated, with a railroad and road connecting it, but miles of what appeared to be swampland separated it from civilization. It also looked like a fishing village, and perhaps he could find a thousand gallons of fuel. Everglades City was closer to their current location, and if they could refuel, closer to their rendezvous with the U-459. The chart also showed deeper water close to the coast west of Everglades, where they would have to drop off the inflatable rubber boats.

Picking up his dividers and a parallel rule, Gunter calculated the course to a point thirty miles off the coast of Everglades City. "Steer one hundred degrees east," he said to the helmsman.

Chapter 16

Monday Night

The two sailors had been summoned to the control room and entered the cramped space to see Gunter and Franz studying a chart unfurled on the small table. Marked with soundings dating back to a British Admiralty survey in 1880, the chart showed a coastline with shallow water extending far offshore, the water depths increasing only a few feet with every additional mile from the shoreline. Near the coast, the chart showed hundreds of small islands that looked like pieces of a jigsaw puzzle that had been randomly thrown onto the paper. Further inland, the coastal plain was dissected by what looked like small rivers draining the interior.

Gunter placed a pin on the map and pointed to it. "This is a small town called Everglades City. We think it's a fishing village. I want to send ashore a raiding party to see if we can capture a boat with diesel fuel. But I need a reconnaissance before risking a fight. You two are the only ones in the crew with English that might pass. I want you to go ashore and find out what's there. We need at least a thousand gallons of diesel to get to the rendezvous with U-459," he explained. "Look for a situation where a few men could seize a boat and bring it out to water deep enough for us to come alongside and make the transfer."

"How are we going to get in?" asked Peter, the older of the two crewmen. He was not surprised by the mission. The loss of fuel caused by the depth charge was known throughout the submarine.

"The only way is to row in with the rubber boat. Unfortunately, we can't get any closer in than six miles. We'll be in only fifteen feet of water at that point, and scraping bottom. It will take you about two hours. We thought about seizing a fishing boat to get you in, one working the shallow Gulf, but we don't want to alarm the natives and lose an opportunity."

"Six miles?" Alarmed at the prospect, Adolf could feel the submarine rocking in the slight chop as it drifted offshore.

"That's one way. Round trip is double," said the XO. "Row in, tie up, go to town, and row back. Shoot a flare after you've rowed out for the same time it took you to row in, and we'll look for you. Cheer up; at least you'll get a chance to go to a bar and get a beer."

"Look for a lighted marker near the coast. There's a channel marker at the end of the pass, and the chart shows a red light flashing every four seconds. They know a submarine can't get in that close, so they probably haven't turned it off. From there, you can follow the channel markers up the river to Everglades City," Gunter instructed.

"That's it, then," he continued. "Get ready to go. I want to see you dressed in black, with stocking caps and scarves in ten minutes." He was not optimistic about these two successfully making a twelve-mile round trip in the inflatable, especially at night, but the possibility of refueling was worth losing them and the boat. If they couldn't find and seize enough diesel fuel to meet the U-459, they would all be dead or in an American prison anyway.

The U-boat edged into the shallow water, and three of the crew quickly dragged the inflatable boat up through the foredeck hatch, inflated it with a foot pump, and prepared it for the trip to shore. A long row in calm water, the journey would be even more challenging by a steep chop formed in response to the offshore breeze. Peter and Adolf stepped into the craft and shipped the oars, looking at the small compass and the distant light of the Everglades City lighthouse. The boat tended to row in circles, having no keel or hull shape to impart any directional stability. They embarked with caution, having limited experience in small boats, and on inland lakes. But their presumed ability to pose as Americans overrode the need for seamanship in their journey to the marsh adjacent to Everglades City.

Fortunately for the two non-mariners, a tailwind and a following sea aided their journey to shore, the oars required more for steering than propelling the unwieldy boat. Less than two hours after seeing the U-boat reverse and back into deeper water, the inflatable raft drifted ashore at the edge of the Everglades City waterfront. The occupants of the rubber boat quickly stripped off the dark clothes they had worn for the voyage, removing khaki work clothes and boots from a waterproof duffel bag. Pulling the raft into the marsh, they quickly cut reeds of grass and covered the inflated pontoons, concealing the boat but leaving a stake to mark the location when they returned. Trying to keep their boots free of mud that would make a casual observer wonder why two men looking for work had been slopping in the water, they reached the shell road and started walking toward a wooden dock at the edge of town. Peter's pocket watch showed twenty one hundred hours, a time of day when they could expect a few men and women to be killing time in the waterfront bars, happy to talk to anyone on the next barstool. They had three hours for conversation with the local shrimpers, laborers, waitresses, and anyone else who was looking for someone to listen. Gunter had told them to embark on their return by midnight so the submarine could be offshore and submerged in deep water by daybreak.

As they neared the town, the two German sailors saw the waterfront curving away in a shallow crescent, with the barnlike structures of the fish and shrimp markets lined up along the dock, lit up by a thin string of electric lights resembling Christmas decorations. At the end of the seafood-processing plants, and separated from them by a vacant lot, was a white building with a screened veranda that came down to the waterfront. A neon sign said S APPER IN, and an Old Milwaukee beer sign showed through the window. Music from a jukebox emanated from the screened enclosure that was filled with tables, about half of which were occupied.

"Looks like the place to start. I hope those Amerikaners are drunk enough to talk freely," Adolf said quietly.

"Maybe we can find a girl who wants out of here and convince her we can give her a job in Tampa. That used to work for me in London when I was in school. I would say I owned a company in Kaiserslautern and that she should show up next Monday. "

"They believed you? Who would move to Kaiserslautern from London?"

"They were getting tired of working behind a store counter, and I promised them a job as a secretary. Worked about half the time. I wonder what they thought when they showed up in Kaiserslautern at the courthouse. That's the address I always wrote down." Peter laughed at the memory. Those were good days, before the approaching war had compelled him to return to his family in Frankfort. At the urging of his father, he had joined the Navy. Ending up in U-boats was his own fault, the result of a drunken night after basic training, ending in a promise to his barstool neighbor to become a submariner. To his dismay, the next morning the U-boat lieutenant had found him asleep in the barracks, reminded him of his oath, and hustled him off to the U-boat CPO to sign up as a torpedo man in training. The cruise to the Gulf of Mexico had sounded exciting at first, but a month confined in the narrow steel tube had caused him to reassess his worst concept of hell. It couldn't be any worse than the voyage so far from Lorient.

Their story was to be that they had come south, looking for work, and had come to the end of the road in Everglades. Peter hoped they could find out where there might be a diesel boat with enough fuel to be worth stealing. He knew enough about the submarine's predicament to be concerned about the prospect of spending the duration of the war in a Georgia POW camp. If the American camps were half as bad as the stories he had heard of the German camps, it would be a brutal existence. The typical shrimper or fishing boat only held about one hundred gallons, and they needed at least ten times that, so they needed to find something larger. Perhaps one of the small coastwise craft that delivered supplies from Naples and Key West, or one of the offshore fishing boats that targeted tuna one hundred miles out.

Sitting at a corner table, Eddie noticed two white men in their late twenties, thin and distinguished by their pale skin in a country where almost everyone was burned to a deep brown. They sat at the bar, and the taller one ordered two Schlitz beers, lighting cigarettes with a shared kitchen match.

The bartender took two cans out of the ice chest, opened them with a church key hanging from a chain, and put them on the bar with a dish of unshelled peanuts. "Fifty cents," he said.

"I got it," said Adolf. He reached in his pocket for the change Gunter had given them when they left the U-boat, pulled out a handful of quarters, and gave two to the bartender. The package of coins had all been quarters, eliminating the need to look at them closely. Picking up the beer, he drank half of it in three swallows. It had been two months since they had been in a beer garden in Lorient, drinking all they could before the U-boat motored out to sea. The alcohol created a pleasant sensation in his head, and he reminded himself to slow down—it would be easy to slip up if he drank too much. Turning toward the crowd he noticed the dark man, with two missing teeth and a scar, looking at them with an open expression. Adolf nodded to him, slid off the barstool, and walked over to the table.

"How are you doing?" he asked, practicing the idiom he had learned on summer vacations at his uncle's house in the hill country of Texas, near New Braunfels. Not quite the drawl that was characteristic of the deep South, but a thin, clipped speech.

"Doin' fine," replied Eddie unsteadily. "Have a seat. Can you spare me the money for a beer? I left my wallet at home."

"OK." Adolf went back to the bar, returning with another Schlitz. "We came down from Georgia. Worked at a poultry plant up there, but got tired of chickens. Heard there might be some work on the railroad down here that pays better. "

"How come you're not in the service?" asked Eddie. "You don't seem to be 4F."

"They haven't found us, and we haven't gone looking for them. Guess sooner or later we'll be in front of a draft board. Not in any hurry to fight anyone, anywhere. In the meantime we need to eat."

Eddie coughed, then tilted back the can. "The railroad was finished last year. Only work right now, besides fishing, which you don't look like you know how to do, is on that oil rig east of town."

Peter had wandered over, plopping down in another chair at the table. "Hi," he said to Eddie. "Are you from here? We would be glad of some help to find work. Didn't know there was any oil in Florida; thought it was all in Texas."

"There isn't any yet," Eddie replied. "They're looking to find some. I represent them here in Everglades City. Anyone goes to work at the rig goes through me."

"What kind of work? I never saw an oil rig before. How do they dig a well, anyhow?"

"Mostly carrying, lifting, pulling kind of work. The crew that know what they are

doing is from Oklahoma and came with them, or they been training them. But they need people to do the heavy work, loading supplies, pumping fuel, mixing mud, carrying pipe. Any dumb ass can do it, but you need a good back." Eddie looked at their hands. Pretty obvious that neither had been doing any kind of outdoor work. But if he got them on the rig and they lasted a week, he would get a day's pay for finding them, and if Joe ran them off that, wouldn't be his problem.

"I guess we can do that. Where is this contraption?" asked Peter, trying not to twitch at the mention of fuel.

"Out west about three miles. This here river goes from here up to a dock that the boats and barges use to carry supplies and people, then a board road across the swamp for about half a mile after that. All the supplies come in barges and have to be unloaded onto the dock, then moved up the road in wagons. A lot of bags of mud, fifty-gallon drums of diesel, and sacks of cement. Never saw anyone use stuff so fast."

"Who would we see?" asked Adolf. "And how would we get there?"

"There'll be a barge coming through in two days carrying diesel fuel. They burn a lot and need a resupply once a week. You could ride up the river with them. If I say you are OK, you see Joe and he'll put you on."

"Do you think we are OK?" asked Peter, waiting for the shake-down.

"I want two days' pay. One day each. Joe will take it out of your first week's pay and hold it for me. You need to tell him that's what we settled on, and that Eddie sent you."

"Sounds high. How about one day for both of us? We are dead-ass broke after hitching down from Georgia."

"Two days is it. Someone else will be in tomorrow." Eddie had no idea if anyone else would be in for weeks, and the rig was short-handed as always. He had convinced Joe to let him find people in return for a day's pay, which Joe would hold out for him. It had worked out well, with about one man a week being hired to replace those who quit, got run off, got hurt, or were found by the law. These two seemed a little strange, maybe desperate, and it wouldn't hurt to put the touch on them for two days' pay for the pair.

"OK. We'll be here in two days. How do we get on this barge?" asked Adolf.

"Let's see. This is Monday. The barge will be going past here on the way up the river Wednesday afternoon. Meet me here, and I'll run you out in my boat. I'll tell the captain you are new roust-abouts. That's what they call them that carry stuff. The drilling crew is called roughnecks." Eddie happily estimated how much rum he could buy for two days of someone else's pay, and walked out the door and down the road to the dock where his skiff was moored.

"That's all we need to know," Peter said to Adolf. "Let's get go-ing. It's going to be a lot harder to row out than it was to come in." They returned to the inflatable raft as quickly as possible without seeming to be in a hurry. Stepping into the rubber boat, Peter pushed it away from the mangroves into the channel. "Start rowing," he said softly.

"Damn!" Adolf's oar skipped over the water, hitting the side of the boat as he pulled back without lowering the blade into the water, causing him to fall backwards onto the rubber floor.

"Quiet. Get us out of here, and I'll start pulling too. Right now I'm steering us." Peter held an oar along the side of the boat, using it as a rudder to guide them into the channel. Minutes later, he turned to face astern, picking up the other set of oars and rowing in tandem with his mate.

As they reached the open Gulf at the end of the protected channel, clearing the islands and shell banks that had sheltered them from the surf by islands, the offshore breeze that had carried them in was now directly in their faces. A two-foot chop occasionally crashed over the blunt bow, soaking them and swirling around the bottom of the boat.

Peter looked at his watch. Twenty-four hundred and ten minutes. Six miles to go. And making about a half a mile an hour with the headwind and the opposing waves.

"We won't make it by daybreak like this," he said. "Any ideas?"

"Let's go back and steal a boat with a motor. We can sink it when we get out. They'll think someone left early to go fishing."

"OK. I don't know what else we can do. We can't row six miles against this headwind."

Turning the inflatable around, they quietly rowed back to the mangrove bank they had departed thirty minutes earlier.

"Just tie it up. We'll pick it up on the way out in whatever we get." Peter commanded. He wasn't officially in charge, but Adolf didn't argue.

Reaching the shell road, they started jogging toward the wooden dock that marked the downstream boundary of the Everglades City waterfront. The appearance of two headlights prompted them to dive into the adjacent marsh and lie face down in the shallow water. They resumed their progress as the taillights of the truck disappeared around a bend. As they approached the dock, they returned to the water, wading under the dock and examining the boats.

"This'll do." Peter paused next to a lapstrake skiff with an outboard motor, sixteen feet in length. White with a stained mahogany interior, built with round bilges and a plumb bow, it seemed to be a fishing boat built for fun, maybe belonging to one of the guides. Floorboards kept the feet of the crew dry. A small plaque on the bow stated, "Lyman Boat Works." It steered with a tiller on the motor, and there was no water in the bilge. Lifting the small gas tank, Peter said, "It's almost full."

Adolf scrambled over the side as Peter cut the line securing the craft to the dock and pushed it out into the river. "There's no oars or paddles."

"Lift up a floorboard and use that. We have to get at least around the bend before we can start the motor."

Adolf wrenched up two of the floorboards that ran from bow to stern, handing one to Peter and beginning to quietly paddle. Another truck passed, headed north, but the road turned away from the dock and the headlight beams missed the small boat drifting toward the west. As they paddled past the first bend in the river, making them invisible from the town, Adolf started to giggle uncontrollably, the aftereffect of three beers and an overdose of adrenaline. Peter slapped his ear. "Stop it. We've still got a long way to go."

Wrapping a cord around the motor flywheel, Peter pulled hard. The motor spun but no ignition followed—the noise of the spinning cylinders just died. Four more tries had the same result. Peter stood up, looking nervous and listening for the sound of pursuit from the dock, set after them by the owner noticing someone had stolen his skiff. Hearing nothing unusual, he sat down and looked at the engine. A small bulb on the fuel line felt full of air. Squeezing it, he pumped several times until it felt firm and he could smell the odor of gasoline from the carburetor. Trying again with the rope, he was rewarded with a cough and then the sputter of the motor. Relieved, he turned the tiller to head the boat west downstream and follow the channel markers through the islands to the open Gulf where they would pause to pick up their rubber boat and secure the bowline to the skiff.

Clearing the lee of the last island, the wooden boat met the open Gulf and plunged into the oncoming waves. The seas were only about two feet high, but that was sufficient to send a constant shower of spray over the small foredeck. As they continued to confront the seas head on, the skiff started filling with water, losing buoyancy as the bow lifted sluggishly to the next wave. Periodically, green water would come on board when a three- or four-footer slammed into the boat.

"Bail with that can," Peter ordered. "I'll keep steering." Adolf bailing constantly, and Peter tried to steer at an angle to the waves, reducing the tendency of the bow to pitch downward. He gave that up when a rogue wave almost turned them sideways to the seas and came close to capsizing the small craft. But Adolf managed to keep up with the boarding waves as they slowly motored out to the rendezvous spot where they expected to meet the U-boat.

Peter guessed that the small motor was driving the boat about six miles per hour. Using the handheld compass they had been issued, he navigated to about where he guessed they had pushed off from the submarine. He could be five miles away if there was a current he hadn't counted on, or if he had misjudged their speed, or if the compass was faulty. But hoping the flare would be visible for a sufficient distance for the lookouts on the conning tower to see it, he ignited the handheld signal as Adolf collapsed on the floorboards, flexing his sore arms. Arching into the sky, the orange flame blinded them momentarily as it hastened upward toward the stars. The wind had died down, and the skiff floated on a calm sea. Adolf had managed to bail out much of the water, and they were no longer in danger of sinking. Relaxing but nervous, they looked around for a sign of the U-boat.

Looking west, they noticed a dark shape approaching without lights. It blocked out the stars on the horizon, a white bow wave becoming evident as it came nearer. It was a large ship, not a boat, but that was all they could discern in the darkness. Suddenly a spotlight illuminated the drifting boat, blinding them, as they waved their hands to indicate no hostile intent toward the intruder, American or German.

Then they heard the distinctive noise of the submarine engines, muffled by the underwater exhausts, diminishing as the ship approached them. A hail in German greeted them from the conning tower. "Hello, stand by to tie up along the lee side."

Ropes were tossed from the foredeck to the skiff, which was pulled in and protected by rope fenders from the steel hull. Exhausted, the two men clambered up the sloping side of the U-boat and stood on the deck. Still squinting from the searchlight, they peered up at the conning tower, where they saw Franz motion them to ascend the ladder and descend into the hull. The seamen on the foredeck opened a hatch and deflated the rubber boat, folded it, and lowered it into the hull.

"So how did you commandeer this boat?" asked Gunter.

"We couldn't make it back to the U-boat by rowing. The tide had started to ebb, and the offshore wind had picked up. We would have been going backward. So we went back to Everglades and saw this boat tied up along the river dock. Thought no one would think it was stolen by Germans, probably by a rumrunner."

"Good. We can use it to send in another party if we need to. What did you find out?"

"Didn't find out much about fishing boats. But they are drilling an oil well west of town. That burns a lot of diesel, and they get a supply barge three times a week to refuel. The next one is due in two days, with a few thousand gallons of fuel. It will come in the channel, then head up the river past the town to the dock near the rig. They've built a board road from the river to the rig location. Found out a lot from a man named Eddie, who thinks he is going to hire us."

"Did he say how much fuel this barge carries?" Gunter asked.

"He didn't. But they resupply once a week. It the rig engine is the size of a big truck motor, it would burn about thirty gallons an hour, five thousand gallons a week. So if the barge comes once a week, it would have to bring at least five thousand gallons." Peter had made the mental calculations on the ride back in the rubber boat. It would be more than enough to refuel the U-boat and make the rendezvous with the U-459.

"That would do it," Gunter mused aloud. "The problem is how to get the barge to the U-boat. If we can get alongside, we can transfer it. Get some sleep while I look at these charts and talk to Franz."

Turning to the XO, he ordered, "Anchor that skiff with plenty of line, and put a light on it. No one else should be out here tonight, and the light will let us find it again. Then go west twenty-five miles and submerge. We'll come back after dark in two days when that diesel barge is supposed to show up, pick up the skiff, and send in a raiding party.

Franz looked at the chart of the southwest Florida coast. An inland waterway of bays and sounds existed from Tampa Bay south to the Withlacoochee River, replaced further south by unconnected harbors at Naples, Everglades City, and other small towns. A barge would presumably be loaded at a terminal in Tampa and travel south in the protected water until it reached Sanibel Island. From there, it would travel south along the coast, turning inland at Everglades City to travel upriver to the board road dock.

"I don't see how we can reach it going on the way in to the oil well," he said to Gunter. "It will be inland for half the way, then probably hug the coast in water too shallow for us to board it from the U-boat until it reaches Everglades City. And it will be moving too fast to board from either a rubber boat or that skiff they captured."

"I agree," said Gunter. "We can't seize it while it's offshore. We're going to have to get a party on board and take control after it goes inland, then take it out to sea where we can bring it alongside and transfer the fuel. "

"That leaves two choices. We can take in a landing party in the rubber boats and wait for the barge on the river bank, then board from the boats in the river as it goes upstream. Or we can land a crew north of Everglades City who can go overland to the rig, then seize the barge when it docks at the rig and turn it around. That would mean we have to take care of the rig crew somehow—they'll only be half a mile from the dock and will be surprised to see the barge leave without the supplies being unloaded."

"I think we would have a better chance taking it at the dock by the rig. If it's moving, the barge could run aground while we are taking it, and we might not be able to get it off. Start making plans to land a party. If the barge is due to arrive in two days, we need have them ashore in forty-eight hours." It wasn't a great plan, and it would mean sending men through an unfamiliar swampy terrain. But Gunter couldn't think of anything better.

Chapter 17

Monday Night

Watching the door in the mirror behind the bar as she rinsed and dried cocktail glasses, Maria saw two men she didn't know walk down the sidewalk, heading toward the east end of Riverside Drive. Unusually pale-skinned for these latitudes, they both walked with a rollicking gait, characteristic of months at sea flexing muscles to adjust to a constantly pitching deck. *How could a man stay indoors on the sea?* she wondered.

The two strangers disappeared from the sliver of the sidewalk that she could see through the door, replaced by a newcomer who pushed open the door and entered the bar, looking around uncertainly. Wearing expensive outdoor clothes, which Maria recognized from the windows of Abercrombie and Fitch and the other exclusive outdoor stores she had passed by on her afternoons in Manhattan, the fisherman smiled at Maria and stepped toward the bar. In his late forties, tanned from golf and tennis, he had the mannerisms of someone accustomed to getting what he asked for. But beneath the habitual ease in his movements, he appeared visibly shaken. His face was pale beneath his tan, and the expensive wristwatch he wore on his forearm slid back and forth as his hand twitched.

"Hi," he said. "I was in the other night but you had left. They told me they had a new bartender from Queens. That must be you, right?"

"That's me," she answered. "And I know you from the newspapers. You are John Wase, president of AmCan. I saw your picture a few months ago with the president, something about converting factories to war production."

"That's right; we retooled two factory lines to make the size can for C rations. Troops in the field eat a lot of Vienna sausage. I'm on my way back from Jamaica where I was looking at a bauxite mine—that's where we get our aluminum from. And I stopped to fish for a couple of days. I don't feel too good about enjoying myself when we're in a war, but life goes on. Last month I was in Miami fishing on a boat called the Neptune—the two guys that own it are working nights in a factory that makes airplane engines but were glad to make a few bucks taking me trolling. Paid for a bottom job."

"My husband thinks he should be in the Navy. But Pride Oil convinced him he should stay—that he would do more for the war effort finding oil than as a rifleman."

"He's working on that well they're drilling east of town? Charlie Pride told me about it last week, before I left. How's it going? Did they find anything?"

"They're close, but no word yet. Jerry says they'll know something in a few days. He's out at the rig right now. Want something to drink? This is a bar, you know."

"Thanks. I'll have a martini. Can you make one of those?"

"I'm from Queens, not Everglades City. Dry?"

"That's it. Thanks."

"You seem kind of shaken," Maria said. "Lose a big fish?"

"Sometimes being in a position of really knowing what's going on isn't always a good thing. I have a son on a Navy destroyer. I found out that he's going to be in a bad place in a few days. Every other Navy parent in the country knows that their son is where something terrible can happen, but they don't know if today is any worse than last Tuesday or next Thursday. I do. But that's all I can say."

"I'm sorry. I have friends from back home in the Navy. I hope they're OK. One was on the Ferris last month when it went down, and we assume he's dead. I don't know about the others. I'm glad Jerry is not in any danger, but I wish every other wife could feel the same way."

Signaling to Maria to refill his glass, John Wase recalled yesterday's telephone conversation with his contact in the Pentagon. He kept in touch with the general officer, a friend from Yale who was now in the Army Reserve. Assigned to logistics, the general was desperately trying to prod the industry leaders he knew to convert factories from windows to bombsights faster than they believed possible.

"We're going to take the Marshall Islands," he had told John. The Pacific fleet is sending every ship that is operational, and so are the Japanese. The naval battle looks to be the biggest surface engagement since Guadalcanal."

John hadn't mentioned his son on the Shiloh, a destroyer that he knew was headed to the western Pacific. His friends and contemporaries tended not to convey their feelings about the dangers their sons were in. Most were military and industrial leaders and had boys in their twenties, recently finished with college and at a prime spot in their lives to be Army captains or Navy first lieutenants. He was going to get considerably richer from this conflict, but he recoiled from the thought of what was happening to triple the demand for aluminum cans.

Maria set his drink, dry with an olive, down on the bar and brought his thoughts back to the barroom of the Turner Inn. "Where do you go from here?" she asked.

"I'll be here another few days; then I'm taking the train back to Grand Central. How about you? I have a private car if you and your husband are finished here and want to return with me."

Maria remembered the opulent private cars of the millionaires being connected at Grand Central Station. They resembled yachts on wheels, with curtained windows that didn't completely shut out a view of white tablecloths, heavy furniture with expensive coverings, and shining crystal. Riding back in one to New York would be a dream. John Wase had said "if you and your husband are finished," so he wasn't trying to get Maria alone for a couple of days. At least not openly.

"That sounds like fun," she replied. "I'll ask Jerry when he gets back. Maybe we'll be ready in time."

"I could use the company. And it would get Jerry back to report to Charlie Pride faster. I hope this well hits. A new play in Florida would take a lot of pressure off the Texas fields and could be transported by barge up to the Delaware Valley, safe from the U-boats."

"Do you have family besides your son?" Maria asked. She liked the man, who was friendly and respectful in spite of being one of the richest and most powerful people in the country.

"Yes, Katy, my wife, is in New York making sure the war doesn't slow down the social scene. She is pretty upset that it isn't safe to go to Europe this year and had no interest in coming to Florida. We have no other children besides David, my son who is in the Navy. How about you?"

"No children. Jerry and I have only been married a few months. My parents both live in Queens, along with more relatives than I can count or want to know. We have some good eggs in our family, and some who would break your head for looking at them the wrong way. My uncle, Ignatius, owns the bar where I used to work. He's been like a second father, offering me help and keeping me out of trouble."

John Wase finished his drink and stood up, leaving Maria a five-dollar bill for a dollar drink. As she started to get change, he said, "Please keep it. You took my mind off things for a little while. Let me know if you want that ride back to New York City. I'll be at the Mangrove Lodge until Friday."

"Thanks," she replied. "We probably won't make it. I don't think Jerry will be through with the well by then. But I appreciate the offer and the conversation, and the tip." She smiled goodbye as he nodded and turned for the door.

Chapter 18

Tuesday

Jerry stood on the rig floor and watched a small pile driver pound iron pipe into the marshy soil. The hammer rang out every fifteen seconds, giving him a headache. After about an hour, the pile driver stopped, and a charge of dynamite was lowered down the hole, connected to a pair of wires. The wires were tied around a stake at the surface, and the machine was loaded on a flatboat and moved through to a point about five hundred yards away.

In the distance he could see one of the swamp buggies rolling slowly though knee-deep water, a man standing on the back and pushing yellow cylinders secured to sharpened spikes into the soft soil. The cylinders were listening devices, recording sound waves reflected from underground layers of rock when the dynamite was exploded. They were linked together by a wire cable feeding from a spool. The swamp buggy followed a straight path that had been clearcut though the swamp, allowing the jugs, as the yellow cylinders were called, to be laid down in a straight line. The arrival of the seismic crew in Everglades City had provided new work for the local labor force, cutting trees and clearing brush, but nothing on the scale of building the board road.

"What are they fixing to do?" asked a man carrying sacks of cement from the wagon, looking up at Jerry.

"Shoot a seismic line," Jerry replied. They're going to explode the dynamite in that hole they just drilled, and listen to the echoes in those yellow jugs. That tells us what's under the ground two miles deep, and where we might drill next."

"How much dynamite they going to blow?" asked the laborer. He was a new man, hired from Everglades City the week before. The arrival of the brown shrimp season had caused some unexpected attrition in the rig work force. Three men who had saved enough money to repair their nets and buy gasoline for their boats had left to take advantage of the yearly appearance of the shrimp, forcing Joe to bring on replacements.

"About fifty pounds," said Jerry. "It will make quite a geyser when it goes off."

The line ran from the drilling location to the southwest over Maggie's property. The data would be recorded and sent back to New York, where the geophysicists would carefully examine every foot of the line, looking for evidence of another reef. It provided a view of what was two miles below—not a clear picture, but often sufficient to identity features deep in the earth that might be worth the investment to drill.

The rotary table turned, turning the iron pipe, and drilling mud was pumped down to whoosh out the center of the bit, then return upward to the surface where the mixture of mud and rock fragments flowed onto the shaking metal screen. The circulating mud took about two hours to carry the cuttings to the shaker, so the rock fragments told an educated eye what kind of geologic formation the drill bit had encountered two hours previously.

The screen was covered with pearly white translucent pieces of rock with small brown veins. Jerry picked one up and scratched it again a small square of glass, leaving no mark. He took a small magnifying glass, suspended from his neck by a string, and looked at it closely.

"Anhydrite," he said to no one. The Lake Trafford Anhydrite was the layer of earth directly above the Sunniland Limestone. Calcium sulfate, deposited during the Cretaceous Period on a salt flat in shallow water, had been transformed into a mass of white rock hundreds of feet thick. Jerry had seen cores from West Texas drilled through anhydrite, intriguingly pretty but featureless. He imagined that if they bothered taking a core at this point, they would see something similar. The Sunniland was less than a hundred feet below the bottom of the well, he realized, nervous excitement taking hold as he entered the notation on his well log. A discovery worth millions or a dry hole that had cost Pride three months of drilling were the possible outcomes. Success or failure would be apparent within another day. Continuing to watch the seismic crew, Jerry's attention was distracted by a call from the driller.

"I think we're getting a drilling break." The rate the drill bit was descending into the earth had suddenly increased, indicating that it was cutting through a different type of rock, one easier to grind up with the bit's rolling teeth.

"What's the depth?"

"Eleven thousand, seven hundred feet," said the driller excitedly. In charge of the levers and knobs that controlled the drilling progress, the roughneck knew that was the expected depth of the Sunniland Limestone.

"OK. I'll start catching cuttings every fifteen minutes." Jerry wanted a detailed record of the changes in the ground-up rock fragments as they drilled into the Sunniland, something he would use to reconstruct the geology of the reef they hoped to find filled with liquid crude oil. Picking up a few of the cuttings that had been separated from the drilling fluid, he saw nothing but the white of anhydrite chips. Pulling his boots clear with each step through the muddy soil, he made his way to the cookhouse. Careful to stay out of Eileen's way as she finished cleaning up after the noon meal, he poured a cup of coffee from the pot sitting over a low flame and relaxed at the wooden table. The roughnecks had enjoyed their dinner an hour earlier, which was fortunate since Joe would want everyone on the rig floor when they drilled into the reef. This was the most dangerous part of drilling the well—an inflow of gas, a loss of drilling mud to caves in the reef, or a kick that drove the drilling mud back up the well faster than it was being pumped down could all result in a loss of control with potentially disastrous consequences.

He was interrupted by a shout from the roughneck raking cuttings from the surface of the shale shaker and putting them in a barrel for disposal.

"Hey, Jerry, some brown rock coming up the hole!"

Picking up his coffee cup, Jerry closed the screen door and tramped back to the shaker. No rush; the cuttings weren't going anywhere. His flashlight showed a few flat dark brown shards among the white anhydrite chips. He picked out a handful, then returned to the drill shack, sitting down at the small metal desk he had set up next to Joe's.

The dark brown fragments had thin, black, wavy stripes, and the magnifying glass showed a network of tiny pores. He picked up a small bottle of hydrochloric acid, drew a milliliter with an eye dropper, and squirted it onto one of the shards. It fizzed slowly, bubbling on the surface like a flat bottle of Coke. He would study these more closely with the microscope in his room at the Everglades City hotel, but he knew he was seeing samples from a tidal flat deposited on top of the reef, similar to the mud flats found today in Florida Bay. He expected the mudflat to be only a few feet thick, so if the bit had penetrated it two hours ago, the well should now be going down into the top of the reef. Jerry realized he was seeing part of the earth no living creature had seen for one hundred million years.

Joe entered the drill shack, his curiosity piqued on hearing the roughneck shout out the news of a change in the cuttings. Jerry's excitement caused him to stutter slightly as he answered Joe's question before it was asked. "We'll know something today. I'm going to want to go back and call Mike Woods as soon as I have something to tell him."

"Got it. Hope we found something after three months in this goddam swamp." It was kind of a treasure hunt, like discovering a sunken ship on the seafloor and crawling inside with a diving helmet on, wondering whether it contained gold coins or building stones. Joe tried to act nonchalant, but the excitement caused him to pace excitedly, looking out the window at the rotating drill pipe.

A continuous chart unrolling from a device on the wall recorded the rate of penetration, how fast the drill bit was going through the layers of rock, and the concentration of natural gas escaping from the mud. The gas meter had been reading zero, but suddenly the needle jumped to the right, signaling that methane was bubbling out of the drilling mud as the pressure dropped.

"Make sure that the flare is lit," Joe called out to the driller. "That's a good sign," he said to Jerry. "Means there's some oil or gas down there if it's coming up in the mud."

As Jerry shown a light on the shaker surface, he saw that the dark brown chips had been replaced by small pieces of gray and light brown rock. Some showed small crystals like a geode, and some had recognizable images of shells and coral. Using a magnifying glass, Jerry could see small pores, resembling a tiny sponge. Oil did not occur in large caves or underground rivers in the earth, but in pore spaces too small to see with the naked eye. Putting the samples under an ultraviolet light, he saw them glow in the dark.

"It's a reef, with porosity, and it contains oil," he told Joe. "I'll stay till tomorrow morning, then go back and call it in. We've got some work to do to see if it's going to make a well or not, but we know we've found pay."

The well was about on schedule, the last two weeks marked by an increased frequency of demands to call Mike Woods. Pride had invested several hundred thousand dollars, and the refinery in Delaware desperately needed crude oil. Jerry knew that Mike was asked once an hour now about the progress on the well, by Mr. Pride, the government, the board of directors, and the refinery manager. He talked to Joe more than Jerry, to find out how the drilling operation was going. But now he would want a detailed description of the geological results. He would be pleased.

Chapter 19

Wednesday

Tired from a sleepless night spent analyzing new cuttings every fifteen minutes as the drill bit continued to bore down into the reef, Jerry returned to Everglades City at dawn and called Mike Woods from the pay phone in the train station. As he expected, Ellen answered.

"Mike Woods office." Mike didn't expect his secretary to be there when he arrived before daylight, but Ellen had adapted her life to his schedule, coming in before the rest of Pride's office workforce showed up.

"Hi, Ellen. This is Jerry. Is Mike there? He wanted me to call him with the well results."

"He's not in. He had to go to Washington for a meeting, along with Mr. Pride. Took the early train. But he'll be back later and wants to talk to you. He said you'd probably call in and to tell you to wait in Everglades City until he can call you back."

Jerry made the mental transition from the noise and urgency of the rig floor to the priorities of the head office of Pride Oil. He had been ordered to wait, and so he would, in spite of desperately wanting to return to the rig and see what had been brought up and dumped in the shale shaker. "OK," he told Ellen. "I'll wait in the hotel lobby. He knows the number."

"When are you coming back?" she asked.

"Maria and I will be back as soon as the well is down," he replied. "I'm looking forward to walking up to the thirty-ninth floor and seeing your smiling face."

"Take care," she said. "See you soon."

Jerry spent the morning examining the cuttings with a microscope, scanning them with an ultraviolet light, and breaking them apart with tweezers. The microscope showed tiny pieces of coral and clam shells, bound together with crystals of clear calcite and dolomite. He confirmed his initial impression that they had encountered a reef with porosity and oil and then worked on the drilling log, sketching symbols and depths onto the linen paper.

"We've found oil," he told Maria, hugging her. "Right where I expected. I'm sure this is going to be the beginning of a new oilfield, the first in South Florida. "

"I'm not surprised," she said. "My husband, the wildcatter."

Exultant, Jerry thought about the months spent studying the geology of South Florida, examining the logs from other wells, interpreting the gravity and seismic surveys, and mapping the location of the potential reef. He knew the odds were against discovering oil. Only about one in ten wildcats were successful. He was going to be a great geologist, he decided. One hundred percent success so far.

"Don't you need to get back to keep catching the cuttings?" Maria asked.

"'I'd be back there right now, but I've been told to wait for Mike Woods to get back from Washington. He wants to talk to me. I'm going to finish looking at these this afternoon and draw up the drilling log while I'm waiting for him to call me. I'll leave as soon as I talk to Mike, either on the supply boat or the fuel barge if it's too late for the boat. The roughnecks will keep catching samples, so I can look at them when I get out there."

"When do you expect this well-drilling endeavor will be over?" she asked.

"In about two weeks. We have about another two or three hundred feet to drill. Hopefully we'll be logging at the end of the week." He had explained logging to her during the long trip south, teaching her how a well was drilled. After the drill bit penetrated an oil reservoir, the drilling mud prevented any oil from escaping to the surface, with only trace amounts in the mud and on the cuttings indicating the presence of a potential oil field. An instrument that recorded electrical resistivity had to be lowered into the well on a wire cable to determine the presence of water or oil, recording what they called an electric log.

"What's in the newspapers?" he asked Maria. The supply boat brought a daily paper to Joe at the rig, but he didn't share it until he had read it thoroughly, which usually took him three days.

"Mostly the war. Guadalcanal has been completely captured. The Army has invaded Africa. There have been a lot of tankers sunk by U-boats in the Gulf. Do you think they could come ashore and attack us here?"

"No, they only have about fifty men on a U-boat, and they're all sailors. There is some concern in Texas that there may be Nazi sympathizers onshore that they are contacting. Haven't heard anything like that here. And no reason for them to land in a swamp. The US Army couldn't beat the Seminoles, and I doubt the German Army could, either."

Jerry said this lightly, but he was aware of the magnitude of the tanker sinkings from his conversations with Mike Woods. So far over thirty ships had been sent to the bottom of the Gulf of Mexico, impacting the flow of bunker oil, diesel, and gasoline to the ships, aircraft, and tanks that were useless without it. A secure supply of crude closer to the northeast refineries became a high priority to the logistics officers in Washington, who had pushed through the red tape to have the Sunniland well drilled as quickly as possible. When he thought about the U-boats, Jerry was somewhat surprised they had gotten the rig safely across the Gulf without any incidents. It could have come by rail, but moving it from Louisiana by barge had saved time and money. Maybe the barge's low silhouette had prevented it from being visible to a periscope.

"Let's go have dinner at the Mangrove Lodge. After a week of Eileen's cooking, even though it's good, I could use something a little more upscale, like with a martini first," Jerry suggested. "The Turner Inn can bring me a note when Mike Woods calls, and I can call him back from there."

"I'd like that," Maria replied. "We can have a drink, even though it's early."

"OK. I have some more work to do on these cuttings, and then let's walk over. "

Seated at a waterfront table on the screened porch overlooking the river, Jerry tasted his martini approvingly, ice cold and very dry. The wealthy men and a few women who could afford to travel to the southern tip of Florida and spend a week on guided fishing trips were mainly from the north and accustomed to good booze. The room was about half full, with one table occupied by three men in their early fifties, dressed in expensive outdoor clothes and talking about their morning on the water. Two were unfamiliar, but Maria recognized the third as John Wase, her customer from the Turner Inn bar the previous night.

"Who did you go with yesterday?" the most sunburned man asked.

"I went with someone named Eddie," replied the slender, balding man sitting next to him. "They warned me that he had worked here before and they had to let him go because he would get drunk and not show up. But with the shortage of men today, they gave him another chance. They said he does know how to find fish and that he seemed to be sober during the day lately. We met up at dawn, and we went up to the Ten Thousand Islands."

"How'd you do?"

"Well, we ran up there in about thirty minutes, and he started poling along the mangrove creeks. He ties a gold spoon to my line, and the first bend we came to, he tells me to cast it within a foot of the bank. I threw it about three feet away, and nothing. He says a foot, not a yard. So I throw it again and it goes into the tree and I lose it. So he ties on a new spoon and throws it twelve inches from the edge of the mangrove roots. Bam! A twenty-four-inch redfish. He says, 'They hide in the roots and wait for bait to swim past. They won't go out more than a foot from the edge, because they usually don't have to and because a shark or a gator might get them. So you have to get the spoon into their feeding range.' He poles some more, and motions to another bend. That time I managed to get it about a foot from the bank, and Bam! Another redfish. We did that all morning. When I could get it close enough to the bank, I caught a fish. When I didn't, nothing. He knows what he's doing."

"Did he stay sober?"

"Pretty much. I could see him nipping on a flask when he thought I wasn't looking. But he got through the day and cleaned the fish fine. I was going to book him again for today, but he said he had something to do for that oil well they're drilling upstream."

Half listening to their conversation, John Wase looked around the room and recognized Maria sitting with Jerry and watching the river traffic. He nodded to her and said to Jerry, "I'm John Wase. You must be the geologist working on the Pride well. I stopped by the bar at the Turner Inn last night, and your wife, Maria, made the best martini I've had since I left New York City. I told her I'd be happy to have both of you go back to New York with me. I'll be leaving Friday. There's an express train that will include my private car."

"I'm Jerry MacDonald, and thanks for the offer. That would be a great way to travel. But I think we'll be here for about two more weeks."

Later, after grilled redfish and corn from one of the small farms further north, Jerry looked affectionately at Maria. "As soon as the well is finished, we'll be heading back to New York," he said thoughtfully. "Guess we'll have to travel with the rest of the world and not in a private car. When we return, I'll need to close out the file on this well; then we're heading to Maracaibo. Think about what you want to do while we're in the city. Maybe go to the theater. I think Maracaibo is a nice little town, but everyone will be speaking Spanish. So we should take advantage of New York while we're there."

The waitress approached them before Maria could reply, handing Jerry a message from the Turner Inn. Mike Woods was back in his office and wanted to talk to Jerry immediately. Jerry asked if he could make a collect call from the restaurant and was handed a telephone on a long cord. Evidently it was a common request from the businessmen who frequented the Mangrove Lodge.

Mike Woods was delighted but wanted precise information he could digest and pass on. "How many feet so far?" he asked.

"It looked like we had penetrated about one hundred feet when I left this morning. We're expecting three hundred, so we are about a third of the way down."

"What's your estimate of the porosity?" This was critical to knowing how good a discovery they had made. If the pore space constituted only one percent of the rock, there wouldn't be enough to hold a significant amount of oil.

"It looks good. I've been looking at the cuttings this morning with the microscope I have in the hotel room. About ten to fifteen percent. I'll have some thin sections made when I get back to New York to get a better number. But I don't think it will change much."

"Excellent. What's the rig doing now?"

"Drilling ahead. No gas kicks, but about two hundred units on the geolograph. They think they can get to the base of the reef without making a trip to change the bit."

"Anyway to keep this a tight hole?" Pride Oil had leased thousands of acres in the area, but they still had Roger and other landmen negotiating with landowners, from large corporations to small farmers and homesteaders, to lock up more. Tom Price and his compatriot had already shown up, reacting to the news in the trade journals of Pride's plan to drill the well. They had been run out of town, but if word of an oil discovery got out, the money expected to sign a lease would climb dramatically as competition increased overnight.

"Not really. The night tour came in this morning with me. Joe warned them to keep quiet and threatened them with their jobs, but I'm sure they are already talking about it. But we will keep the porosity and thickness data tight, and the electric log when we get it."

"Have you called out SunTex yet? They're the company we've contracted to run the electric log."

"No, Joe asked me to call them as soon after I talked to you. They'll have to bring a unit from Oklahoma, drive down, then load onto a barge to get to the rig. It'll take them a few days. It will take the rig about two days to get to the base of the reef, then Joe plans to circulate and condition the hole until SunTex gets here. The hole looks good. It's hard rock, so he's not worried about sticking. And no evidence of any lost circulation. "

"OK. Good job, Jerry. What are your plans now?"

"I'm going back out tonight to keep logging the cuttings. They need me there to call the base of the reef so they can TD the well. I'll come back in and call you after we get through the Sunniland and we're ready to log."

"Thanks for the update. I'll pass on what you've told me about what we know so far. Mr. Pride and the Pentagon both keep calling. Your news should keep them satisfied for at least an hour. Good luck."

The supply boat had already left for the rig when Jerry finished his phone conversation with Mike Woods, so he waited for the barge that was due later that afternoon. Sitting on the front porch of the Turner Inn with a duffel bag that held clothes and some drafting supplies, he watched the river impatiently. The barge had not arrived by dusk as expected, delayed by some unknown event of weather, cargo, manpower, or mechanical misfortune. But finally, he could see a white running light over the mangrove trees, changing direction as the vessel navigated the twists and turns of the channel. The barge rounded the last bend from the Gulf, pushed upstream by a small tug manned by a captain and a deckhand. A bow wave washed into the mangrove banks as it navigated the twisting channel, the tug's propeller kicking up the mud bottom. Over the last two months, repeated intrusions into the narrow river by the flat steel bow of the barge had widened the channel by knocking down the trees on the inside of the curves and washing away the roots so they collapsed into the open water. What had been a tight squeeze was now wide enough for two barges to pass side by side. The tugboat slowed and coasted alongside the riverfront dock, allowing Jerry to step aboard. He tossed his gear into a corner and sat down on an uncomfortable bench in the cabin, anticipating that they would tie up at the board road dock about midnight. The roustabouts arriving in the morning would unload the drums of diesel and sacks of cement before the barge started its voyage back to Tampa.

Chapter 20

Wednesday Night

The U-167 proceeded cautiously, the night lit with starlight but no moon, neither land nor another vessel visible on the horizon. The man on the bow cast a lead weight on a knotted rope to measure the depth, a throwback to sailing ship days. "Twenty feet," he called back in a quiet voice, then threw the line again.

"Dead ahead slow," Gunter told the helmsman below. The U-boat drew fifteen feet, and they were in danger of running aground. But the tide was coming in, and they were still six miles from the mangrove coast. The mission of the ten men in the raiding party was to find their way to the shoreline, make their way inland to the rig, seize the barge and tugboat, and take the barge out to the U-boat. It would be barely possible before the arrival of daylight made them visible to either the shore dwellers in the town or to nearshore fishing boats. They had to get closer, but the bottom continued to slowly shoal.

Gunter had met in the control room earlier with Franz, Peter, Adolf, and Karl, a seaman who had joined the submarine for the first time when they left port. Karl was about thirty years old, in excellent physical condition but with a small potbelly resulting from the inactivity of the cruise, and an open but wary look. He had been assigned to the submarine as the closest thing to a marine, trained to command the sailors in an infantry role if needed. A veteran of the Polish invasion, he was unsentimental in his politics, committed to the Reich but not a fervent supporter of the Nazis. His routine duties were those of an ordinary seaman, assigned to the maintenance of the U-boat, not fighting the specialized naval armament. The only one on the submarine who understood what killing someone hand-to-hand was like, he viewed the torpedoing of unwary ships as somewhat lacking in courage.

All five men looked at a chart of the coastline and a tourist fishing map that Peter had picked up in Everglades City.

"We have to go tonight," Gunter announced, trying not to let the uncertainty in his mind show on his face. "The barge is coming in, and we don't have enough fuel to last another week and keep the batteries charged. We'll send ten men, four in the skiff and three each in the rafts. Karl, you will need Peter and Adolf. Pick another seven men who can fight and know how to handle a machine pistol. It looks like there is a small stream here, north of the river. You can follow that east until it ends, then it looks like the mangroves give way to grass and cypress islands. You'll have to walk about a mile to the rig. Some of will be wading through the swamp, but maybe you can find dry path through at least part of it."

"Try and take control and not have any gunfire, if you can. If you have to shoot, you have to shoot, but that's likely to alert the townspeople in Everglades City and make it more difficult to get the barge back to the Gulf. There should be plenty of chain and cable around to immobilize whoever you find. The barge and the tugboat pushing it should be at a dock on the river connected to the rig site by a board road, according to Peter and Adolf's conversation with this Eddie. There should only be two or three men on it. After the situation at the rig is under control, send a few men down to the barge to take over from the crew, and make them help you get it down the channel and out to the Gulf. When you are ten miles out, shoot off one flare and we'll find you. Questions?"

"How do we find the rig in that swamp?" asked Karl. "We could traipse around in there for days."

"It's the highest thing around, and lit up at night. You can see the light at the top from Everglades City," Peter pointed out. "We can find it. The hardest part is walking though that marsh grass. It's growing in about two feet of water on a muddy bottom."

"If we fire one or two rounds taking over the rig, people will think it's someone hunting gators or jacklighting deer. But if we get into a firefight, we're going to get the police coming up from Everglades City." Adolf said this in a matter-of-fact voice, without a solution. But it was true that if resistance materialized and alerted the civilians downstream, police coming up the river would make it impossible to get the barge downstream without a struggle, and the sounds of further gunfire would bring still more police and perhaps military response.

"No reason to have any resistance. The crew is working, not expecting anyone to bother them. No reason for them to have any weapons." Gunter knew this was wishful thinking, but hopefully with some truth to it. A group of civilians should surrender quickly when surprised by a party of ten trained and armed military personnel.

Karl had become more familiar than he ever wanted to with the U-boat crew during the voyage from Lorient, watching their reaction to fear and response to an insult as he thought about who he might want for any landing operation. The list of individuals he would want for a raiding party was clear in his mind, and he went forward to tell them to prepare and arm themselves.

"Eighteen feet!" They had gone a mile since the twenty-foot depth had been called by the seaman casting at the bow. At this rate, they could go about another mile before the bow would start to hit the bottom in the trough of the waves.

"Get the boats on deck, and bring the skiff alongside. Make fast a towing bridle from the stern of the skiff to the first raft, then the second," Gunter ordered. "Tell the landing party to form up on the foredeck and be ready to cast off. If we hit bottom, I want them off quick, because we're going to start backing off right away."

Karl yelled an order below to the assembled members of the raiding party, who scrambled up the ladder to the top of the conning tower, then climbed down the metal steps to the deck. Two crewmen opened a hatch in the foredeck, taking out the two rubber boats with oars. This time they would be pulled by the outboard skiff seized by Peter and Adolf, aided by a following sea. The voyage in should take less than an hour.

"Sixteen feet."

"Go another kilometer, then stop," Gunter ordered the helmsman. "Karl, when we stop, that's it. See you at dawn with some fuel, I expect."

The journey in was uneventful, the outboard motor on the skiff chugging without interruption, pulling the two rubber boats at a steady five-knot pace. Shutting down the noise of the motor to an idle when they were inland of the maze of mangrove islands and in a channel paralleling the coastline, the boats moved slowly toward the mangrove coast. The chart and the tourist map showed a small creek with an entrance about a half mile north of the Barron

River. Using the lights of Everglades City as a marker, they steered toward the coast, aiming for what they thought was the location of the creek, guessing at their distance from the mouth of the Barron River. They could easily be too far north or south when they reached the coastline.

"How are we going to find this creek?" whispered one of the sailors, a heavyset man showing the scars of bottles and fists in waterfront bar scraps. "I can't see a damn thing."

"Hopefully there will be a gap in the trees," the man seated next to him responded quietly.

"If there is more than one gap, how do we know it's the right one? We could spend the night out here if we're wrong."

Karl looked at the tourist fishing map, sketched by hand with coves, shell banks, and other fish-attracting structures marked with names like Tarpon Hole or Speck Reef. The creek was named Boudreaux Bayou, presumably after some French-speaking explorer who had passed this way. The sketch showed a continuous shoreline from the Barron River to the creek, unbroken by gaps in the little tree-like symbols that presumably represented mangroves.

"Steer south," he ordered the man steering the skiff. "We want to hit south of it, then row north until we see an opening. It should be the only place where the tree line isn't solid."

The skiff pulled the two rafts north, parallel to the mangrove-lined coast, moving at the pace of a slow walk. Peering ahead in the darkness, lit by stars and absent any moonlight, Karl noticed a small, sharp decrease in the elevation of the shoreline. The height of the mangrove trees was remarkably even, controlled by growth and hurricanes, resembling a well-groomed hedge on a country estate. The apparent decrease was caused by the intervention of the creek entrance. The trees on the opposite bank were about two hundred yards further away, giving the impression of an apparent change in height. The channel became visible as a ribbon of water glimmering in the starlight, an enticing pathway into the mangrove forest. Karl ordered the skiff abandoned and moved two men to each of the rubber boats. The rafts turned and rowed east into the shallow river, soon finding themselves in a dark tunnel of overhanging branches, navigating by pushing off the shores as they slowly crept up the bayou.

The waterway meandered east, a narrowing channel between banks formed by mangrove thickets, black in the dim starlight. The boats almost turned west at times as they followed the twisting stream, working their way against the ebbing tide. The crew brushed mosquitos from their exposed faces, their heavy clothing and boots protecting the remainder of their bodies from the ravenous insects. The mangroves gave way to the grass savannah as the bayou narrowed and shallowed until the lead raft was forced to stop, the bow resting against the grass. The lighted derrick of the rig was visible a mile to the south when Karl stepped out of the boat, his feet reaching a muddy bottom in waist-deep water. The marsh grass was about two feet high above the water, making it impossible to see ahead, with only the derrick visible above the reedy tops. He pulled out a compass and took a bearing, almost directly south.

"We have no choice but to wade through this stuff to the rig. It's about a mile, a good walk. Form two columns, and if one finds a shallower or drier path, we'll merge. Keep your weapons out of the water. And observe silence discipline." The men were all from the streets of German cities, used to the sea and able to subdue their panic when attacked in the cold depths of the ocean. But aside from Karl, none had spent time in the wilderness. Walking through the night swamp, half submerged in water and unable to see anything but the dim shadow of the man ahead, induced a sense of panic they struggled to control. Only their training and the engrained habit of obedience to their officers drove them out of the boats.

Swamps and marshes in the northern latitudes are relatively benign places. One can drown by being immobilized in mud or quicksand, or drop exhausted from trying to traverse the mix of water, mud, and grass on foot. Over the centuries, few people tried to move on foot across the coastal estuaries of the European rivers or the swampy shorelines of the mountain lakes, instead utilizing a variety of watercraft. But when unavoidable, a march did not come with the expectation of perishing from the predations of the local fauna.

Tropical swamps, filled with water the temperature of a man's blood, are exponentially more dangerous. Cold-blooded predators are able to move and thrive year round in the warm waters. Alligators, crocodiles, flesh-eating piranhas, and carnivorous snakes are the origin of legends, stories of men and women being dragged away and eaten alive. Without the annual freezing temperatures to keep them in check, these animals control the food chain of the lowlands, competing equally with the mammals that dominate in colder environs. Accustomed to the delta of the Rhine, the German sailors stepped out into a hostile environment that was beyond their wildest expectations. They also encountered an enemy who had adapted to life in the warm marshlands, able to survive and prosper from hunting and fishing.

Peter led the left column, cautiously putting a foot ahead to test for firm bottom before putting his weight down. A small open lagoon appeared to offer a chance to see a little further ahead. He tread carefully into the area of open water, partially filled with green lily pads, and noticed a floating stick about five feet long. It appeared to be a tree branch that had fallen from one of the cypress islands. Moving into the open water and approaching the stick, Peter felt a sharp pain on his upper arm—as the snake, a water moccasin slowly crossing the lagoon with a sinuous motion—felt Peter brush against it. The serpent latched on, closing its fangs that carried venom into Peter's veins and resisting Peter's efforts to dislodge it. Twisting and thrashing, the snake flailed the water until the man behind it slashed it in half with a knife.

Karl looked at Peter's face in the dim moonlight, recognizing the onset of shock and paralysis. He wouldn't be able to walk another hundred yards as the venom spread into his arm muscles.

"You'll have to stay here. We'll tell the Americans where you are, and they'll send help and a doctor. You can spend the rest of the war eating Hershey bars in a camp. Good luck." Karl waved the other eight men ahead.

Peter pulled himself onto the marsh grass at the end of the lagoon, finding a piece of firmer ground, perhaps an old tree stump. The venom had spread up his arm to his chest, causing his breathing to slow, his chest struggling to move and force air into his lungs. No one in the landing party had known to tourniquet his arm or tell him to lower it below his heart. He looked up at the stars, then around the lagoon, fighting off panic as he saw a pair of close-set red eyes coming closer. He felt a powerful set of jaws close on his leg as the alligator pulled him under water, drowning him and hiding the body in a hole at the bottom to be eaten later.

Eddie's still was located in a cypress stand about a quarter mile from the rig, on a small island originally formed by floods overflowing the creek bank and depositing sediment to form a small area of dry ground, now covered with decaying cypress leaves. He had built it years ago, and its proximity to where Pride Oil wanted to drill their well turned out to be convenient. The still had been upgraded with copper tubing, new buckets, and metal flashing stolen from the rig, hidden in the swamp when no one was looking, and retrieved after dark. The crew knew Eddie was a moonshiner, wandering off and coming back with the smell of shine on his breath, but they had no idea where he went. No one ever asked the location of someone's distillery. They wouldn't tell you, and it was better not to know. If the revenue service found it, or someone stole the shine, you didn't want to be one of the people who could have talked. Moonshining in Florida was a more casual business than in the North Carolina mountains, but the practitioners were still violent men pursuing a banned trade. Eddie made a few gallons a week, consuming about half of his product when he couldn't afford store-bought rum, selling the rest to an establishment in Immokalee that offered it along with beer and liquor smuggled from Cuba.

Lighting a fire to heat a new batch of mash, Eddie twitched when he heard a sucking sound from the marsh. It was repeated, along with rustle of grass and the snap of small reedy stems as someone pulled a boot from the muck. Several people were trying to make their way through the sawgrass, sinking into the mud with each step and struggling forward. Eddie pulled the burning sticks from the fire and pushed them under water, leaving the rest to stay dry and be relit sometime in the future. The still was carefully covered with grass and cypress branches, invisible even during daylight. Unless someone looking for it knew exactly where it was, it would not be found.

A quarter moon had risen, and Eddie could make out a group of about ten people sludging through the swamp, dressed in black overalls and caps, faces blackened and carrying what looked like Thompson submachine guns. Could be federal revenuers, he thought, armed for an anticipated fight. They didn't appear to be casual looters who would back away if they found the still occupied and defended. The interlopers struggling through the mud had invested too much in arming themselves and in making their way laboriously across the swamp to be interested in a few gallons of moonshine. Maybe they were a search party looking for a fleeing murderer. As he watched, the file drew closer to his hidden distillery, forcing Eddie to crouch behind the stand of small cypress trees. He decided they were headed toward the rig, not his clandestine liquor production, which in his mind meant they had their minds set on trying to steal something. He wasn't sure what. The payroll was kept in a bank in Everglades, and the specialized equipment would be difficult to carry off, much less sell. But it was obvious now that they were headed toward the drill site and would get there in about an hour.

Eddie swigged a swallow from one of his bottles and thought about what to do next. He didn't want to get in front of some armed men. Feeling more confident that his still was not their objective, he considered warning the rig crew. If they were alerted, maybe they could deter the robbery, and maybe there would be a reward for raising the alarm. He decided that going to tell Joe was better than hiding. The marsh had a few high spots that he had connected with logs, forming a pathway he used to carry his stolen supplies from the drill site to the still. Hopping from a patch of dry grass to a half-submerged log to a patch of broken limbs, Eddie was able to reach the rig floor in minutes, carrying the shotgun he always bore in the swamp for defense against snakes, gators, thieves, revenuers, and nosy tourists.

"Joe! Someone's coming to rob you!" he called out when he arrived.

"What the hell are you talking about? There's no one coming. I can see down the road to the dock from here, and there's no one on it." Joe was irritated and on edge. They had encountered oil, the riskiest part of the drilling. The drilling had slowed down, and he was having to consider pulling the pipe from the hole to replace the drill bit. That meant losing the ability to control the well by manipulating the pressure until the pipe was run back to bottom, increasing the possibility of a blowout.

"They're coming through the marsh. About ten of them. With Thompson's. Black clothes. Will be here in about an hour, the way they're getting stuck in the mud."

Joe looked closely at Eddie. Was this a hallucination, he wondered? But Eddie tended to just get passed-out drunk, not conjure up things that weren't real. In any case, he decided, he needed to know what had brought Eddie to such a state.

"Jacque, go with Eddie and see what's out there." He didn't need the derrick man for another hour or two, the slow pace of drilling delaying the need to hoist more pipe to the top of the steel tower and connect it to the rotating string in the hole. Jacque was not in his usual position at the top of the derrick, but sitting comfortably at the corner of the rig floor on a chest full of short sections of pipe.

He nodded, asking Eddie, "What direction are they coming from?"

Eddie was reluctant to answer. He knew that although Jacque and the others didn't know the exact location of the still, if they found out, it would be a tempting refreshment stand for the rig crew when Eddie wasn't around. But now that he had come back to the rig and warned Joe, he was stuck. "Due north," he said without any expression.

Jacque went into the drill shack to retrieve the rifle he used to collect pelts. He had been disappointed in the population of fur-bearing animals here, less of them and less valuable than in the swamps around his native Houma. But he managed an occasional bear or bobcat. He motioned Eddie to the pirogue, a small canoe-like craft he had built in his spare time to navigate the marsh, with a flat bottom for stability and shallow draft. Jacque had spent his life in the wetlands of south Louisiana, and the Everglades weren't all that different. The marsh could be traversed quickly by paddling up the small channels, then sliding the pirogue over the grass flats to the next open water, minimizing the time wading in the muck. He paddled quietly, Eddie pointing the direction. Half a mile from the rig, the sound of feet being pulled from the bottom startled them both in to sudden silence.

"Verdammt nochmal!" a man swore as his boot came off and stayed in the muddy substrate, leaving him barefoot and feeling a stick of pain as he stepped down onto a small broken branch.

"Ils sont Allemagne!" Jacque whispered, reverting to the native French he had learned as a child. *Where in the hell had Germans come from?* he thought. They seemed to be a disciplined party, as the leader pushed the bootless man ahead, not allowing him to grope the bottom for his lost footwear.

"Switch places," he ordered Eddie, planning to start paddling the double-ended boat back to the rig. Eddie tried to comply, but fell over the side with a splash. He quickly climbed back in, and they both lay on their backs, looking up at the stars and hoping the low freeboard would make the pirogue impossible to see in the dark. They heard the sounds of movement from the trudging men stop.

"Wer weib? Lasst uns gehen!" Karl ordered them to keep moving, having no time to delay and find the source of the splash. Maybe it was an alligator. They had seen more than one as they rowed up the river and waded through the marsh grass, red eyes glowing in the night. Seeing the lighted derrick a thousand yards ahead, and hearing the sounds of heavy machinery operating at full tilt, the landing party plodded ahead, moving away from the floating pirogue as they headed directly toward their objective.

The pirogue drifted silently away, Jacque paddling slowly on a winding channel. "Does this channel connect to the canal next to the board road?" he whispered to Eddie.

Eddie nodded his head. "We go another hundred feet, then into that patch of mangroves. There's a small channel that cuts it, you can't see, but we can make it through. That will connect up to the canal, and we can get back to the rig without them seeing us."

A few minutes later, as a cloud obscured the thin moonlight, they tied the small craft to a stake at the edge of the raised clearing that was the site of the drilling rig, hastily climbing out and running up the staircase to the rig floor.

"Eddie's right. There are five to ten armed men coming this way through the marsh, speaking German!" Jacque spoke quietly but rapidly, nervousness evident in the hoarse tone of his voice. His father had volunteered to fight in France during the Great War. One day he had boarded the train with two friends from the tiny village south of New Iberia, returning years later to tell young Jacque terrifying stories of the savagery of the German troops they had fought, images that had sprung to life in Jacque's mind when he had glimpsed the shadowy shapes of the invaders struggling through the boggy marsh. Back in Houma, Jacque had heard the rumors of U-boats in the Gulf south of the Louisiana coast. If the Germans were this close, why would they not land troops ashore? He convinced himself that this was the beginning of an invasion.

Joe was forced to believe they had really seen an armed party approaching the rig. He wasn't sure if Jacque could really recognize German, but he couldn't disregard it. He had read the newspaper stories about the U-boat carnage in the Gulf, enough stories being printed in spite of the government's effort to suppress accounts of the mayhem, and he knew there were enemy ships within sixty miles of where he was standing. He had heard of several saboteurs being captured in New England, trying to blow up power lines and bridges. If the German Army had invaded Poland, why wouldn't their Navy send a few raiders ashore to cause some havoc? The war was not only happening in Europe and the Pacific, but also off the coast of Florida and Louisiana. But he had no idea why they would want to attack an oil well in the middle of nowhere. Maybe they wanted to delay or prevent the Americans from having oil much closer to the northeast than Texas, the same reason Washington so much wanted this well to be a discovery, he thought. In any case, they would probably all be dead unless they could do something.

"Pull ten feet off bottom and circulate!" he ordered. This meant moving the drill bit above the bottom of the hole, while continuing to pump mud down the well. The well would be in a stable condition, and while normally monitored constantly, it could be neglected for a while if necessary. "Turn off the rig lights. I know most of you have a gun somewhere around here to shoot critters and gators when I'm not around, even though you're not supposed to. Bring all the firearms you have, and all the ammunition, and meet me in back of the mud tanks."

There are times when drilling an oil well that progress slows to a crawl, with hours required to drill through another foot of dense limestone. It was common practice for the driller to let the crew wander off if they stayed nearby, able to know when they were needed by the height of the large pulley suspended in the derrick. If Joe was in town for a break or to talk to the head office of LT Drilling, the crew often passed the time shooting rattlesnakes, gators, ducks, and other wildlife, some for food and some for fun. Eileen took the ducks and made a stew if they had enough. Joe knew about it, and didn't bother looking under the cookhouse or behind the piles of cement sacks for rifles and shotguns. They were against Pride company policy, but he wasn't worried about anyone getting shot. If there was any liquor around, he would have been more concerned, but there wasn't. He viewed the guns as much less of a threat to the enterprise of drilling the well than drunkenness.

Karl watched the rig lights dim and go out, accompanied by a diminished noise from the rig engine and a cessation of the clatter of rotating pipe. He swore under his breath, knowing that somehow they had been detected. He looked at the stars, his years at sea enabling him to quickly find Polaris and know they were still headed almost due south. Still struggling through waist-deep water, it would not be easy to move the final distance to the cleared marsh occupied by the drill rig. Pulling their feet from the sucking mud one boot at a time, the raiders continued toward the staccato bark of the idling engine, now about five hundred yards ahead.

"Let's speed it up," Karl ordered. "They know we're here, and unless they run, we can expect a fight. They probably have some kind of weapons to be this far out in the woods. If they do run, it will be to the barge, and we'll have a fight there. So let's get to the rig first and take control. Don't shoot unless I give the order. If you do shoot, put it on single shot and maybe it will sound like someone poaching alligators or deer."

Adolf looked at the intervening swamp between them and the derrick of the drilling rig, now evident as a crosshatched pattern against the starlight as his eyes adjusted to the absence of the rig floodlights. "I hear them talking," he said. "Someone sent them off to gather firearms and reassemble." The sounds of Joe's orders had carried across the stillness of the evening.

"Very well. Keep moving in two columns." Karl swore under his breath, aware that now a fight was likely to be inevitable. He was confident that nine men who were used to working together in a military unit could easily defeat a group of civilians, backwoodsmen or not. But he also knew that extensive gunfire would alert the police in Everglades City and make it impossible to move the barge through the town to the Gulf.

Joe sat on the ground in the mud behind the tanks, surrounded by the roughnecks on the night tour. The laborers who carried sacks of mud and lengths of pipe had departed on the boat for Everglades City, leaving only the skilled practitioners of oil well drilling to operate the machinery overnight, as well as Eddie, who seemed to have missed the boat back to town. Joe had been due to go into Everglades City himself, but had let the boat depart without him so he could talk to Jerry. There were seven of them. Four had been hired since the rig arrived, including Big Slough and Eddie. Bobby and Jacque were Cajuns, coming from Houma on the barge with the rig. All were outdoorsmen, raised in the semi-wilderness of the rural south during the Great Depression, by families who subsisted at least part of the year on what could be hunted and killed—deer, squirrels, rabbits, and birds. They walked in nervously, carrying a variety of guns, a collection of lever action rifles, shotguns, a 1903 Springfield Armory 30'06, and a couple of revolvers. Everyone had a few boxes of ammunition. Big Slough had brought a collection of otter traps, steel jaws that would be chained to a tree root and would break the back of a fur bearing animal.

"OK," Joe said. "We can't leave—the boat has gone, and the barge isn't here yet. We have to assume they are here to destroy the well and will kill us if we get in the way. We could surrender and let them blow up the rig and the wellhead, but they may kill us anyway. I want to fight. They are used to fighting. But we know the swamp and they don't."

He looked around, asking, "Any other ideas?"

No one spoke. Then Bobby said, "Might as well make it hard for them."

Joe nodded, assuming a lack of dissent was agreement, and is-sued more orders. There was a risk that this was an expedition of biologists from a northern university studying the biota of the marsh at night, but he didn't think so. "Eddie, take that dry path to that still I know you have out there. That'll be east of them. Jacque, you take the pirogue and go back out; you'll be west. See if you can pick off one or two—that should slow them down some." Joe knew that neither would have any compunction about shooting another human being—both had been arrested for doing just that but had been re-leased for self-defense. The two men grinned and set off.

"Big Slough, take these traps and set them in a line across the edge of the location, as far out as you can go. The rest of you pile up some of these bags of mud and get set," he continued. He knew that Germans had to be stopped before they reached the dry land of the drilling pad. The group of Cajuns, trappers, and fishermen who had paused their previous lives to drill an oil well had guns and knew how to shoot. But they were undisciplined and had never been trained in small unit tactics. Joe was certain that while the approaching Germans were sailors and not infantry, their effectiveness as a team in small arms combat exceeded that of the men sitting around him.

Fifteen minutes later, Jacque lay motionless in the pirogue, looking up at the stars performing their great circular procession around the North Star. He lifted up the paddle periodically, silently dipping it into the dark water to propel the tiny craft to the north, west of the column of the German landing party. He could hear the splashing of a number of humans moving through shallow water, which also helped to keep him oriented. He was apprehensive, but thought the raiders were easy to track compared to a white-tailed deer moving through the hardwood cypress swamps of the Atchafalaya Basin. The pirogue lay slightly west of their intended march toward the rig, and they should shortly pass about fifty yards east.

He was startled by a muffled scream, not an animal but definitely a man in pain. Lifting his head over the gunnel, careful to cover his face although the stars were the only relief from total darkness, he saw the group of men circled around something splashing in the water, perhaps a companion. They pulled him onto the grass at the end of the small pond they were moving through, then continued toward the rig, now a clear shadow against the sky. Rolling over on his stomach in the pirogue, Jacque rested the Army surplus rifle he had bought at a store in New Orleans on the gunwale. It was a bolt action

30'06, powerful enough to kill an elephant if the shot hit the right place. Jacque sighted on the third man in the column and quickly pulled the trigger, then lay flat again in the pirogue. Learning from boyhood to shoot before the game he was pursuing vanished into the cypress swamp, he was usually able to hit a turkey at one hundred yards with a snap shot. This time, the hard thunk of a bullet impacting flesh and a grunt told him he had hit his intended target. He imagined the U-boat sailors wildly looking for the origin of the bullet, but not seeing the rifle flash, having no target to shoot at in return. They had all been looking at the rig and hadn't noticed the small canoe-like craft drifting closer and killing one of their number.

Got one! he thought, still lying flat on his back in the pirogue. *Wonder if I should go back or stay here? Probably hunting's better right where I am. Wonder how Eddie is doing?*

Eddie carefully stepped from a small patch of marsh grass that he knew had a minimal foundation of composted peat, enough to provide a stepping stone without sinking into the water, to a cypress log trapped against one of the grass islands. The pathway was quick and dry, but only to someone who knew where a footstep resulted in a chance to push off and move forward and not a plunge into chest-deep water. He reached his still minutes after leaving the rig.

Building a complex network of piping, vats, and collection devices intended to produce ethanol alcohol from sugarcane mash was an endeavor that took knowledge and enterprise. Having invested both, Eddie had situated the still to conceal it from unintentional visitors like fisherman and hunters, as well as law enforcement and thieves who might target his place of business. An escape pathway, a series of semi-dry patches of marsh and haphazardly placed logs, led to a rowboat tied in a small lagoon, which was connected to a labyrinth of creeks flowing to the Barron River. Eddie figured he could always hold off an intruder with a few well-placed shots, which would allow him time to get to the rowboat and escape downstream if they didn't run or he hadn't managed to hit them.

The still was surrounded by a crude dike of burlap bags, piled two deep, an effort Eddie had made to keep water from seeping through on a high tide. It wasn't successful at all, the water flowing through the mud-filled sacks to inundate the small island and forcing him to periodically rebuild the apparatus. But although it had failed as a flood-control device, it provided a foundation for natural camouflage, marsh grass sprouting through the network of fiber to form a grass wall. Eddie lay on his stomach behind the berm, seeing the silhouettes of human figures against the starlight accompanied by splashes and grunts. Four men were plugging along in a single file, close enough for him to distinguish the submachine-gun-like weapons they were carrying.

The last man in the column passed the still, and Eddie let him proceed another twenty yards, then shot him in the back of the head. The Germans were looking ahead at the derrick now becoming apparent through the darkness, and no one saw the flash of the 30/30. Eddie lay flat on his stomach behind the embankment of burlap and mud, waiting for a burst of machine pistol fire to pound into the barrier. He heard some muffled yells in a language he did not comprehend but guessed to be German, but no returning fire. Both groups of men continued toward the rig, their increased pace evident from the shorter interval between splashes.

Chapter 21

Wednesday Night

The tugboat shifted to reverse, churning up a mixture of mud and shell fragments from the bottom of the Baron River, and the barge gently collided with the board road dock. Floodlights from atop the pilothouse turned the scene into daylight as the deckhand leaned over and looped lines around the cypress pilings. Jerry slung the worn leather strap of his duffel over his right shoulder, picking up a satchel of papers in his left hand, and started trudging down the wooden platform. The sight of the derrick suddenly disappeared, the Christmas tree effect created by lights strung along the framework vanishing in the darkness. *Must have blown a fuse,* he thought, still hearing the engine idling as the pumps forced mud down the drill pipe. Not alarmed, he continued shuffling slowly, letting his eyes become accustomed to the dim starlight, carefully watching for water moccasins resting on the warm boards. Cold-blooded animals, the snakes sought out warmth from anything heated by the sun, lying motionless after dusk until the cypress planks cooled off.

SUNNILAND

Bam!

Jerry couldn't tell what kind of firearm had just been discharged, but it sounded sharper than the shotguns he occasionally heard the crew used to kill ducks. *Maybe a rifle,* he thought, wondering why one of the crew had gone into the dark swamp to shoot at anything. Even if they managed to kill a deer, they wouldn't be able to find it until morning, and it was more likely that an alligator would drag it away in the darkness. Concerned that it might have been aimed in his general direction, he crouched and ran quickly to the edge of the dry ground surrounding the wellsite, having seen no one when he arrived.

"What the hell is going on? Where is everyone? Who's shooting at what?" Yelling loudly and expecting a response, Jerry instead felt a hand on his arm, holding his bicep and pulling him to the ground.

"Shut up and lie still," Joe said quietly. "I don't know why, but there is a party of armed Germans, probably from a U-boat, coming at us. Eddie and Jacque are out there to slow them down. That was Jacque's '03 Springfield."

Crack! The sound of a round from a different weapon came from the same general direction.

"That was Eddie's 30/30," said Joe. "Should have two less Germans now. Have you ever shot a gun?"

"You don't grow up on a farm without knowing how to shoot. Mostly varmints. But I went pheasant hunting whenever I could," said Jerry.

"OK, take this." Joe handed him a revolver he kept in his desk, mostly in case a show of force was needed. He had been glad to have it at other times and other places in the world, but he'd never had to use it.

"Don't shoot unless I tell you they are coming," he continued. "Eddie says they're dressed in black. Don't shoot anyone from the crew. And don't point the gun at someone unless you intend to shoot them. Don't think that just waving it at someone is going to make them do what you want!"

With the rig noise diminished for the first time in weeks, Jerry became aware of the nighttime cacophony of sounds in the swamp, splashes and grunts by the alligators, the scream of a distant cougar, and the rustling of small animals moving through the brush. It was an unfamiliar environment, more primal than the dusty plains of western Oklahoma, an environment yet unchanged by human intervention. Usually the noise of the machinery, the floodlights turning the rig floor from night to day, and the constant movement of the crew mitigated the feeling of isolation. But now, with the lights off and the sounds of the swamp that were usually drowned out by the machinery—aware that an armed group of men was planning to attack them—he started to shake. Joe grabbed his upper arm and squeezed it hard, causing Jerry to wince.

"Settle down or you'll be dead. Just sit here, don't move, and start shooting people dressed in black when I tell you to."

"OK," Jerry said, feeling the bruise on his arm and ashamed of his reaction. "Where do you want me to be?"

"Go lie down on the ground next to the mud pits. And for Christ's sake, don't shoot me."

Jerry sat by the mud pits, deciding he would wait until there was a more imminent danger before lying flat on the wet ground. Mud from the bottom of the well was flowing into the pits, carrying small amounts of oil, gas bubbling out with a smell of rotten eggs. Normally, a vacuum system would have been turned on, degassing the mud and carrying the methane and hydrogen sulfide to a flare. Joe didn't want the light from a flare, positioned to the side of the dry land pad and rising fifty feet, illuminating the wellsite. And turning off the lights had also cut the power to the vacuum pumps. So the gas bubbled from the surface of the mud into the atmosphere, making him slightly dizzy as he sat on the ground directly below the open surface of the pits. He looked at the flare stack, a vertical pipe steadied by steel guy wires. He checked the revolver that Joe had handed him. And he wondered if would be able to kill a German sailor before the sailor shot him.

Karl stepped onto a cypress root, then slipped off and dropped into a deep pool, sinking over his head before his feet touched bottom. Panicking, he pushed to the surface and paddled toward the grass at the far side of the small area of open water. The bottom began to slope upward, and he could raise his machine pistol above water as he waded toward the grass. He turned around and saw Heinrich, a heavyset man who was carrying two bandoliers of machine gun ammunition as well as the heavy gun, cautiously put his left boot into the pool. Plunging to the bottom, he fought to push off the soft, muddy substrate, but weighed down by the armament Karl had ordered him to strap to his overalls, he could not reach the surface. A violent churning motion slowed and then ceased as Heinrich inhaled water and drowned. A shorter, husky man bringing up the rear of the column began to unsling his weapon and release the web belt that carried ammunition and grenades, wanting to dive down and rescue the machine gunner, but he stood motionless as Fritz ordered: "Don't drop it in the water. We'll have to move on and leave him. Go to the left around this pool and make sure you've got a foot on the bottom before you step off."

That left five men and himself, Karl realized. One to a snake, one to drowning, and the Americans had shot two. They were still a few hundred yards from the rig. Three futbol soccer fields, or one hole of the game the Americans and Scots liked, called golf. Or a long rifle shot, a distance at which only a skilled marksman could hit a man-sized target with a rifle. Their forward progress had slowed considerably, as the men cautiously tested the bottom of the swamp and searched the grass islands for reptiles. Continuing to plod slowly forward, they came to a large, shallow pond, illuminated by starlight, an open area directly between them and the last stretch of marsh grass at the edge of the drilling pad. Karl considered working around the edges, using the marsh grass for concealment, knowing the watching Americans would easily be able to shoot them in the open water. He looked at the watch on his left wrist, the hands and numbers glowing with phosphorus and allowing him to read the time: one o'clock. Two hours later than planned. He realized that that even if they were successful in quickly overpowering the rig crew and seizing the oil barge, dawn would be breaking as they navigated downstream through Everglades City and into the Gulf. They had to move.

"Go straight across," he ordered. "Head for the derrick. We don't have time to go around. Form a line abreast and expect some resistance."

The file of U-boat expeditioners, now down to six, accompanied Karl across the pond, preparing for a final assault on whatever defenses the rig crew had been able to prepare. Wading in waist-deep water, their feet sinking into the muddy bottom and threatening to pull their laced boots from their feet, they moved by stepping forward and then pulling hard on their back leg to extricate the trailing foot from the mud. This caused their leading foot to sink six inches deeper into the muck, making it even more difficult to pull out during the next step. But there was no other way to move, so they laboriously trudged across the open water.

"I hope there are no more snakes or gators in this little lake," Adolf spoke softly, his voice trembling.

"Silence!" ordered Karl in a fierce whisper. "They'll fire at any voices. Move on."

As they began their traverse, an explosion of water in the middle of the pond startled all of them. Bright silver flashes reflected the starlight, and a curtain of shimmering tiny mirrors rose and fell to the surface of the brackish lake. All was still; then the performance was repeated closer to Karl as he cautiously shuffled across the pond floor. The second time, it was apparent that a school of shiny minnows was being pursued by one or more larger fish. Reminded of trout in an Alpine stream, Karl saw fish rolling in the turbulence as they savaged the school of bait. Startled but not alarmed, he led the column into the center of the feeding frenzy, noting that the gorging fish were not deterred by the wading humans.

Suddenly he felt a bump as a large animal swam past, knocking him sideways and lifting his legs from the bottom. Panicking, he treadmilled furiously until his feet found purchase as he saw the fin and tossing head of a shark move away from him. The shark and two companions circled the fish that were feeding on the minnows, forcing them into a compact school, then dashing in to tear viciously at their prey. Fritz had seen bluewater sharks offshore, following the submarine across the tropical surface of the southern Atlantic, but these were smaller and unfamiliar. They were bull sharks, aggressive predators that could survive from fresh rivers to the salty Gulf, drawn upstream by the presence of food. Responsible for most of the attacks on swimmers and waders on the Gulf beaches, often erroneously reported in the press as the strike of a great white, they were capable of severing a human leg or arm with a single bite of razor sharp teeth.

"Freeze!" Karl called out. Knowing he had led them into the middle of a school of sharks, remaining motionless seemed the only solution. The party had already stopped moving, terrified by the slashing, jumping, slapping bull sharks as they surrounded and herded the smaller fish. Hoping the bait would move on and draw the feeding fish and the sharks to another place, Karl looked at the edge of the pond, seeing nothing at first, and then a red flash.

Bam! This time it was a shotgun. Buckshot skipped across the water, and three pellets at the top of the pattern hit Adolf in the abdomen, knocking him into the water with a trail of blood and stomach contents forming a slick that drifted toward the quieting school of bait. Adolf screamed in pain, then panic.

Marked by a sweeping, forked tail, five feet in length and weighing over two hundred pounds, a bull shark turned slowly and followed the slick toward the column.

"Shoot that shark. Please. Please. Don't let it get me." Even for a man or woman standing on a sunny beach or a pier, the approach of a large shark invokes a primeval fear of a predator that cannot be escaped. Standing in a swampy pond in darkness, panic is inevitable. Some people can suppress it and move; some are unable to think or control their bodies.

"Suppress that fire in the swamp! Forget about the noise!" Karl yelled as he took the sling off his shoulder and aimed his machine pistol at the approaching shark. It was an easy shot, the fin marking the dorsal area only an inch below the water, and Karl fired two rounds into the head. The shark leapt skyward, exposing a white belly, then fell backwards into the water, its body undulating slowly as it sank to the bottom. Turning his attention to the sniper who had killed Adolf, Karl heard the sound of four machine pistols on full automatic, firing back at the red flash of the shotgun. He heard a grunt followed by a splash, as someone hit by a lead bullet fell into the water. After losing five men, the landing party had at least succeeded in killing or wounding one of the defenders, Karl thought with satisfaction.

Jacque had used his shotgun, hoping he could hit more than one of the Germans. The pattern had thrown low, and he had only hit one, causing a disciplined response of machine pistol fire. One round had hit him in the shoulder and knocked him out of the pirogue. The Germans were struggling with an unfamiliar environment, taking casualties from the Americans and the creatures of the swamp, but they had maintained the discipline required to suppress their panic and focus their firepower. Jacque was alive and not mortally wounded, but no longer a factor in the defense against the advancing Germans.

The four remaining German sailors gathered around Karl, scared and disoriented. Adolf was gone, the weight of his boots and web gear having pulled his body to the bottom of the pond.

"We either make it now or we don't. Move as fast as you can toward the shadow that looks like a tall tree. That's the rig derrick. Don't slow down for anything. We will have to hope the Americans take care of our fallen comrades." Karl started walking across the pond, pushing himself, knowing that if he lost another man he couldn't hope to seize the barge, fearing that it was already impossible to complete his mission.

The boiling bait and the predators trailing it had faded away, moving beneath the surface to another isolated pond in the Everglades, protein moving up the food chain. Praying there were no potholes in the remaining distance they had to wade, Karl moved out in long strides, hoping that when they reached the grassy shoreline it would be possible to walk on some sort of solid surface. Stepping forward on the flat, muddy bottom, he put his foot down and felt an excruciating pain in his ankle, above the combat boot he wore. The stingray moved off, disturbed by the sole of Karl's boot descending on it without warning. Karl gasped for breath and struggled to remain upright.

"Grab my arm!" he commanded the nearest seaman. "Something hit me; I can walk but it hurts like a sonofabitch. "

The sailor grabbed him under the armpit, holding his machine gun in the other hand. Together, they hopped across the pond, stepping in tandem like two children in a three-legged race at the fair. Reaching the edge of the water, Karl collapsed onto the marsh, motioning the other men to lie flat. He peered forward toward the rig, the shapes of the tanks and other equipment now visible in the starlight about one hundred yards away. No evidence of any defenders, but they would be hidden, taking cover behind the steel walls of the tanks or lying behind the sacks of cement and drilling mud. "When I say go, rush the derrick. Suppress any defensive fire. If anyone surrenders, take their weapons and shoes. If they resist, shoot them," Karl commanded in a soft but authoritative voice. The pain in his leg had subsided to the point that he could limp forward unaided. He rose to his feet, pointing his machine pistol toward the Americans.

Chapter 22

Wednesday Night

Sitting on the front porch of the Turner Inn after her shift at the bar, drinking an iced tea and propping her legs on the porch rail to take advantage of the cool breeze, Maria relaxed. She had gone to work before Jerry caught the barge and was tired after four hours of tending bar and mixing drinks for the waitresses. A few more minutes and she would go to bed. She looked up as the hotel owner, John, came onto the porch and sat in the rocking chair next to her, sipping whiskey from a short glass.

"How was the crowd tonight?" he asked.

"OK. I never have any trouble with the locals who know me now. A few drunks tonight from that little freighter that's tied up at the seafood plant. But nothing serious. They were just having fun."

"Have you been out to the rig? I want to see it, but I haven't been able to get away. Need to take advantage of the tarpon season—it won't last long." John looked at her, trying to decide if she was happy to be in the same part of the world as Jerry or pissed off that she was stuck in a nowhere hotel while he was gone for a week. She seemed pretty happy. He still wasn't sure why a pretty woman whose husband was making good money with Pride Oil wanted to work in the bar. But he was happy to have her.

"No, there's no place for me to stay, even for a few hours. I could stand on the board road like the sightseers Jerry tells me about, but that doesn't seem to be worth the trouble. I would like to see it, but they seem pretty busy and don't need an onlooker standing in the middle of what they're doing."

Some irritation was evident in her voice. She wanted to see the rig, but asking Jerry about it for weeks had not resulted in a boat ride and a tour of the drill site. The operation was still about as familiar to her as the backstage of a circus. Jerry made excuses about it being too dangerous. *How could Eileen make it out and back every day?* she wondered.

"Do they seem to be on track to find some oil?" John asked, looking around for the whiskey glass he had brought out to the porch. "I would think they would know after three months."

The sound of distant explosions filled the silence before Maria could reply. There were three bangs, spaced about two seconds apart.

"Somebody must be shooting deer. It's out of season, but that doesn't make any difference to these guys," Maria offered.

"Definitely gunfire. Kind of late in the day for hunting. Sounds like it was from due east, near the rig. Do you know how to shoot a gun?"

"No, where I grew up, that was what the guys did, and not to shoot ducks. It wasn't a sport but a part of life."

There was a volley of more distant gunfire, ten shots close together. Then more silence.

"I guess they got whatever it was. Maybe a wild pig. Sometimes they come close to the rig, and they're good to eat. Eileen, the cook, is from around here and can make anything taste good. But Jerry says it take a lot to bring them down—they have a thick skull and are tough. They're also pretty fierce if you hurt one and don't kill it; they have tusks that can do some damage."

Maria remembered some pork that Eileen had brought back from the rig one afternoon. Seared on both sides with a lot of spices. It had been delicious. If they had shot a pig, maybe Jerry would bring a slice or two when he came back in.

Another volley of shots, spaced so close together the resultant sound waves merged into a single event, followed the brief silence. "That sounded like a machine gun," said John. "Not sure why any of those guys would have one out there. Don't need it to shoot pigs or ducks. More of a John Dillinger weapon to hold up banks, unless you're in the Army. Wonder how that got out there."

Maria had tensed up, listening to the night sound, waiting to hear more gunfire. She heard a few more intermittent shots, then more silence. Turning to John, she said, "Jerry's out there in the middle of whatever that is. I'm going to go down to the sheriff's office and ask them to send someone out to the rig. This doesn't sound right. Something's going on."

She left the porch and walked the three blocks to the police station. In too much of a hurry to change shoes, she looked down at her slippers, turned brown by the mud of the puddles found in the intersections that interrupted the dry path of the wooden sidewalk. Turning into a building that fronted a section of the sidewalk illuminated like daylight by burning bulbs from hooks hung overhead, she saw a tired looking man, about forty-five years old, bald, and probably more than thirty pounds heavier than when he had joined the force, sitting at a desk. He was reading a magazine with a slick cover and photographs of half-nude women and men with submachine guns, titled *True Crime*. Sensing a visitor, he folded the periodical and slid it into a desk drawer, then turned to greet Maria.

"Hi, Maria. What can I do for you?" he asked cordially. He had been to the Turner Inn bar three nights out of four since Maria had arrived, and liked her.

"Hear all those shots? They're coming from the rig. That's where Jerry is. I want you to send someone out there and see what's going on. Sounds like a warzone."

"I heard it. Was a lot of gunfire. Can't imagine why anyone would be shooting so much in the middle of the night. But there's no one here but me, and I have no one to take me upriver, and if I went I wouldn't know where to look. It sounds like its coming from the rig, but it could be a fight over a still five miles away. But I'll go up the river tomorrow morning and take a look."

"I guess that'll have to do," said Maria defeatedly. "I hope nothing big is happening out there. I'll talk to you after you get back tomorrow about what you found out."

"Sorry I can't do more to set your mind at ease right now," said the deputy. "But that's all I can do. I'm sure it's nothing to do with the oil well. Nothing to steal there that could be carried away."

"I guess so," replied Maria. "Thanks." She waved goodnight and turned toward the door.

The sounds of gunfire kept her awake until two o'clock, when it suddenly ceased. *Too much for a fight between a moonshiner and the revenuers,* she thought. And too long for a dispute between feuding gangsters. In Queens, gunfire was not that uncommon, but it only lasted a few minutes. Disputes were settled quickly. This was going on too long to be explained by anything in her experience.

Chapter 23

Wednesday Night

Holding onto the pistol Joe had handed him, Jerry lay on his stomach behind the mud berm that had been piled up around the rig, a two-foot high levee put in place to reduce flooding during high water. Turning his head while keeping his cheek flat against the mud, he could see Joe and the roughnecks lying belly down in the mud, peering over the berm and aiming hunting rifles and shotguns at the approaching Germans.

"What do you think that shooting was?" he asked Joe. "Us or them?"

"The first shots were Eddie's 30/30 and Jacque's Springfield, then Jacque's shotgun. The submachine gun fire was from them," Joe replied calmly, just stating the facts.

"Then the Germans fired about fifty rounds to our three." That didn't seem too encouraging, even if Eddie and Jacque had been able to see a target and hit it in the darkness, taking advantage of their ability to move and shoot in the swamp.

The man next to him lay flat, holding a pump action shotgun, the steel barrel resting above a brown wooden stock. It looked like the Winchester Model 12 that Jerry had bought in high school, using money he earned carrying pipe and cleaning tanks in the oilfields. A reliable workhorse of a gun, it could kill anything from small birds to large deer or even a bear, depending on the size of the pellets.

"What kind of shells do you have in that?" Jerry asked.

"Twos," the roughneck replied. "Was hoping to shoot some geese or canvasbacks. They'll be good for these guys when they're sixty feet away, but not much further than that."

"What's going to happen?"

"It looks like they're going to rush us. We can hide behind this levee, but they can shoot a lot faster than us. Joe put two guys at each end, spread us out some."

"Ever shot any anybody?"

"Not that could shoot back at me. Just to chase off some guys broke into my barn once. I missed them."

When first deployed under Joe's direction, the five armed men, protected by an earthen wall, were confident they could defend themselves against anyone wading through the marsh. But after the events of the last hour, the Germans now seemed unstoppable, surprisingly surviving the arduous and dangerous trek through the swamp in spite of the natural predators and the sniper fire of Eddie and Jacque. At best, the rig crew could get off six or seven shots against a disciplined team that could lay down a barrage of automatic fire, forcing them to keep their heads down while the Germans advanced unopposed. Jerry crawled over to Joe, saying softly, "I don't feel too good about this."

"Neither do I," replied Joe. "I didn't count on the fact that they would be much better armed. I've been in some skirmishes around the world, bullets and poison arrows fired at me, but never before with professionals. I'm not sure we can stop them."

"Let's haul ass," Jerry suggested. "We can hide in the swamp until they leave."

"Too late. They're close enough to see us if we stand up and run, and the way they're shooting, I don't think they'll just let us go. Whatever they want to do here probably doesn't include having someone out there taking potshots at them. We're better off staying here."

Jerry thought about Maria, a feeling of utter sadness overcoming him. Then a thought jolted him away from his dwelling on how Maria would take the news of his death. "What if they're going to the town next?"

The newsreels in 1940 and 1941 had shown the Nazi invasions of Poland and France, images of dead civilians and burning buildings. Accounts of rape, murder, and the forced removal of the local populations had been vividly described in the pages of the *New York Times* and other newspapers. The Germans had no compunction about killing, either those who actively resisted them or those they deemed undesirable. The accounts of German brutality to the civilians of Europe flashed through his mind as Jerry envisaged black-clad men invading Everglades City, burning buildings and randomly shooting civilians. He could see no reason why they wouldn't do precisely that, causing panic among the shoreside villages of the Gulf of Mexico and forcing the government to send troops to Florida instead of Italy. Hostile navies had sent raiding parties ashore for centuries, a tradition of the Greeks, Vikings, and the British among others. In Jerry's mind, it was a logical reason for the assault on the drilling rig that he now found himself entangled in.

"I've got no idea what they're here for," said Joe. "Can't do anything about it at this point. We've got to take care of ourselves."

Easy for you to say, thought Jerry. *No one in town that you care about.*

SUNNILAND

Heart pounding, Jerry looked up at the stars, trying to calm himself. He noticed the flare tower, a vertical pipe tied to earth by four guy wires, each attached to a metal stake driven deep into the earth. It was positioned at the north end of the rig, to take advantage of the prevailing winds when it was necessary to burn off gas brought up by the circulating mud. The first day after the derrick had been erected, Joe had ordered a windsock raised on a steel rod secured to the top, watching it for several days while the rest of the machinery was put in place and the piping connected. There typically wasn't a lot of wind, nothing like the continuous breeze encountered on the Great Plains, but it seemed to be more from the south when it did blow. Concerned about the possibility of flaring on a calm day, allowing drops of hot unburned hydrocarbons to fall directly onto the rig, he had ordered an additional twenty feet of pipe welded to the top. That had made the tower unstable, shaking in a moderate breeze, so four pad eyes had been welded near the top, with steel cables leading to stakes pounded into the soft soil. It vibrated and shook during the high winds of thunderstorms, but was stable enough with the additional support. And it only had to last the few months until the well was finished.

A bullet rang off a steel tank, making him duck and wondering what would happen when the German submariners charged the drilling rig. He was not sure what they wanted, but he didn't believe that the way things were going he would be alive to find out. The earlier shooting, whether it originated from Eddie and Jacque or from the approaching German seamen, didn't appear to have stopped their advancing. He could still hear them splashing through the shallow water, closing in on the edge of the artificial island that had been dredged up as a foundation for the rig.

Then he remembered what had happened when the well had drilled into the top of the Sunnniland reef. Gas trapped in the po-

242

rous limestone had flowed into the drilling mud, forming bubbles that lightened the weight of the mud column and forcing the driller to carefully circulate the mud containing the entrained bubbles of gas to the surface. As the mud flowed from the wellhead to the mud tanks, the gas effervesced like a shaken bottle of Coca Cola. It swirled above the surface of the mud, a potential bomb if left in place, but picked up by powerful fans it flowed to the flare tower. An electric spark ignited the combustible mixture and resulted in a steady flame, resembling a huge cigarette lighter.

Running back to the toolshed, a portable metal building that had been delivered intact on the barge and placed near the stairs to the rig floor, he picked up a pair of bolt cutters from a box on the floor. Resembling giant pliers with four-foot long handles, they were essential to cutting through the rusted and jammed bolts often found on outdoor machinery. His other hand grasping a sledge hammer, Jerry ran toward the flare tower as the crackling sound of machine pistol fire started to overwhelm the occasional shotgun and deer rifle reports. Putting the bolt cutters around the guy wire nearest the rig, he strained to pull the handles together, frustrated when the blades resisted biting through the steel wire. Lowering one handle to the ground, he struck downward on the other with the sledge hammer, forcing the sharpened jaws to cut through the wire. The flare tower drooped toward the swamp with the loss of one quadrant of support. Jerry rushed to the next wire, severing it in the same manner. The flare tower sagged further toward the edge of the drilling pad, with no support from the direction of the rig. As Jerry moved toward the third wire, a bullet kicked up mud near his shoe, as one of the approaching raiders saw him moving. He sprinted toward the guy wire, dropping the sledge hammer and lying in the mud. Putting the blades around the cable, he squeezed with all the strength he had, feeling the handles move closer together. Another bullet sprayed mud onto his face. Desperately, he hooked one leg around the handle and pulled it toward his chest, and felt the blades slice through the strands of steel wire, releasing the last support that prevented the flare tower from starting to fall over toward the swamp. It sagged toward the north, at first slowly and then with increasing speed, then hesitating with the tip a few feet above the surface of the ground as it rested on the mud levee. The pipe bent but did not rupture, so that it resembled a horizontal cannon barrel, pointed at the approaching Germans.

Crawling back toward the drill shack, Jerry reached the switch to start the generator, risking the attention it would attract. As it chugged to life, belching smoke and causing the lights to flicker on, he reached out and turned on the vacuum fans, sending the gas evolving from the mud tanks down the flare line. Gas had been slowly bubbling from the surface of the mud tanks since the power had been switched off, enough to make him almost pass out. As the vacuum fans cleared out the methane vapors, he was able to think clearly again and remember where the igniter switch was, situated on a panel on the rig floor, eighteen feet above his head. Jerry crawled on his stomach, propelling himself forward by his elbows and pushing with his legs, his face in the dirt. He was invisible for the moment from the advancing submariners, and reached the foot of the ladder reaching to the rig floor. It was only about twenty feet high, but he knew he would be a clear target with starlight shining through the rungs of the ladder.

"Joe! I need to get to the rig floor. I'm going to ignite the flare. Distract them for a minute," he shouted hoarsely, hoping none of the approaching men could understand English. He heard a faint "OK" in response, and waited.

Joe reached into a steel toolbox he had been sitting on and withdrew a short red cylinder, resembling a chair leg. Twisting the end, he ignited the handheld flare and threw it toward the approaching men. As it arced across the sky, illuminating the area in a white light. Jerry waited for it to hit the ground and extinguish, then pounded up the latter while the German's night vision was momentarily destroyed. Crawling across the steel-plate floor to the control panel, he reached up and pushed the igniter switch.

Karl and his remaining four men had crossed the rest of the swamp to the dry land surrounding the rig. "Let's go!" Karl shouted, trying to ignore the searing pain from the stingray wound in his leg. Rising to their feet and running toward the rig, they fired short bursts at the top of the mud levee, forcing the Americans to keep down. No answering fire came from Joe and the roughnecks, unable to return fire without exposing themselves to the hail of German bullets.

'Keep firing!" Karl yelled. "Keep their heads down."

The Germans advanced at a run, approaching to within twenty yards of the edge of the machinery-filled space, intent on crossing over and shooting the survivors. There was no intent of taking and securing prisoners now. Karl knew they would have to fight to get the barge downstream through the town, and he wanted to do it before dawn. He didn't want to waste any time tying up captives.

The Germans heard a sharp clicking noise, followed by a blinding flash. A fireball of gas, forty feet long, growing from a point to a broad front, exploded from the collapsed flare tower toward the running Germans. They fell to the ground, seeking a respite from the intense heat as the flare covered the surface of the ground. It was not a temporary flash, but a sustained, burning flame fed by the gas that continued to evolve from the drilling mud, setting the weedy brush on fire as it roared. As it crossed the bank into the marsh, the water boiled, then evaporated, the muddy bottom near the shoreline steaming.

The five German sailors who had survived the voyage from the submarine to the shoreline of the Ten Thousand Islands, then managed to stay alive during the slogging march through the swamp, now died instantaneously. Their flesh caught fire and the superheated air filled their lungs. The ammunition they carried exploded, sounding like firecrackers, small sparks visible through the flame. Their clothing burned and the charred corpses collapsed onto the ground, reduced to skeletons as the flesh turned to ash and smoke.

"Turn it off, Jerry!" Joe shouted. "I saw three or four of them for a second before the flare reached them. They're gone. Let's see how many are left."

Jerry climbed down the ladder and turned a valve over the mud pits, diverting the gas to a small vertical pipe over the pits, sufficient to dispose of small amounts of gas when the flare was being repaired. It would suffice for a few hours until the situation was stabilized. The flame blasting over the water went dark as the supply of gas was eliminated, the starlight showing the bubbling subsiding as the water temperature rapidly fell.

"Don't shoot, but don't move for a while!" Joe shouted in the voice he used to call orders to the top of the derrick when an Oklahoma tornado was approaching. "Let's see what happens, and if any of them are left. Keep your heads down."

A few minutes passed, broken only by the normal sounds of the swamp. An owl hooted and an alligator coughed, but there was no sound of men moving through the water. Joe decided that at least the immediate threat had been stopped. No telling what else was out there. He needed to check on his crew.

"Sound off!" he said loudly.

"Yo!"

"Je suis ici!"

"Here!"

"I guess that's everyone here with you and me, Jerry," Joe said. "We'll have to wait and see about Eddie and Jacque. Everyone get back to the rig and behind some cover. Turn the lights back on and aim them over the swamp. We'll wait until morning to see what we've got."

Chapter 24

Wednesday Night

The U-boat drifted in a moonless night, hatches open to give the crew fresh air, recharging the batteries. A stalled cold front in the Gulf had formed a low pressure area to the northwest, resulting in a stiff twenty-knot southeast wind and two-to-six foot waves. The cylindrical hull of the submarine rolled in the choppy water, not enough to cause discomfort to the crew long accustomed to the motion of the vessel, but enough make to those on deck and atop the conning tower brace themselves. The four lookouts nervously searched for aircraft or the white bow wave of an approaching vessel, but none were expected. The chance of a plane spotting the dark hull, only a few feet awash above the surface, was minimal after dark. Gunter wasn't worried about enemy aircraft. He was worried about the diminishing level of his fuel tanks, dropping further as the engines turned generators that sent current to the batteries. And he was worried about no radio contact with the BDU, the U-boat headquarters in Lorient, France. But at least a quiet night on the surface was giving the submariners a chance to repair the damaged communication equipment.

Four men on the foredeck were working to repair the radio antenna, soaked from the occasional wave that broke over the deck. The depth-charge attack had knocked the transmitting device loose from the conning tower, but the guy wires securing it to the hull had held, preventing the entire contraption from sinking to the bottom of the Gulf. Cannibalizing steel from the damaged railing of the gun turret, they were welding a new support mast, a kneeling figure concealed behind a mask of dark glass holding the torch in one hand and a welding rod in the other. His coworkers tried to conceal the bright light of the welding torch was as best they could with a heavy tarpaulin, stretched from the conning tower to the bow but flapping in the stiff breeze. Some escaping light might still act as a beacon to a cruising airplane, alerting them to the presence of some human activity occurring on the waves of the Gulf. But radio contact with the U-459 was a necessity. The successful theft of a diesel-laden barge would still not provide them with enough fuel to return to Lorient.

The flame from the welding torch vanished as it was extinguished, and the repair party stepped back from the mast they had constructed. It was a crude replica of what had been fabricated and installed by the skilled machinists in Germany, but it would suffice to support the antenna, a slim rod that held the transmitting wires. It had been repaired with cable torn from interior lighting and other appliances that provided creature comforts they would have to do without until the submarine returned home.

"We're ready to hoist this up and attach it to the conning tower," one of the men announced to Gunter. "But we're going to have to weld for a few minutes without the tarp hiding the flame. No way we can cover it up while we're attaching this."

"Proceed," Gunter ordered. "We'll have to take the chance."

A cable was passed from the conning tower to the repaired mast, attached by turnbuckles. It went over a sheave atop the conning tower to a waiting group of seaman on the afterdeck. Muscle power would be quicker to raise the mast than routing the cable to a motorized pulley, and adequate for the task at hand. "Pull!" ordered Gunter, and the men on the afterdeck grasped the steel wire with gloved hands, passing it along hand over hand. The mast was pulled upright, the base quickly spot-welded to the deck and metal braces made one with the side of the conning tower. Stabilized, the welder then added more steel to make the mast an integral piece of the submarine. It might not withstand a depth charge, but it would withstand the onslaught of the ocean's energy unless they had to remain on the surface during a hurricane.

A rope was thrown over the crossbar at the masthead, and one of the smaller sailors was pulled to the top in a bosun's chair. The antenna, about ten feet in length, was passed up, trailed by a wire cable that attached to a connection on deck for the radio.

"Make sure you don't pull on the wires," ordered the radio operator, who had come on deck to superintend this part of the operation. "Careful, there."

Steadying himself against the mast as the submarine rocked gently in the swell, the seaman held the antenna erect, sliding it into the attached clamps. Bolted securely, it swayed slightly but showed no evidence of fracturing or coming loose. He attached the trailing cable to the mast with smaller clamps as he was lowered to the deck.

The radioman eagerly seized the cable and screwed the watertight connector to a port on the side of the conning tower, then went quickly below to turn on the radio. They could hear the buzz and static varying in pitch as the operator turned the knobs, searching for a signal from BDU.

A faint click interrupted the signal, familiar to everyone on the bridge deck as Morse Code. A series of cheers rang from the steel hull as word was passed forward and aft that the radio was working. The crew was accustomed to danger and isolation. But the thought of drowning in the open Gulf, with no one aware of when or where they had died, awoke all of them at least some nights. The radio operator wrote down the signal, translating the dashes and dots to letters and passing it to Gunter. "We can receive. This isn't for us; they're trying to contact the U-153. But at least we got the signal. Should I try transmitting?"

Transmitting was a risk, as it would be evidence of their presence in the southeastern Gulf, but was unavoidable. "Send the identification signal," Gunter ordered.

The radio operator tapped out a signal. He waited in silence, then tapped again. A few more minutes of silence. Then an answering series of clicks.

"They're acknowledging us," he answered. "Do you want to code a message to send?"

"I'll prepare one," answered Gunter. He disappeared into his cabin, closed the curtain, and unlocked a box containing the code machine. Thinking carefully, he wrote a message by hand, then entered it into the machine, writing down the resulting letters and destroying the original message.

"Send this," he ordered, handing the coded message to the operator.

The radioman looked at the message, then began operating the telegraph key, sending a series of dots and dashes that reflected from the ionosphere and reached the tower of BDU on the Atlantic coast of France. Finishing, he relaxed and waited for a reply or further orders, relieved to be able to perform his duty again. He had tried repeatedly to reach another U-boat with makeshift antennas but had received no response. But this repair was sufficient not only to contact other U-boats, but to actually reach Donitz's headquarters.

Gunter took a deep breath, the relief in his expression evident to the officers and men occupying the crowded control room with him. He was still commanding a damaged vessel in enemy waters, and nearly out of fuel, but at least he could expect some help. He left the radioman to await a return signal and ascended to the top of the conning tower, looking to the east for some sign of the approaching barge. It was critical the barge and submarine met before the sky started to lighten in the east. Without cover of darkness, the U-boat would be an easy target for a cruising airplane as they pumped fuel from the barge to the U-boat tanks. There was no sign of the barge, but Gunter's vigil was interrupted by clicks of Morse Code, indicating a response from BDU that would require decoding. He hoped it would say that the U-459 would be able to meet them within range of the little fuel that they still had on board. Gunter was beginning to feel that the landing party was not going to show up with the captured fuel barge.

The low-lying coast of southernmost Florida is only a few feet higher than the sea, and sunrise occurs as a red ball ascending above the horizon, uninterrupted by hills or mountains. Foretold by a lightening of the eastern sky, light sweeps across the marshy land south of Lake Okeechobee, then races westward onto the Gulf of Mexico. Mist rising from the swamps and lakes may make the new morning hazy, scattering the light but not impeding the approach of the day. Land is below the horizon for an observer ten miles offshore, invisible and undetected.

The U-boat idled along at two knots in thirty feet of water. No preparations were made for diving, since in this depth the top of the conning tower would still be visible while the keel rested on the sandy bottom. Gunter looked west, away from the sky turning from pitch black to gray, then back toward the coast of Florida. The lookouts had been ordered to maintain absolute silence all night, listening for the two series of three closely spaced shots that would alert them to the presence of the hijacked barge. The sky quickly grew more luminous, and the presence of a stick-like mast betrayed the presence of a vessel hull down below the horizon.

Gunter considered going in another few miles; perhaps the mast was the radio antenna of the tugboat pushing the captured barge. But that would risk the U-boat being trapped during daylight in shallow water unable to maneuver, much less submerge, to avoid an American aircraft. A decoded signal from BDU during the night had left open a slight possibility of securing fuel from the U-459, a chance to save his vessel without refueling from the barge. Reluctantly, he descended the ladder into the bridge space and ordered, "Proceed due west at six knots."

"We're going to have to leave them, if they are still alive," he said to the XO. "Prepare to submerge when we have 150 feet of water. We'll spend the daylight hours underwater, then head south at hull speed on the surface tonight."

Chapter 25

Thursday Morning

The supply boat tied up at the river dock the next morning, and the captain was surprised to see a drilling rig with no activity, the engine silent, and the drill string motionless. He noted that the flare tower, easily visible from the dock, wasn't visible in the early light. An unusual passenger, a trim man wearing a suit and a hat more suited for a northern city than the Florida Everglades, was the first up the road to the rig. He moved quickly, crouched over and moving in zigzags, acting like someone who has been shot at in his lifetime. As he approached the drilling location, he saw a middle-aged man in red coveralls with a metal hat standing on the rig floor, twenty feet above the surface of the shell pad, looking north over the swamp. Two men in a small canoe-like boat were paddling toward a body in black clothing floating face down in the water. Another was sitting at the edge of the rig floor, his shoulder bandaged but conscious and alert. A fifth man, dressed in cleaner khakis than his companions, was watching a dial over a large metal tank. The visitor approached him first, assuming from his dress and apparent technical focus that he must be the one in charge.

"Hello, are you responsible for this operation?" he asked.

"No," Jerry replied. "Joe, up on the rig, is the tool pusher. I'm the rig site geologist. Who wants to know?"

"My name is William Banner. I'm with the Navy Department. What's happened here?"

"Some Germans attacked us last night from the swamp. The crew shot several, a couple died from drowning and alligators, and I burned five with the well flare. But we have no idea why us, or what they were looking for. What are you doing here?"

"You got attacked by a German U-boat crew. That's a German Navy uniform on that guy in the water. We have been anticipating some landings—we expect they are running low on supplies, and remote areas like this would be easy for them to raid onshore for food or medicine. And they might want to shoot up and burn down a small village just to try and cause some panic. Four of them landed on the other coast near Jacksonville last year, saboteurs who were headed out around the country to blow up railway yards and bridges. One of them turned himself in and we caught them all. They were electrocuted. Maybe the Germans saw this oil well as critical to the war effort and wanted to blow it up."

"Has it happened anywhere else?" Jerry asked.

"Can't say. It is all classified. We don't want it in the papers. Which is why I'm here and need to talk to all of you. Tell the man in charge to call everyone in."

Fifteen minutes later, Banner was talking to the assembled crew. "You were attacked by Germans, all right. I'm sure you can tell that from the uniforms and weapons, so I won't try to convince you otherwise. There's been a lot of U-boat activity about fifty miles off-shore, sinking tankers. For some reason they sent a few men ashore to take over this oil well. I have no idea why, instead of raiding one of the smaller fishing villages where there might be more supplies and medicine. But as far as you are concerned, it did not happen. The American people think the homeland is safe and that there is no threat of attack here. If they think otherwise, they'll demand troops, planes, and boats we don't have to protect the coast. We need all those in the Pacific and Europe, not in South Florida."

"What do you want us to do? All that shooting is going to make for a lot of questions in town," said Eddie.

"Here's your story. Four guys escaped from Raiford last week, stole a car, drove to Marco, then stole a boat. Two of them were on death row, the others both in for murder. They took off in the boat, pretending to be fishermen, then got lost when it got dark. They saw the rig lights and apparently thought they could kill all of you, get some food and gasoline, and head back into the swamp. If they could have survived in the swamp, no one could have found them. But you all were able to take care of them.

That's your story. If I hear one word about Germans, I'll find out who was talking and you will be imprisoned under the Sedition Act. Understand?"

Banner spoke as a man who was accustomed to being obeyed and was not surprised at the lack of reaction from the rig crew. He didn't really believe they would never tell some version of the truth, but if they could give some version of shooting escaped convicts for the next couple of weeks, and varying tales of Germans trickled out after that, it wouldn't get much attention. That would keep it out of the papers and Washington. And talking about shooting escaped convicts would make them all heroes as much as shooting Germans.

After telling the crew to keep their mouths shut about Germans, Banner walked out to look at the collapsed flare and the remains of the incinerated bodies. The path of the flame was evident from the scorched weeds on the drilling pad and the burned marsh grass at the edge of the swamp.

Looking at Jerry, he said, "How did this happen?"

"I cut the support wires, then ignited it. A lot of gas had built up over the mud pits when we stopped the generator and cut off the vacuum pumps. It made a pretty big flame, enough to burn everything twenty yards into the marsh."

"Not too many situations where you can improvise a flame thrower. Good thinking."

"We had to do something," Jerry said. "Eddie and Jacque could do some damage to them while they were trying to wade through the swamp, but once they were on dry land, they would have overrun us pretty easily. Shotguns against machine pistols."

"How long have you been out here?"

"About three months. The well is just about finished. I'm going back to New York when it's done."

"I've seen oil wells, but just ones that were finished with a pump jack on them. Never been around one when it was drilled. This is pretty heavy machinery. The size of that turnbuckle is bigger than anything on a battleship."

"Yeah, it's pretty thick steel everywhere. The shooting didn't do anything but make some small dings." Jerry pointed to a few small indentations in a tank, not even close to penetrating the metal.

"Well, I've got to get back to town," Banner said. "I need to get back to Washington. They sent me down here to wait for something like this to happen. I heard all that racket last night and thought it might be a U-boat raid. When they hear the story at the Pentagon, maybe they'll send more of the Navy after these subs."

"I'm coming too," said Jerry. "My wife is in town. Don't know what she thinks was happening last night."

After the ride back to Everglades City with Banner on the supply boat, Jerry climbed the stairs to the second floor of the Everglades Hotel, opened the door, and stumbled into their room with exhaustion. He was knocked backwards by Maria's fervent rush to hug him.

"What the hell went on out there last night?" she cried. "We all heard the shooting, too much for anyone jacklighting deer or hunting gators."

"I'll tell you. Can you get me a scotch?"

Maria crossed to the small cabinet they used for a bar, taking out a bottle and two glasses. "I'll have to go get some ice. Be right back."

"Don't bother. I'll drink it neat. Yes. I'm not supposed to tell anyone what really happened, but I have to tell you. I killed four men last night."

"Who were they? Were they trying to kill you?"

"They were Germans from a U-boat. I don't know why they were coming after us, but they were. I'm lucky to be alive. If Eddie and Jacque didn't know how to shoot and move around in the swamp, I wouldn't be. There would have been too many of them left when they reached the rig."

"So what did you do?"

"I figured out how to collapse the flare so that it pointed toward them, then ignited it. They burned to death."

"You really burned those guys to death with the flare?" she asked.

He had done what he had to do, Jerry thought. He was glad to be alive, and glad the Germans who had tried to kill him were dead. That they had died didn't bother him, although the image of the flaming, struggling human figures was stuck in his mind; the memory of the smell of burning flesh impossible to forget.

"Yes. I shouldn't feel bad at all. But I've never killed anyone before. It's a different feeling. I wonder who they were. A guy from the Navy came out this morning on the boat and told us they didn't want people panicking about raids from U-boats, so the official story is they were escaped convicts. But they were speaking German and wearing German Navy clothes. And they had what looked like German submachine guns."

"That's about it," continued Jerry. You have to promise not to tell anyone else. We must say they were escaped convicts, not German sailors. But they are all dead, and all of us are OK. Jacque got shot in the arm, but he will be fine. The Navy is sending out some people to clean up, using the excuse that the prison doesn't have the boats to work in the swamp."

Maria pushed Jerry onto the bed, took off her dress, and lay down, embracing him. Later, sitting up and covered to her waist with a sheet, she said, "I have cousins in Queens who have killed people for a lot less reason, and I can't tell anyone. You felt bad for missing the war, and the war came to you. But no one will ever know about it. If we just made a baby, you can tell him about it when he's ten. But what happens now?"

"I have to see this well down. We should be back to drilling tomorrow. Joe has them fixing the flare, and there was really no other damage to the rig. The crew is taking tonight off, then will be back out tomorrow. SunTex will be coming out to log in a couple of days. We should have about another week to go before we run pipe. So I expect we'll be on a train to New York in about ten days."

"Good. I've had enough of small-town life for a while. Nice people, but not much happening. And hard to get good pasta."

"Do you want to go home? I can finish this by myself. Now that we're into the Sunniland, I'm going to be spending most of my time on the well anyway."

"Hell no. I've been here this long. I want to see what happens at the end of our little adventure."

The only person whose opinion Jerry cared about knew what had happened. Maybe someday he could tell their children. But right now he needed to get his mind back on the well that had discovered a new oil field.

The story about the escaped convicts was widely accepted in southwest Florida, aided by a visit from the warden at Raiford Prison. He talked to the newspaper editor in Everglades, describing a story of a harrowing chase of desperate killers, similar to the tale being publicized by Banner. He described the gruesome murder of a family in Sebring, where the murderers had stopped to rest and get some food, embellishing the details. The story quickly spread throughout Everglades City, causing the townspeople to regard the rig crew as fearless frontiersmen who had defended themselves in the wilderness against an attack by savages to good effect. It led to free drinks and a few offers of work after the rig left. Impressed by being part of a secret operation and gratified by the respect they encountered walking down the street, the crew had stuck to their story of escaped convicts, at least so far. As the tale was told and retold by the roughnecks, the number of escaped prisoners increased, with each of the crew singlehandedly dispatching at least three in hand-to-hand fighting. Eddie told the story of sneaking up behind wading murderers one at a time, cutting the throat of each unaware escapee so silently that the others didn't know that one of their number was no longer with them.

"See this knife?" he would say to the avid audience in the Snapper Inn bar, showing a large skinning knife that he kept razor sharp to flay muskrats. "Pulled it across their throats, one at a time. It's so sharp it took the head off one of them. Left it behind and went after the others."

"First time you've said anything about cutting anyone's head off," said a skeptical woman at the end of the bar. "I've heard that story about five times now. Next you'll be choking them without a knife."

"Shut up or I'll choke you," Eddie blustered. "You weren't there. And that's what happened."

The woman, tired from waiting tables all day at the Mangrove Lodge, turned to her drink and was silent. She had known Eddie all her life, and there was no arguing with him after a few drinks. He just got mean. She saw Eddie put down his empty glass and look expectantly at the other patrons, hoping for an offer of a refill. Sure enough, a newcomer to the bar, a visiting fisherman from the north who had enjoyed the story, told the bartender to give Eddie whatever he wanted.

Chapter 26

A Few Days Later

On a night with a new moon, the U-boat motored slowly on the surface, propelled by one of the two engines and using every possible adjustment to maximize fuel economy. The battery-charging system was silent, ventilation was turned off, and hatches were open on deck. The gun crew was sitting on the metal deck plates, still warm from the tropical sun that day, scanning the sky for American aircraft. They would have to fight if sighted—there was no longer any capacity to submerge if they were detected by a cruising plane, executing a search pattern over the approaches to the Gulf.

They cruised slowly toward the rendezvous point with the re-supply submarine. BDU had radioed the coordinates two nights ago, moving the U-459 further into the Gulf, but unwilling to risk not being able to resupply the other U-boats that needed fuel. They were expected fifty miles southwest of the Dry Tortugas, about one hundred miles from their current location west of Cape Sable. At five knots, that would take about twenty hours. They barely had enough fuel to get there and would arrive with nearly empty tanks, close to converting from a warship to a piece of drifting scrap metal. Their heading was south southwest, a course that would send them between Key West and the Dry Tortugas. That would be risky, but the U-boat did not have the fuel to head further offshore, and if they couldn't submerge, there was no advantage to seeking deeper water. Gunter's plan was to pass Key West before dawn, taking advantage of darkness to conceal them from ship traffic out of the port and Navy base, but they would still be exposed for sixteen hours of daylight after sunrise.

Rather than the whine of an airplane engine, they heard the chugging sound of an inboard motor, pushing cooling water out through the exhaust on a small boat. Staring hard through light-gathering Zeiss binoculars, the lookouts spotted a dark shape becoming apparent to the west, a bump in the horizontal plane where sea met sky. The bump became the outline of a shrimp boat, nets suspended from masts, rising above the horizon to their west. It was running without lights, far offshore from the shrimping grounds. An odd place to be during wartime, exposed to the well-known U-boat threat, and seemingly without any commercial reason to be there.

"Silence," Gunter ordered quietly. "They might hear the engine, but they might not. We don't need to let them hear any German words."

"Should we take them?" asked the XO. "They might have a few gallons of fuel."

"No, that sounds like a gas engine," said one of the lookouts. "Boat's too small for diesel." They let it continue, passing a few miles to their west, headed roughly in the direction of Tampa.

The shrimper was named Blondie, after the girlfriend of a former owner. Painted across the stern and printed on the documents, the three fishermen who had owned it since had not bothered to change it. The boat was to make a living, not a toy, and the name had little significance to them. The current owner and captain, Luther Merrill, hadn't gotten enough gasoline to shrimp since the war started. But he had found enough to make a voyage from Havana to Tampa, carrying contraband rum. He was running at night to avoid the Coast Guard, who were focused on finding submarines, but not averse to seizing a load of rum if the opportunity arose. Maybe half would make it back to the customs dock. The shrimping gear made a good cover, but running at night was even better. He made the voyages alone, both to reduce the chance of loose talk by a mate in port that might get back to the Coast Guard, and to avoid sharing the proceeds. Lashing the wheel during the daylight hours, he managed a few hours of sleep once he had passed north of Key West. Running at night demanded attention to stay on course, so he had been standing in the wheelhouse for several hours, drinking coffee spiked with some of the rum stored in barrels below deck.

Looking to the east, he saw a dark shape pass in front of the stars. It looked like a small building gliding over the sea. Luther had spent years shrimping out of Key West, near the Navy base, and recognized the conning tower of a submarine moving slowly over the surface of the Gulf. The direction of motion was toward the south, toward the Key West Navy base. He estimated it was moving at about five knots, less than hull speed, showing no lights and not acknowledging his presence. Setting down his cup of coffee and rum, he looked at a chart in the dim light of the instruments and estimated they would be at the Navy base well before dawn.

Why would it be moving so slowly? he wondered. Moving on the surface at night was standard operating procedure for US Navy submarines, recharging batteries and submerging during the day during the peacetime drills he had witnessed. But they moved quickly, running engines at three-quarter speed to power the battery charging system as well as the propellers. This was unusual. Luther knew about the German submarines' presence in the Gulf. He couldn't think of a reason why a US sub would be cruising so slowly, so a U-boat seemed a likely possibility.

He held course, hoping not to perceive a change in the shape of the conning tower that would indicate the vessel had changed course toward him. The strange shape continued with the same direction and speed, either not aware of his presence or ignoring it. Thirty minutes later, it had disappeared into the night.

Well, I hope the Coast Guard don't come out for an eye witness accounting and find the rum, Luther thought to himself as he picked up the radio microphone. Putting it down, he decided to wait a couple of hours—the U-boat might be monitoring the American ship-to-shore channels and turn around. About four o'clock in the morning, he turned on the radio.

"Blondie calling US Coast Guard."

"You are supposed to be observing radio silence."

"Just saw a German U-boat on the surface."

"Oh! What's your position? And what is its course?"

"I'm eighty miles southwest of Cape Sable. It's going south southwest at about five knots."

"Are you sure? That's crawling."

"I'm sure. It took about a half hour to pass me. About ten miles away."

"OK. I'll pass it on. Take care."

Luther turned off the radio with relief. There would be a truck waiting for him tomorrow night at Little Manatee River in Tampa Bay, with two hundred dollars in cash. It would get him through the rest of the year.

Gunter stood on the bridge as dawn broke, watching the approaching airplane. It dropped to several hundred feet above the sea's surface, heading straight for the submarine. A torpedo dropped from the cradle suspending it under the plane's fuselage, churning toward the U-boat. The submarine's slow speed made evasive turns impossible, so accepting the inevitable, he knelt down over the open hatch and shouted below: "We are going to take a torpedo. Get on deck if you can!"

Scared men emerged from the open hatchways, one flying into the air as he was shoved skyward by his companion on the ladder below him. About ten men were on deck when the torpedo pierced the steel exterior side of the U-boat and exploded, tearing apart the starboard fuel tank and the pressure hull. There was no following fire, the only benefit of the lack of fuel—the starboard tank was empty. But the explosion had created a gaping hole the diameter of a Volkswagen, and the U-boat sank quickly as the warm waters of the Gulf rushed in. Gunter was killed instantly from the explosion, as were the sailors who had escaped from the hatchway and had been staring at the wake of approaching death, locked in place on the forward deck. The remainder of the crew drowned in the steel box in which they had voyaged from Germany, trapped in a maze of pipes, bulkheads, and the machinery that operated the submarine and its weapons.

The plane circled and flew back over the sinking submarine, marking the position. The water depth was relatively shallow, about one hundred feet. The hull of the submarine was clearly visible as it rested on the bottom in the clear water, the top of the conning tower only fifty feet below the surface. It would be a popular fishing spot after the war. Shaking his head, the pilot thumbed open his microphone: "Sank one U-boat. No visible survivors, no oil slick, position sixty miles west of Key West. Not sure what they were doing here. They were cruising southwest at about five knots during daylight on the surface."

"Good work. We think it was the U-167. Not sure why they were there, but good that they're gone."

Chapter 27

Jerry studied an electric log spread out on the table in the screened porch that served as a dining area for the crew's lunch, drinking Eileen's coffee and calculating the volume of oil contained in the Cretaceous reef. It was a South Florida morning in late spring, the cypress trees shedding pollen and the shoots of green marsh grass replacing the burned area. Clouds were building up to the east, heralding a likely thunderstorm later in the day. He could see bubbles rising in an area of clear water, signaling the presence of an alligator moving along the bottom of the small pond, disturbing the bottom sediment and releasing marsh gas that rose to the surface.

A couple of days of uninterrupted drilling had resulted in the bit penetrating the bottom of the reef, signaled by a change in character of the cuttings as the bottom of the well went through the bottom of the Sunniland formation and into the Punta Gorda Anhydrite. The reappearance of the white, pearly sulfate mineral in the cuttings marked the bottom of the reef. Oil had continued to be circulated up with the drilling mud, and it was evident that the entire reef was full of crude from top to bottom. Jerry had ordered out a well-logging truck to conduct an electric survey of the entire well.

The SunTex truck, driven south from Oklahoma and loaded onto a barge in Everglades, had carefully navigated the ramp onto the river dock, then inched its way up the board road to the wellsite. It was an odd looking conveyance, a large spool of wire cable at the back of a cabin filled with electrical instruments, sitting on the frame of what appeared to be a heavy duty dump truck. A young man appeared to be in charge of three others dressed in blue coveralls. He introduced himself to Jerry.

"Mr. MacDonald? I'm Andrew, the logging engineer. We're here to run a wireline log for Pride. I was told to report to you."

"That's me," Jerry replied. "Go ahead and rig up. I'm going to want to sit in the cabin with you while you record the log. Everyone around here knows we hit pay, but we're going to keep the log tight, so I'll expect you to leave me the only copy."

"Will do," replied Andrew. He was used to the secrecy surrounding wildcat logging and wasn't surprised. The logging crew had been enthusiastic and eager to be involved in the initial discovery of oil in Florida. Their drive south had taken on a holiday air, a welcome change from the Oklahoma prairie. They had reached Everglades City the night before, staying at the Turner Inn and visiting the bar after supper, tended by a pretty woman who had introduced herself as Maria. Two other customers sat on stools, gazing at the new arrivals with the importance of someone who has information to share. An hour later, the SunTex contingent had heard the details of the desperate fight between the rig crew and the escaped prisoners, including the story of the flamethrower created from the collapsed flare tower. Andrew looked at Jerry MacDonald with awe, hoping for some conversation about the encounter. But Jerry seemed totally focused on what they would find out logging the well.

The truck had backed up to the rig, the crew unloading a set of cylindrical pieces of pipe they screwed together and then attached to the wire cable. Winding around a set of sheaves, the assembly was lowered into the opening in the rotary table, then to the bottom of the well, two miles deep, as the cylinder on the back of the truck revolved and the cable unwound in smooth coils. Sitting beside Jerry in the cabin, Andrew said, "We're on bottom. Starting to log up."

The pieces of pipe that were now passing upward through the Sunnniland Reef emitted an electric current into the formation, which passed through the rock and back into the wellbore, detected by an electrode on the tool. It was recording the electrical resistivity of the formation. Since oil did not conduct electricity and salt water did, a rock full of oil would record a higher resistivity than one filled with salt water. The more oil, the higher the resistivity. For years, this had been a qualitative indicator of the presence of oil or gas, and whether a well had indeed encountered hydrocarbons or only a reservoir full of salt water. But last year, a scientific paper had described a method to actually calculate the percentage of oil and water. Jerry had read the paper so many times he had memorized it and was anxious to apply the technique to the electric log from the Sunniland.

As the logging tool emerged from the wellbore, Andrew handed Jerry an accordion of paper showing the resistivity recorded from the bottom of the well to the top. Signing a ticket that acknowledged that the work was completed and that he had received the log, Jerry left the SunTex crew to rig down their equipment and embark on the board road back to the moored barge. He quickly walked down the wooden walkway to the cookhouse, carrying the paper log, some pencils, a slide rule, and a notebook. Sitting down where he could count on some solitude and relief from the rig activity to make some calculations, he began to determine the volume of the oil they had discovered.

Some of what he required he had already determined: the porosity of the reef by painstaking microscopic examination of the cuttings, the electrical resistivity of the salt water in the well, the estimated temperature. He started looking at the resistivity of the Sunniland reef, busily making notes with his pencil and moving the center of his slide rule feverishly. His results confirmed that the tiny pores in the reef, cavities created by growing coral over one hundred million years ago, were almost entirely filled with oil. That meant the five-hundred-acre subterranean reef contained over one hundred million barrels of oil. They would only be able to pump out about half of that, since the remainder would stick to the rocky matrix of the limestone and not flow to the wells. It was a tremendous discovery, one that would have gained attention even in Texas or Louisiana.

Joe had left him alone to work his pencil and slide rule, anxious to know the results of the three-month-long endeavor that had brought him to the Everglades, but knowing that Jerry needed to concentrate. But seeing him look up and smile, Joe walked over to the table, opened the screen door, and stood inside.

"Well?" he asked.

"Order some casing. We're going to run pipe," Jerry replied. There was still an expensive process to be finished in order to complete the well. It required putting seven-inch pipe called casing into the hole, cementing it to the rock on the side of the borehole, and putting a pump jack on top. The decision to spend this final amount of money depended on the volume of oil that had been discovered. As small amount, although scientifically interesting, would not pay for the cost of finishing the well, and it would have been plugged and abandoned, as nine out of ten wildcats are. But this well was one of the exceptions that not only would make a huge profit for Pride Oil, but would allow them to finance the dry holes that had found little or nothing.

"I knew it!" Joe shouted. "Congratulations! I could tell from the drilling breaks and the gas cutting the mud that it would be a keeper. I've already got the production casing on the way, figuring you would be telling me this."

"You were right," said Jerry. "There will be a lot more wells to follow up this one in the next couple of years."

"How long are you staying in Everglades City?" asked Joe.

"I'm heading back to New York City tomorrow," said Jerry. "I've got to show the log to Mike Woods and Mr. Pride. I expect I'll be there for a few weeks; then they want me go to Maracaibo in Venezuela."

"You did a good job for us," Joe said as he shook Jerry's hand before walking out the door.

Chapter 28

Tampa was a different kind of city in 1947, a variant among the mid-sized metropolises found in the southern part of the United States. A cottage industry of hand-rolling cigars from Cuban tobacco had evolved into a major pillar of the local economy, supporting an immigrant Cuban community located in the suburb of Ybor City. The University of Tampa had evolved into a four-year college, giving the city academic credentials that had more impact on local pride than on the overall industry of higher education. The city had been founded at the head of the best natural harbor in the state of Florida, an estuary fed by several rivers that rising sea levels had turned into a protected bay, separated from the Gulf by barrier islands and deep enough for oceangoing ships to travel up to the city docks. Rail cars delivered phosphate mined from pits in central Florida, derived from the bones of vertebrate animals that had lived millions of years in the past, to be loaded onto ships for delivery around the world. Freighters and tankers, many bearing the logo of the hometown Lykes Brothers shipping line, steamed up from the Gulf entrance to the docks south of downtown. The economy was

booming with the postwar demand for phosphate, jobs were plenti-
ful, and shoppers filled the downtown streets near the shore of the
Hillsborough River.

Maggie stepped onto the sidewalk outside the Tampa department store, her arms filled with purchases, looking for her driver.
With the end of the war, gasoline was no longer rationed, and she
enjoyed the weekly car trip up Highway 41 for shopping that was
not to be found in Fort Myers. Not a fashion queen, she still liked to
read the New York magazines and dress like the models portrayed in
their pages. The shoes, makeup, dresses, and hats she desired were
only to be found in Tampa and Miami, and she preferred the drive
up the coast over traveling the Tamiami Trail across the Everglades.
Moving permanently to the larger city entered her thoughts every
time she returned home, but her children were happy with the school
in Everglades City, and she enjoyed the new house she had purchased on Riverside Drive. The Turner Inn where she had cleaned
rooms and made beds had been her latest acquisition, purchased on
the untimely death of her friend, John, the owner. Her life was occupied with managing her business, raising her family, and enjoying
her wealth. When she had first arrived from her island homestead,
there had been few people willing to befriend her, tagging her as
white trash. Her accent, dress, and manners had led to rejection by
the residents who already called Everglades City home. Today, she
was the first lady of Everglades City, in demand for social events at
the Mangrove Lodge, president of the Garden Club and benefactor
of causes mostly related to children. It was as much a home as she
ever knew, and she doubted that the socialites of Tampa who lived
in the mansions along Bayshore Boulevard would welcome her in a
similar fashion. She often thought about the afternoon visit several
years ago that had changed her life.

Maggie heard a knock on the door of her small house in the fall of 1943, after the LT drilling rig had left Everglades City and the talk about the fight with the escaped convicts had subsided. She worked the early shift at the hotel and had arrived home for a late lunch. The children were still in school, and she enjoyed the time alone to practice her reading while she ate bread and cheese. The newspaper had become intelligible to her. She read it daily, looking up unfamiliar words in the dictionary that Maria had bought her as a parting gift, more interested in the local news about Collier County than the accounts of the fighting in Italy. Putting down the paper, she opened the door and greeted Roger Sanders, who was standing on her small porch. Roger had adapted his dress somewhat to the southern climate. He still wore a hat, but it was made of straw that was considerably cooler than the wool felt he had worn on his head the first time she had seen him.

"Hello, Maggie," he said, greeting her with affection. He had good news and looked forward to the effect it would have on her. "Can I come in and talk to you for a bit?"

"I'm always glad to see you," she replied. "You helped me when there was no one else. Of course you can come in. Want a glass of water? I don't have anything else."

They sat across from each other in two of the four chairs that Maggie had purchased to complete her kitchen, along with the secondhand but serviceable wooden table. Roger sipped water, then said, "The seismic line we shot shows there is likely to be a reef, like the one where we drilled that last well and discovered oil, under your property. We want to drill a new well on your land."

"What does that mean? I don't live there anymore," she had replied.

"We leased the mineral rights from you. That means we have the right to drill a well on your property, and if we find oil, you get one-eighth of what we sell it for. But you still own the surface rights, which means that if we want to move a rig on your property to drill, we have to pay you for the use of the land. And that's what we want to do."

"You've been good to me. Go ahead and drill. I sure hope you find something, especially if I get some more money from it."

"We want to put the drill site near your house. It's high and dry, and will save a lot of money compared to building another fill pad like we did on the first well. Your landing is also on deep water, so we can bring in the barge without having to build a board road. We can put it next to your house, but if you want to sell us the house, we'll buy it, tear it down, and put the well in your yard."

"I won't miss that house at all," Maggie said. "We just struggled to stay alive. Now that I'm in town, I'll never, ever go back. I'd be glad that you bought it."

"We'll give you five thousand dollars for the house, the rights to build a drilling location on your property, use of the waterfront, and a place to put tanks if we make a discovery. How does that sound?"

Maggie gulped and stuttered. "You're not fooling with me, are you?"

"No, I'm serious. Come over to the courthouse with me and make your mark. I understand you're learning to read and write, though, so you might want to sign your name."

Maggie hadn't been out to the homestead since 1944, when the well came in at one hundred and ten barrels a day. It was followed by two more, one at two hundred barrels a day and the other at one hundred and fifty. It gave her a monthly check of nine thousand dollars.

The reefs that formed the oilfields in the Sunniland trend were hundreds of acres in size, but not continuous, resembling small hills buried deep underground. For those fortunate enough to own the land above these subterranean reservoirs, a cascade of riches beyond their imagination fell on them. Two or three wells, each producing oil and providing the land owners with one-eighth of the proceeds from the sale, gave the fortunate few incomes of tens or hundreds of thousands of dollars every year. Those whose land covered the area between the reefs earned nothing. It was a strange situation for families who had lived side by side for generations, farming, fishing, and ranching. Some were suddenly looking at the merits of an Oldsmobile compared to a Cadillac, while their neighbors were still scratching out a living from fishing and trapping. Maggie Eversby had been one of the fortunate ones.

The red Cadillac pulled up to the curb on Ashley Drive, and the uniformed driver greeted Maggie while he opened the trunk and relieved her of her packages. He wore a black suit and a visored hat. The apparel looked somewhat incongruent with his face, deeply tanned from growing up in the tropical sun, and missing two teeth that were evident when he smiled at his mistress. But it was obvious he was proud of the clothing and wore it carefully, avoiding a puddle near the curb when he stepped out.

Maggie opened the front door on the passenger side and sat down. She found riding in the back seat boring. She couldn't see out the windshield, and she didn't like talking to the back of someone's head. The custom of her rich friends was to sit in the back, making it obvious they were being driven by a chauffeur rather than accompanying a husband or a friend. But not Maggie.

"Let's go home, Eddie," she said.

Bio

Stephen O. Sears grew up in South Florida, boating and fishing off the Florida Keys and in the Everglades. He studied geology at the University of Florida and earned a PhD in geochemistry from Penn State. Following a career as a petroleum geologist with Shell Oil in Texas, California, and Louisiana, Sears joined the faculty of the LSU Petroleum Engineering Department in 2005.

Sears' interest in the German U-Boat campaign originated in 2001, when he was on an oil field vessel that discovered the sunken U-166, on the Gulf of Mexico seafloor in mile-deep water near the wreck of the torpedoed freighter Robert E Lee. The author of over forty technical, scientific, and general interest publications on geology, engineering, and higher education, Stephen Sears lives with his wife, Barbara, in Mandeville, Louisiana

Made in the USA
Coppell, TX
25 May 2020